THE GUILD CODEX: SPELLBOUND / ONE

THREE MAGES
AND A MARGARITA

ANNETTE MARIE

dark owl
fantasy

Three Mages and a Margarita
The Guild Codex: Spellbound / Book One

Copyright © 2018 by Annette Marie
www.annettemarie.ca

Dark Owl Fantasy Inc.
PO Box 88106, Rabbit Hill Post Office
Edmonton, AB, Canada T6R 0M5
www.darkowlfantasy.com

Cover Copyright © 2018 by Annette Ahner
Cover and Book Interior by Midnight Whimsy Designs
www.midnightwhimsydesigns.com

Editing by Elizabeth Darkley
arrowheadediting.wordpress.com

ISBN 978-1-988153-23-0

BOOKS BY ANNETTE MARIE

THE GUILD CODEX

The Guild Codex: Spellbound

Three Mages and a Margarita

Dark Arts and a Daiquiri

STEEL & STONE UNIVERSE

Steel & Stone Series

Chase the Dark

Bind the Soul

Yield the Night

Reap the Shadows

Unleash the Storm

Steel & Stone

Spell Weaver Trilogy

The Night Realm

The Shadow Weave

The Blood Curse

OTHER WORKS

Red Winter Trilogy

Red Winter

Dark Tempest

Immortal Fire

THE GUILD CODEX

CLASSES OF MAGIC

Spiritalis
Psychica
Arcana
Demonica
Elementaria

MYTHIC

A person with magical ability

MPD / MAGIPOL

The organization that regulates mythics and their activities

ROGUE

A mythic living in violation of MPD laws

THREE MAGES
AND A MARGARITA

KEEPING A JOB involves a few simple rules: Arrive on time. Work hard. And don't assault customers.

I forced a polite smile as the woman at table six snapped her thick fingers even though I was already hurrying toward her, a tray of drinks weighing down my arm. She jabbed fuchsia claws at her meal.

"My pasta has no *meat*," she declared in the tones of an offended Victorian governess.

I looked at her plate. The pasta did in fact display a shocking lack of poultry, considering it had arrived at her table with an entire grilled chicken breast. I knew, because I'd seen the busboy carrying it. Streaks of creamy sauce smeared the plate's edge.

I looked at her tablemate's meal. Oh hey, more Alfredo. And wow, that was a mighty big pile of grilled chicken sitting on top, which the other woman was eating at maximum speed as though she could make it disappear before my poor waitress brain calculated the disparate mass.

"This is *unacceptable*." The woman waved a hand to draw my attention away from the suspicious heap of meat. "I hope you don't expect me to pay for a meal that's missing the main ingredient!"

Shifting the heavy weight of my tray, I gazed at her wordlessly, then turned the same stare on her co-conspirator. Did they really think I'd never seen this scam before? When they started to squirm, I refocused on the chickenless woman and smiled brightly.

"What was the problem again, ma'am?"

"My—my meal has no chicken!"

I *tsked* playfully, like we were all in on the joke, and winked at the other woman. "Your friend must have a lightning-fast fork, then! You didn't even see her swiping the chicken off your plate."

Forcing a laugh, I stepped back, the three cokes, two beers, and iced tea wobbling on my tray. Six thirsty customers only a table away watched me with begging eyes, and I could practically see my tip shrinking the longer they waited.

The chickenless woman gawked at me, rusty gears turning behind her close-set eyes. I'd called out her stupid lie and given her an easy escape. All she had to do was shut up and steal some protein back before her friend ate it all. No free meals for her today.

But instead, she swelled like a bullfrog and pointed a pink claw at my chest.

"What are you implying?" Her voice rose, cutting through the cheerful babble of the busy café. "I told you my meal arrived without any chicken. Are you calling me a liar?"

Why yes, I was. "I must have misunderstood," I said soothingly, lowering my voice as though that would cancel out her increased volume. "I assumed you were joking because your chicken was obviously dumped onto your friend's plate."

"How dare you!"

Ah, okay, I probably shouldn't have said that. "I'd be happy to have the kitchen grill up another chicken breast for you at no charge."

"I'm not paying for this meal. After your rudeness, we're not paying for anything!"

"I see. In that case, I'll have to fetch my manager." With my free hand, I pulled the chicken extravaganza out from under the other woman's fork.

"What are you doing?" she demanded.

"She said you weren't paying for anything, so I'm—"

"I'm not finished with that!"

"Are you planning to pay for it?"

Fork still poised in the air, she looked at her furious companion. More spinning gears. These two women probably hadn't thought this hard since kindergarten.

"Put that plate back!" the first woman barked. "And get your manager over here immediately."

I returned her meal, my drink tray wobbling again. The imaginary tip counter hovering above the thirsty table was now in negative numbers. I'd be paying *them* for their drinks.

"I'll send a manager," I muttered as I turned away. "Don't pig out on your free meals."

"Did you just call me a *pig*?"

The offended shriek silenced every conversation in the café. Oh, hell. Grimacing, I swung back to face the woman. "You must have misheard—"

"I didn't mishear anything!" she straight-up screamed. "You called me a pig! Where is your manager?"

"Um." I glanced across the tables, the dinner rush halted by the spectacle. No managers in sight, but at my panicked look, another server zipped into the kitchen. "Let me just—"

"We're leaving. I won't pay to be mocked and insulted." The woman shoved to her feet, frothing at the mouth with vindicated rage. Her companion shoveled one last mouthful of chicken down her gullet before scrambling up.

"If you could just wait one moment," I tried again. "A manager will—"

"Out of my way!" Her fat hand shot out and shoved my drink tray.

It flipped up, dumping all six beverages onto my chest. Liquid drenched my white blouse and glassware shattered on the floor, spraying shards over my legs as ice cubes skittered under tables.

Anyone who's known me for more than an hour has an inkling of my temper. And by inkling, I mean I might as well wear a flashing sign that reads, "Firecracker Redhead, Beware." Or, if you're my ex-boyfriend, it reads, "Don't Stick It in Crazy Gingers."

I try my best, okay? I keep my mouth shut, I smile real polite, and I let the managers give free meals to every scamming asshole because "the customer is always right" or whatever.

But sometimes I react before I think.

Which is why, as ice-cold liquid gushed down my front, I whipped my dripping tray right into the woman's smirking face.

The plastic hit the side of her head with a shocking *crack* and she stumbled backward, then fell on her well-padded butt.

Her mouth hung open, eyes bugged out, coke and beer and a hint of iced tea speckling her cheek.

If the restaurant had been quiet before, now it was silent enough to be a new dimension.

"She pushed me first," I announced, my voice echoing in the silence. "You all saw that, right?"

At my thirsty table, a middle-aged couple gave small, hesitant nods and one guy grinned, shooting me a thumbs-up. I could feel a hundred eyes on me as, my blouse and apron dripping, I reached over the woman and picked up the two Alfredo plates, stacking them on my empty tray.

The woman stared vacantly, but I knew better than to think I'd literally tray-slapped some sense into her. Once her shock wore off, she would start howling. Or wailing. Fifty-fifty chance.

"I didn't call you a pig," I told her. "But I should have called you a liar. You lied about your meal, then you assaulted me. I'm going to have to ask you to leave."

Her face purpled, eyes bulging even more.

"On the plus side," I added cheerfully, "you're getting your food for free, just like you wanted. Have a nice day, and please never come again."

With the two Alfredo plates on my tray, I waltzed past her, ignoring the ice cube lodged in my cleavage. Whispers erupted at every table as I counted in my head.

I got to three before the noise erupted. Wailing. I knew it.

A manager flew out of the kitchen, and her glare blazed hot enough to grill some chicken all on its own. Wincing, I ducked through the doors into the back. The moment I appeared, the two line cooks whooped.

"Right in the face!" Neil laughed, waving a spatula at the door's small window where he'd no doubt plastered his nose as soon as the shouting began. "Wow, Tori, are you insane?"

"Why do people always ask me that?" I muttered as I set the tray down on the counter and checked my bare legs and sandaled feet for glass shards.

"I can't believe you—"

"Tori."

I flinched. The café owner stood at the end of the kitchen, her arms folded and her expression as black as her coffee. My innards melted with dread, but I straightened my shoulders and strode confidently toward her. In the dining area, the chickenless wonder had switched from wails to shrieks.

"Mrs. Blanchard, I can explain—"

"Did you hit a customer?"

"She pushed me first."

Blanchard nudged her wire-rimmed glasses up and pinched the bridge of her nose. "Tori, I've told you more than once that if a customer is antagonizing you, fetch a manager."

"I was trying to, but she—"

"I warned you last week after you called one of our regulars a half-plucked buzzard *to her face*—"

"She kept calling me anorexic! Every time I walked by—"

"I warned you," Blanchard repeated, speaking over my protests, "that you were on your final chance. You're a hard worker, and I've done everything I can to accommodate your … issues … but I can't employ a server who attacks customers."

"Custom*er*," I corrected in a dejected mumble. "Only one. I won't do it again, I promise."

"I'm sorry, Tori."

"Mrs. Blanchard, I really need this job. Please, give me one more chance."

She shook her head. "Leave your apron. You can pick up your last check on payday."

"Mrs. Blanchard—"

"I need to help settle things down in the dining area." She stepped around me. "Please use the back door on your way out."

As she walked away, my shoulders slumped. The noise had quieted, meaning the manager had probably offered all kinds of apologies and gift cards to the poor assaulted woman. I tried not to imagine the look on chicken lady's face when she learned the crazy server had been canned.

"Aw, man," Neil said glumly, joining me beside the dishwasher. "Sorry, Tori. Sucks that she fired you."

"Well," I said heavily, "I'm not really surprised."

I untied my apron, then fished the half-melted ice cube out of my blouse and flicked it into the sink.

"Uh, Tori? Your, um, bra ... is showing."

"Yeah, that happens. Ever hear of a wet t-shirt contest?" I scowled. "That wasn't an invitation to stare."

He jerked his eyes up. "Aren't you supposed to wear white bras with white shirts?"

"Are you a fashion expert now?" I didn't admit he was right, or explain that my white-shirt-friendly undergarments were in the laundry. Neither did I glance down to see how visible my pink bra with little black hearts was. I didn't want to know.

After digging my tips out of my apron—a measly twenty-two bucks since I'd only been an hour into my shift—I handed the drenched fabric to Neil. "Well ... guess I'll see you around."

"Yeah. Stop by and visit, 'kay?"

"Will do," I lied. Like I could ever come back here after clobbering a woman with a drink tray.

With a half-hearted wave, I stopped in the breakroom to grab my purse and umbrella, then exited through the back door, as instructed. Rain pattered the asphalt, making the muddy puddles dance. Skirting the reeking dumpster, I followed a narrow alley to the main street.

Chipper music rolled out of the café as a couple entered. The brightly lit windows were warm and inviting, and everything looked back to normal as a server stopped at a table to unload steaming plates for eager customers.

The cool rain peppered my face and diluted the ugly brownish splotch on my chest, but I didn't open my umbrella. If my pink bra was on display, then I was committing to the show, damn it. Wet shirt all the way.

Turning on my heel, I marched down the sidewalk. It was a long walk home, but at least it would delay the inevitable moment when I'd have to inform my landlord I'd lost my job … again.

2

UNLOCKING the apartment door, I poked my head inside. "Justin?"

No answer. Heaving a sigh of relief, I locked the bolt, shoved my purse into the closet, and kicked my sandals onto the mat to dry. My bare feet squeaked on the linoleum as I walked down the short hall into the main room, a cramped kitchen overlooking it. The drooping blue sofa had seen better days, and carefully folded bedsheets and a blanket sat on one end.

Piled in front of the window were four battered cardboard boxes that contained all my worldly possessions. Grabbing the overflowing laundry basket off the top of the pile, I carried it to the narrow closet where the stacked washer and dryer hid. As I loaded my laundry in, I mentally reviewed my bank account. Would my last paycheck cover the rent? Maybe … if I didn't eat for the rest of the month.

Washer loaded, I stripped off my work clothes and tossed them in, then started it up. Returning to the boxes, I selected my last clean bra—hot red with lacy embellishments, normally reserved for special occasions—then dragged out a pair of yoga pants and pulled them on.

As I lifted out a top, the clack of the bolt echoed down the hall. Yelping, I yanked the shirt down, barely getting it in place before a male head poked out from the hall, eyebrows high in surprise.

"Tori! You're home early."

"Hi, Justin." I managed a smile. "How was work?"

He was still in uniform—dark blue slacks and a button-down shirt emblazoned with the police emblem on the shoulder. Normally I loved a man in uniform, but I could only appreciate it so much on Justin. Not that he wasn't handsome with his hazel eyes and close-cropped brown hair. It's just, you know, he's my roommate. And my landlord. And my older brother.

"Tiring," he admitted. "I hate the early morning shift, but I have my fingers crossed for that promotion."

"I'm sure you'll get it."

He unbuttoned his uniform, stripping down to the plain black t-shirt he wore underneath. "What happened at work? Your top is on backward, by the way."

I looked down. Crap, it was.

"How come you're home so early? Are you sick?"

"No …" I muttered, tugging at my ponytail.

"Tori," he groaned. "Not again. You got fired, didn't you?"

I nodded.

He puffed out a breath. "What happened this time?"

I told him the story through his bedroom door as he changed clothes. While talking, I pulled my arms into the baggy striped t-shirt and turned it the right way around. Justin reappeared, his scowl made more severe by the short beard he'd grown at my suggestion. It had been a great call. He looked way more policeman-tough now.

"She shoved you and spilled all your drinks? They should have thrown her out!"

"They might have … if I hadn't whacked her upside the head."

He sat on a tall stool in front of the kitchen counter that acted as our dining table. "How do you do it, Tori? If there's a crazy customer within ten miles, they always end up in your section."

"Maybe I bring out the crazy in people." I flopped onto the sofa. "Maybe it's *magic*."

He rolled his eyes.

"Or aliens," I suggested. "Or … magic aliens!"

He snorted but didn't argue with me. No matter how often he refused to engage in the topic, I would keep ragging on him until he got his head on straight. I couldn't believe my own brother had become a *magic* conspiracy theorist. I'd believe in aliens first.

"I'm sorry, Justin," I said more seriously. "I'll get another job ASAP so I don't miss any rent payments."

"I've told you every month since you moved in that you don't need to pay rent. I'm happy to have the company."

"Living downtown is expensive as hell." I didn't add that my presence here over the last eight months was preventing his steady girlfriend from moving in with him. Plus, he was putting up with all my crap cluttering his one-bedroom suite.

"Cheer up, Tori. You've found a new job after each …" He trailed off, maybe realizing that pointing out how I'd blown six jobs in eight months wasn't encouraging. "You'll find another one in no time."

"Yeah," I agreed listlessly.

He glanced into the spotless kitchen—my small contribution to the household that I held to like a Lysol-worshipping nun—then threw me a grin. "Let's order in tonight."

"I should save my money since—"

"My treat." He grabbed his phone off the counter. "The usual?"

"Sure," I agreed guiltily. I would extra-clean the bathroom tomorrow to make up for it. He'd be able to eat out of the sink if he wanted.

While he called in the order, I unearthed my laptop from beneath a stack of socks waiting to be folded. Settling onto the sofa, I flipped it open and fired up my browser. Unsurprisingly, I had the job posting website bookmarked.

I'd lost my job, but I'd have another one within a week even if I had to sell my soul to get it.

PAUSING in front of the display window, I took a deep breath and smiled at my reflection. Smile, relax. Smile, relax. I needed to appear perky and confident, not bedraggled and exhausted. My hazel eyes, identical to Justin's, looked dark as coal, but the dusty glass couldn't dull the vibrant red of my hair. I scrunched my ponytail with one hand to revive the curls, but it was hopeless.

I stepped back from the window and squinted at the sky. Bright sunlight sparkled merrily, and the breeze carried the salty tang of the ocean, only a few blocks north. People strolled up and down the charming redbrick sidewalks, passing old-fashioned streetlamps and storefronts nestled in tall Victorian-style buildings. Gastown was the oldest neighborhood in the city, a popular tourist destination full of cafés and restaurants.

Across the redbrick intersection was one such café. The yellow patio umbrellas resembled a garden of monster-sized flowers, and servers in cute periwinkle blouses bustled among the tables. The place was packed even though it was only four o'clock—too early for the dinner rush, but no one had told this café that.

Busy was good. Busy meant lots of staff.

I practiced my smile one more time, then crossed the street and entered the air-conditioned interior.

"Hi," I greeted the hostess brightly. "Is your hiring manager in today?"

"Yeah," the girl replied in a bored drone. "I already called her. You can wait there with the others."

She pointed. Two girls my age, dressed in chic business casual attire, stood off to the side, holding folders just like mine. *Their* résumés probably weren't full of one- and two-month server stints, with no references to show for any of them. Goddamn it.

I joined the girls anyway, and when the stocky, middle-aged manager finally appeared, looking overheated and unfriendly, I patiently waited my turn.

"Thank you so much for seeing me," I said once the other girls had left. "I can see you're busy and I won't keep you. I just wanted to drop off my résumé."

I passed her the single sheet, which she skimmed without enthusiasm.

"We do have an opening and if we're interested, we'll—" She squinted. "Winnie's Café? That was your last employer?"

My stomach twisted. "Yes, that's correct."

"Tori Dawson ..." she murmured as though digging through her memory banks. She dropped her arm, my résumé hanging at her side. "I'm sorry, I don't have a position for you."

"But you just said ..."

The manager glanced distractedly into the café before focusing on me again. "Look, hun. Maybe you should try a different industry. I don't think hospitality is for you."

"What are you talking about?"

She shrugged. "You've got a reputation. Unless they're living under a rock, no restaurant manager in downtown will hire you."

I wilted. "Really?"

"Maybe you'd do better in retail." She handed my résumé back. "Shipping/receiving might suit you."

"But ... I'm bad at retail too," I finished under my breath since she'd already walked away. Stuffing the paper in my folder, I trudged back to the street. Passersby jostled me and I ducked into a shady spot beside a brick wall, staring blankly at the cute shops across the road. Most retail jobs were too slow-paced for me. Bored Tori got herself into a lot more trouble than Busy Tori. Another hard-learned lesson.

If no one in downtown would hire me as a server, what would I do? Either I ventured out of downtown, which would require an expensive transit pass and long commutes, or I applied for a starter position in something completely new. But with no experience—or tips—the pay would be too shitty for me to ever afford a decent place of my own. I'd be stuck on Justin's couch for another eight months. That, or I'd have to quit college once the semester was over.

Groaning, I massaged my temples. No giving up. I'd apply at the last few places on my list and hope their managers were the rare rock-dwelling types, then head home and come up with a new game plan. I would figure this out.

As I stepped away from the wall, the cool sea breeze gusted down the street, carrying a swirl of dust, leaves, and litter. Skirts flew up and café umbrellas tottered precariously—and a sheet of paper hit me square in the face.

Swearing, I snatched the paper off my nose and examined it in case my skin required sanitation from the contact. I was about to toss it away—I know, littering is bad—when I recognized the layout of the text. It wasn't difficult. I'd been staring at job postings all week.

Maybe one of the prim and perfect applicants from the café had dropped it. Fat chance I'd land a job anywhere they had applied, but I still scanned the paper. Only three listings graced the page. The first was an entry-level bank teller position in the heart of downtown. Yeah, no. I was many things, but "quiet" was not one of them, and every bank I'd ever set foot in had been silent as a cemetery at midnight.

The second position was for a receptionist at a law firm. Were law firms quiet? I'd never been in one—kind of surprising no one has sued me yet, come to think of it—but I was sure they fell in the same "quiet, dignified, stick-up-their-asses" category as banks. So, also a no.

I squinted at the third one. Bartender? I didn't have much experience, but I'd manned the bar a few times at various restaurants. And bartenders, unlike servers, had more freedom to tell rude customers to shove their bad attitudes where the sun don't shine.

But … the address. Turning eastward, I gulped. The place was firmly situated in the Downtown Eastside, a large neighborhood that half the city was too terrified to set foot in.

Pulling my phone out of my purse, I looked up the address. Hmm, okay, so it was on the west edge of the Downtown Eastside—not as bad as I'd thought. In fact, it was barely six blocks away, though outside the safe charm of Gastown. Maybe far enough away that they wouldn't have heard about Tori Dawson, the Server of Doom and Despair. It was worth a shot, and as the saying around here goes, you miss one hundred percent of the shots you don't take.

Feeling hopeful, I stuffed the paper into my purse, tucked my folder under one arm, and strode east. Just follow the redbrick road.

Disappointingly, the red bricks ended after a quarter block, but the three- and four-story buildings with cute shops continued to border the street. Just when I was starting to feel pretty good about things, I passed a shopfront with empty windows. Then another. Within a block, the doors were blank and the windows covered. The number of pedestrians dwindled to a handful, and they walked quickly.

Chin held high, I lengthened my stride, my strappy but comfortable sandals slapping against the sidewalk. Could I run in these if I had to? Probably. Fear was a great motivator.

I wasn't scared yet, but as I hurried past a heavy-duty chain-link fence with barbed wire on top, I started to doubt myself. Maybe I should go back. What shops there were had thick bars over the windows. Even if I was safe enough in broad daylight, what about late-night shifts—assuming I got the job?

I replayed the café manager's declaration in my mind. *No restaurant manager in downtown will hire you.* Screw that. If I needed to carry pepper spray to and from work, then so be it.

Increasing my pace, I strode toward the next intersection. I had to be close, but all I saw was a bike shop called "BIKES" and a tattoo parlor with bars across the windows *and* the door. Pulling out my phone, I checked the map again, then rounded the corner, walked twenty yards up the street, and stopped.

A black door stood in front of me, tucked into a shadowy nook with no overhead light. Faded print in Ye-Old-English lettering declared, "The Crow and Hammer." Painted beneath was a black bird with its wings spread ominously, perched on an ornate mallet.

The cube-shaped building featured barred windows on the second and third floors. Its northern neighbor was a shorter building with boarded-up windows and construction tape across the doorway. On the other side was a cramped parking lot with a dumpster and two cars. My gaze returned to the painted crow with its flared wings.

Breathe in. Breathe out. Okay. I could do this. Stepping into the shadowed alcove, I reached for the door.

3

BEFORE MY FINGERS touched the peeling paint, an overwhelming urge to turn around washed over me like a bucket of ice water. I didn't want to be here. The need to walk away—or better yet, run away—roiled through me like a physical sickness. I wanted to be *anywhere* but here and if I didn't retreat now, I would … what? Get eaten by a boogeyman on the other side of the door?

Damn, since when was I such a chicken? Teeth gritted, I grabbed the handle and yanked the door open.

My bad case of nerves passed the moment I stepped inside, but honestly? The interior wasn't any more reassuring than the exterior. Heavy beams in the ceiling, wood finishes, and dim lights gave it that dark English pub feel, and it was much smaller than it appeared from the outside, with enough tables and bar stools to seat maybe fifty people. The chairs were cast around like a stampede had charged through the front door, and though it was clean-ish, a strange smoky smell hung over

the place. Not cigarettes, not drugs, not wood smoke, but ...
something.

Oh, and did I mention the place was completely empty? It
was early for the dinner rush, but *empty* was not a good sign for
any business.

Since I was too tough—or too stubborn—to sneak back
outside and pretend I'd never set foot here, I soldiered onward.
The door wasn't locked, so that meant they were open, right?
Winding around the scattered chairs, I approached the bar at
the back. Centered on the wall was a massive steel war hammer,
the metal nicked and tarnished, the wooden handle dark. I eyed
it warily, hoping it was firmly anchored in place.

Setting my folder on the thick wood bar top, I tried to peek
through the gaps in the saloon doors behind it. "Hello?"

A muffled voice answered from somewhere beyond the
saloon doors. So someone *was* here. Someone who was busy,
apparently. I waited, shifting from foot to foot. Since I was just
standing there, I nudged the nearest bar stool under the lip of
the bar. Then I reached over and tucked the next one into place.
And since I'd done that, I fixed the other ones too. Much better.

With a peek at the saloon doors, I straightened the nearest
table. What a mess.

The doors swung open and a woman half fell out of the
room beyond. Short, plump, and maybe ten years older than
me, with dark hair twisted into a messy bun and bangs that
were streaked with blue and red. Clutching a stack of folders so
thick they threatened to disgorge paperwork, the woman
looked around wildly before spotting me.

"Who are you?" she blurted.

Was that how she greeted all their customers? No wonder
the place was empty.

I hitched my professional smile into place and grabbed my folder. "Hi, my name is Tori Dawson. I'm here about your bartending job opportunity."

"You are?" She dumped her papers onto the bar top and gave me a frowning once-over. "Walk-ins aren't usually how we …"

"Could I leave my résumé with you?" I asked, flipping open my folder.

"Clara!" someone shouted from the back. "Where'd you go? Oy!"

The glint of panic in the woman's eyes intensified. "Yes, yes," she told me. "Just leave it. I really need someone, but I don't have time to look at anything right now. Tomorrow—"

"Clara!"

"Coming!" she shouted over her shoulder. "I'm sorry— Tracey, was it?"

"Tori."

"I'm swamped. People are arriving in less than an hour and the freezer broke last night and Cooper called in sick again—" A loud crash from the back interrupted her, followed by a man's furious cursing. "Oh god, what *now*?"

She dashed back through the doors, leaving her paperwork. I winced sympathetically. I'd been in her shoes before— understaffed, everything going wrong, and what sounded like an event planned for the night.

As I laid my résumé on top of her folders, noises echoed out of the back—loud clatters and frantic conversation between Clara and the man. I studied the mess. Half the chairs were lying on their *sides* for crying out loud. Giving a mental shrug, I straightened the tables and picked up chairs. In ten minutes, I had the front of the house tidied up and ready to go. Nodding to myself, I returned to the bar and grabbed my résumés.

Clara reappeared, reaching for her folders. When she saw me, she jerked to a stop, brow furrowing in confusion. I pursed my lips. Awkward. I'd meant to be gone by the time she came back.

Eyes wide, she stared at the restored order. "You …?"

"Just helping out," I explained hastily. "I'm on my way now. Good luck with your event tonight."

"Thanks," she mumbled.

I turned away, making a face at the cringyness, and hurried for the door.

"Wait!" Clara sped around the bar, my résumé in her hand. "Do you have bartending experience, Tori?"

"Not much," I admitted as she joined me. "But I know my way around a bar, I learn fast, and I work hard."

Clara nodded as she scanned my résumé. "You have no references."

"Um … yeah."

"Are you busy tonight?"

I blinked. "Tonight?"

"I know it's unorthodox." Her words tumbled together as she rushed to get them out. "But I'm slammed already and we'll have a full house by six. If you can work a shift, I'll pay you in cash at the end of the night—same wage as my last bartender."

I brightened. A paid shift and a chance to prove myself without having to do the whole interview thing? "Sure, I'd love to."

Clara deflated with relief. "Wonderful! Let's get started." She waved for me to follow her. "Tonight's the monthly meeting and everyone will be here. Ramsey and I will handle all the food orders if you can take care of the liquor. I'll help you out as much as I can. Once everyone has a few drinks, it'll settle down, but six to seven will be crazy."

She halted halfway around the bar. "I'm Clara Martins, by the way. AGM."

Assistant general manager? Finally, some luck. I'd handed my résumé to the second-in-charge.

I shook her hand, then she led me into the back. Through the saloon doors was a cramped kitchen with steel counters.

"Ramsey!" she called. "Get over here!"

A tall guy wheeled into the kitchen from the other end—thin, lanky, with black hair buzzed short on one side and the rest falling in spiky locks below his jawline. Chains hung around his neck, and he was wearing more eyeliner than I was.

"Ramsey, this is Tori. She's interested in the bartender job, so I'm having her help out tonight."

Ramsey's mouth twisted. "Is that even allow—"

"We really need the extra pair of hands," Clara interrupted. "And we can see how she meshes with the gang."

She didn't mean "gang" literally, did she?

"Suppose," Ramsey agreed uncertainly. He gave me a look as though measuring how breakable I was. "Welcome to the madhouse."

I didn't get a chance to consider all the possible meanings of his welcome before Clara pulled me into motion. She gave me a top-speed tour of the kitchen, walk-in fridge, malfunctioning freezer, ice machine, and storage areas. Aside from a cluttered office, that was it. Not even a breakroom.

Ten minutes later, I was standing behind the bar with an apron in my hands as Clara zoomed off. Ramsey was prepping food in the kitchen, so I was officially on my own.

I tied the apron around my waist, overlapping the bottom of my white blouse and slim knee-length skirt. Good thing I'd worn my comfy sandals. I shot a quick text to Justin letting him know I'd be home late, then got to work.

First I wiped down every surface in, around, and behind the bar. I located and laid out the drip mats, then hauled a bucket of ice from the back and dumped it into the well. I checked the liquor bottles in the well, tested the soda guns, and located all the basics in the walk-in and dry storage.

With a few pointers from Ramsey, I found the garnish supplies and prepped lemons, limes, olives, mint, and parsley. I couldn't find any garnish trays, so I stuffed them in highball glasses. As I was lining them up in the well, Clara rushed in. Was she ever *not* rushing?

"Oh, good, you're ready, then?" She started tapping the touchscreen on the till. "Everything is on the house tonight, so all you have to do is log what you make."

I hid my disappointment. Free drinks meant no tips. "What's your policy on carding?"

"Oh, you don't need to check IDs. We only serve members." Clara rubbed her hands together nervously, her eyebrows scrunching. "When it comes to new people, they can be … but you'll be fine! Don't let them give you any crap. And I'll be nearby if you have trouble. Just call me if you need help."

Trouble? Maybe she had heard of my reputation after all. I plastered on a confident smile. No hesitation, not when this trial run could win me the job.

Clara returned my smile with one that was more anxious than pleased, then dashed into the kitchen, calling for Ramsey. I rubbed my damp palms on my apron. Setting up the bar was easy. It was the rest I didn't have much experience with. Nerves twisting, I pulled up a webpage of drink recipes on my phone.

The big clock on the wall ticked over to five thirty. The place was still dead. I appraised the tables and dark walls. How many people would they cram in here? A broad staircase in the corner led to the second level, but Clara hadn't mentioned it so I guessed it didn't matter for my job tonight.

The front door flew open and I jumped.

Two guys walked in. I relaxed—they had beards, but not "biker gang" beards. One guy was average—dark hair, a touch of silver in his beard, mid-thirties—and the other was stocky and buff, with the sides of his head shaved and his blond hair combed straight back. Late twenties?

I smiled welcomingly as they approached the bar, but they didn't respond in kind. Instead, they stared at me like I was a five-foot-seven weed that had sprouted from between the floorboards.

"Hi!" I chirped. "What can I—"

"Who are you?" the older one asked sharply.

"I—my name is Tori." When their suspicion only increased, I added, "I'm filling in tonight to help Clara."

As though I'd spoken the code word, they both relaxed.

"I'll have a whiskey sour."

"Bourbon on the rocks."

"Right," I said breathlessly, grabbing two rocks glasses and adding ice. The bourbon was easy, but I overdid the whiskey in the second drink. Oh well, he was getting his non-money's worth. I passed them off, then added the two drinks into the system. When I looked up, the door was opening again.

Another man—fortyish—held the door for a pair of guys in their twenties. The younger two made it to the bar first and—

"Who are you?"

What was it with these people? I wasn't a damn trespasser. They were more territorial than teenagers in a Wi-Fi hotspot.

"I'm filling in tonight to help Clara," I answered, testing my new magic phrase.

Again, they lost their antagonism and ordered drinks—easy ones, thank goodness. The older guy even smiled when I passed him his Old Fashioned.

I hadn't finished adding their drinks to the tally before the next group arrived. Three girls in their early twenties, all very different blonds. One with pale hair in a wavy bob, one with long golden locks, and one with her shoulder-length hair dyed a hideous banana yellow.

Again, I smiled, and again I got glared at until I assured them via the magic phrase that my repulsive presence in their precious pub was only temporary. Two ordered sodas but banana-hair wanted a Long Island Iced Tea that took several minutes too long to make. By the time I passed it off to her, another ten people had gathered behind the girls—all squinting suspiciously at me.

I gulped down my nerves and offered the magic phrase again. I didn't whimper, I swear.

The patrons I'd already served made perfect sense to me—young-ish, single-ish bar-going types—but now I was stumped. Young, old, classy, weird, goth, hippie. A full spectrum of stereotypes was gathering in the pub, and none belonged in the same room together.

Before I got completely overwhelmed, Clara burst out of the kitchen and people shifted over to order food from her. I scrambled to make their drinks, fumbling liquor bottles and forgetting garnishes. For every smile I offered, I got stony stares and scowls in response.

"Who are you?"

"Who are you?"

"Who are you?"

The stupid question kept coming, and I quit smiling. As the clock hit six and half the tables were full, I ducked into the back to get more ice, panting for air, strands of hair sticking to my face. My nerves were long gone, replaced by anger. Pissing people off was one of my God-given talents, but even I had never met such a universally hostile group of people in my life.

I stomped to the ice machine and filled my bucket, barely acknowledging Ramsey slaving over the grill, the deep fryer sizzling. Bucket filled, I shoved through the saloon doors. Clara rushed past me into the kitchen to give Ramsey the next wave of orders.

More customers had gathered at the bar. I dumped the ice into the well and faced them. The three guys were a few years older than me, tall, fit, and handsome. Under different circumstances, I would have flirted hardcore and written my number on their receipt, but instead I had to contain my grimace as I waited for *the question*.

"Heard there's a new girl," the centermost guy said in a pleasantly deep voice, his blue eyes flashing with humor. Like me, he was a full-blown ginger, though his tousled locks were more into rusty-orange shades. "I see the rumors are true."

I thought he might be my first friendly customer when his buddy added, "Fresh blood."

"What do you want?" The rudely barked demand slipped out before I could stop it. Crap. Deep breaths, Tori.

Surprised by my tone, the redhead glanced at his pal—a dark-haired looker with an exotic cast to his features. The third guy was half turned away, waving at someone.

The redhead offered his hand in greeting, giving me a smooth smile. "Aaron Sinclair."

He was the first customer to introduce himself, which might have seemed like good manners except his tone suggested I should recognize his name and commence fawning. Was he a local actor or something? I didn't recognize him.

"Pleasure," I said flatly, not bothering to offer my name. No one here cared who I was. "Are you ordering a drink or what?"

Damn it. That wasn't any less rude than the last thing I'd said. Unfazed, Aaron grinned like I'd challenged him to a duel—one he expected to win—but then the third guy turned to face the bar.

"Three rum and cokes," he said in a smooth voice that, believe it or not, was pleasant. But I almost didn't notice, too distracted by the white scar that ran down his face from his left temple to the hollow of his cheek, cutting across his eye. While his right eye was a warm chocolate brown, the damaged iris was eerily pale as though the color had drained out, leaving only a dark pupil and outer rim.

Recovering fast, I whipped out three rocks glasses, scooped ice into them, splashed in some rum, and topped them with coke.

They took their drinks, but instead of moving off to the tables like everyone else, they slipped onto the three nearest bar stools. Great. An audience. I ignored them as my next customer walked up and demanded to know who I was.

"So, new girl," Aaron said, distracting my count so I overpoured a vodka. "Are you a natural redhead?"

"Are you a natural pain in the ass?" I shot back without thinking. Cursing my runaway mouth, I shoved the accidental double at the customer.

"Confirmation via temper," the dark-haired one remarked.

Ignoring them even harder, I focused on the next wave of arrivals. They were still coming—there had to be over thirty people in here now—and the original wave was finishing their drinks and coming up for seconds. Clara zoomed in and out, her arms full of plates. The more I rushed, the more mistakes I made and my frustration kept climbing.

"Hey, new girl," Aaron called as I rocketed past him with a bottle of champagne for a mimosa. "What do you call it when a ginger goes off the deep end?"

I added orange juice to the mimosa.

"A *ginger snap*. Get it?"

"I've got a better one for you, Aaron," his dark-haired copilot said. "What's the difference between a ginger and a brick?"

Aaron twisted his mouth suspiciously. "What?"

"A brick gets laid."

As Aaron snorted dismissively and the scarred guy snickered, I dashed into the back, searching for a brandy I'd never heard of, which my current customer was *insisting* he always ordered. I dug around in the storage room, finally found it, then raced back out again.

"Hey, new girl," Aaron began again as the impatient brandy connoisseur stormed off with his stupid drink. "We've got a wager going on. Care to settle it?"

"I'm busy." Hunching over the till, I tried to remember everything I'd poured in the last ten minutes.

"We just wanna know what you are. I'm betting an alchie."

My hand stuttered over the screen. I'd been expecting another lame ginger joke. He thought I was a *what*?

"Psychic," the other guy said, but I didn't know if he was talking to me or his pal. The one with the scar rolled his eyes and sipped his drink.

"Come on, give us a hint," Aaron cajoled.

"Could you hurry up?" an older woman snapped at me. "I'm waiting to order."

I shifted away from the guys and hastily entered all the drinks I remembered making, then faced the woman. "What can I—"

"Two Manhattans, and make it snappy, girl."

Her sneering tone was too much for me.

"Are you having a bad day?" I shot back. "Or are you always a hag?"

Aaron choked on his drink. I knew I was losing it, but my temper was pulsing and I couldn't remember the definition of "self-control."

"Excuse me?" the woman gasped.

"*Please*. It's an amazing word used by civilized people everywhere. You should try it sometime."

Her mouth opened, then closed. I folded my arms and waited.

"Two Manhattans, *please*."

I slammed a pair of martini glasses onto the mats, then turned around to check my phone for the recipe. I needed to handle my temper whether these jerks were rude or not. At least I wasn't losing any tips.

Aaron whistled. "That sounded great, Sylvia. You should practice manners more often."

"Shut your mouth, Aaron, or I'll seal it shut."

After skimming the drink instructions, I grabbed the whiskey and vermouth, one in each hand, and poured them.

"You're supposed to mix them with ice first," the woman barked. "Forget it. Just give me two cokes instead."

"I can—"

"Two cokes."

Snarling, I poured the drinks and shoved them across the bar. "Don't choke on the ice." Bitch.

Aaron laughed. "Wow, I think I might like the new girl."

I ignored him, my next customer already waiting. As I struggled with increasingly difficult orders and correspondingly crankier customers, Aaron and his pal kept up a steady commentary, interspersed with more ginger jokes, but at least they made fun of other patrons as much as me. Still, they were *not* helping. I doubted my hair color had anything to do with my short fuse, but either way, I was hitting my limit—and with each new dose of nasty thrown my way, my control slipped a little more.

When a guy snapped at me to hurry, I shorted his vodka and told him I'd water down his drinks until he learned some manners. An old man leered at my boobs and asked if I could add something *special* to his drink, so I poured an ounce of bourbon and filled the rest of the highball glass with grenadine syrup.

"Sweet," I said with an overly girlish smile. "Just like me."

He scoffed at the glass. "Give me a real drink."

"You got what you asked for."

"But—"

"Next!"

He left the pink atrocity on the bar and stalked back to his table.

Aaron cackled. "Hey Kai, how do you start an argument with a ginger?"

"Say anything," the dark-haired guy answered with a smirk. "You realize you're a ginger too, right? You're insulting yourself."

I shot them a furious glare. Why were they making my night worse? Why couldn't they move their sexy asses to a table? The fact they were hot just made me angrier. All that drool-worthy sex appeal wasted on jackasses—well, maybe not the scarred guy. He was possibly not a jackass. He hadn't said much so I wasn't sure.

The three of them looked like goddamn models, but each from a different magazine. Aaron, he might have just galloped across a meadow on horseback, lassoing wild cattle—or beautiful women. He wasn't dressed like a cowboy, but he had the same ruggedness to him. And he had the muscles to back up that impression, with toned biceps and hard forearms displayed by his gray t-shirt.

His buddy Kai could have walked right off a luxury car ad—the guy behind the wheel, adjusting his sunglasses as he casually careened his sports car down a winding mountain road while the camera panned across his face. His tousled dark hair, fair skin, and exotic features could sell anything.

The third guy was trickier. Ignoring the scar, he had amazing olive skin and rumpled dark brown curls, with a cultivated five-o'clock shadow that scruffed up his jaw in the sexiest way possible. Handsome as hell but not too striking, he was the kind of guy businesses used to advertise men's casual clothing—*wear our jeans and you, average man, can also turn females into quivering masses of desire.*

Yep, they were hot shit and, in Aaron's case, totally knew it.

"New girl," he called the moment I had a free second to breathe. "I need another drink."

I angrily wiped up spilled grenadine. Refusing to serve him felt like letting him win. "What do you want?"

"Hmm." He pondered for an overly long moment. "I'll have a margarita—the slushy kind. With a cherry and a little umbrella on top."

I glowered at him. A blended drink? Ugh. Whirling around, I unburied the blender and dumped in ice, then searched for margarita mixer. As more patrons lined up at the bar, I raced into the back, almost crashing into Ramsey on my way to dry storage. I rooted around the shelves, found a can, and hurried back to the bar. Add the ingredients, blend, test the consistency, blend again. Good enough.

I dumped it into a margarita glass and shoved it at Aaron.

He briefly inspected it. "What about the cherry?"

"I don't have any cherries."

"We *always* have cherries."

I growled, then stomped back into the kitchen. In dry storage, I found the monster jar of candied cherries, carried the whole thing back to the bar, unscrewed the top, and pulled one out by the stem. I plopped it on top of the slushy drink and even stuck in a sprig of mint for good measure.

"Happy?"

"What about the umbrella?"

"Forget it."

"It's not a margarita without an umbrella."

A dozen more unfriendly patrons were waiting to order drinks. I started to turn.

"I don't want it if it doesn't have an umbrella," Aaron declared. "Get me—"

My vision went red. Whipping back to him, I grabbed the margarita I'd spent five precious minutes preparing and yelled, "If you won't drink it, then you can wear it!"

And I flung the drink in his face.

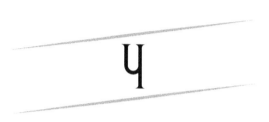

OR, well, I *meant* to throw the margarita at Aaron. My swing was a bit overenthusiastic and his two friends caught a face full of cold slush too. All three guys recoiled as the entire room went silent, every person turning to stare.

A glob of crushed ice slid down Aaron's face and plopped in his lap. "Not cool, new gir—"

"Not cool?" I shouted, slamming my hands down on the bar top. "I've been working my ass off without so much as a thank-you from a *single goddamn person*, and you're jerking me around like a five-year-old with no impulse control. If you so much as open your mouth again, I'll shove my soda gun down your throat and see if you can crack jokes while you drown!"

Shocked silence rang through the pub, just like at the café. Safe to say I'd blown this "interview by fire" but I didn't give a shit. I'd finish my shift because I'd said I would—and because I wanted my damn cash after all this crap—but I was never setting foot in here again.

Everyone gawked, then someone erupted in laughter—Aaron's other friend. With margarita splashed over his scarred face, he laughed so hard he wobbled on his stool.

"I don't believe it," he gasped. "A redhead with more fire than you, Aaron!"

Chuckles ran through the pub as the laughter spread, then conversations resumed like nothing had happened. I stood there, blinking stupidly as I waited for someone to throw me out for assaulting another customer.

The scarred guy recovered from his fit of laughter. "Kai, you weren't recording that, were you?"

"I wish. I'd already be uploading it."

"Hmph," Aaron grunted without opening his mouth. Maybe he was taking my threat seriously.

"A lesson learned, my young Padawan?"

The unexpected voice was so close that I jumped half a foot in the air. A man stood behind me like he'd popped out of the floor. With chiseled features, intelligent eyes, salt-and-pepper hair, and a short beard, he exuded the calm authority of a Person In Charge. With capital letters. I inched back a step, eyeing him. Another handsome one, and though I wasn't normally into older guys, he was definitely yummy.

But he was probably here to throw me out, which made him less yummy.

I cringed when he turned to me, waiting for the scowl, the demand for an explanation, and the inevitable dismissal.

Instead, he offered his hand. "I'm Darius, the GM. Welcome to the Crow and Hammer."

Oh, I was getting my ass booted to the curb by the general manager himself. Lucky me. I took his hand, surprised by his warm, strong grip. "Tori Dawson. Nice to meet you."

"The pleasure is mine," he replied with a sparkle in his gray eyes. "Thank you for your hard work tonight."

I waited for the inevitable "but I must ask you to leave."

He stretched his arm out and scooped Clara out of thin air— or, more likely, snatched her in mid-sprint out of the kitchen. "Clara, we're almost ready to begin, and I think the bartender has earned a break. Are you up for serving drinks after our meeting, Tori?"

"Uh." This conversation was not following my mental script. "Y-yes?"

"Excellent. Clara, set her up in the back for a break, and I'll serve the last few drinks here."

"Yes, sir." Clara grabbed my arm, and the next thing I knew, she'd steered me into the kitchen. "Ramsey, do you have an extra burger?"

"Already cooked one up for her." Sweat shone on his forehead and his eyeliner had smudged. I wasn't the only one who'd worked my butt off. "Hope you like all the fixings."

He passed me a plate with a loaded burger, melted cheese dripping down the thick sesame bun, and steaming fries dusted with seasonings. Clara pulled me into the cluttered office, and I waited with my plate as she unburied a corner of the desk.

"Get off your feet and relax," she told me. "The meeting will take about an hour, then I'll come get you."

"Are you sure? I didn't—"

"Just relax for a bit." She stepped backward through the doorway. "I need to get out there before they start. Help yourself to anything in the fridge to drink."

Alone, I picked up a fry and nibbled on the end, burning my tongue. She and Darius must have been desperate if they were letting me finish my shift. Sinking onto the chair, I replayed the margarita toss in my head. The expression on Aaron's face had been priceless.

I smirked at my burger. Job opportunity lost, but worth it. Who'd want to work here anyway? It was a pub of consummate jerks.

Clara was sweet, I amended. And Darius seemed pleasant enough, though he was probably playing nice to keep me around for the after-meeting rush. As I ate, I pondered the mystery meeting they were hosting. Such a weird group of people. What could possibly unite them for a shared gathering?

I bolted upright in my seat as I figured it out. *Assholes Anonymous.* This was a therapy group for mean people.

Snickering, I relaxed again, wincing at the ache in my back. My feet hurt and my formerly comfortable sandals had rubbed my pinky toes into blistered fireballs. How much longer would this shift last? If it went too long, I'd have a nervous wait at the bus stop.

Burger and fries finished—simple but delicious—I ventured to the walk-in and grabbed an old-fashioned bottle of coke. My dry throat, coated with remnant potato, stuck painfully as I twisted the top. What the hell? Who made soda bottles with real bottle caps?

On the verge of death from dehydration, I searched for a bottle opener. Yeah, I could have gotten water but I wanted the coke, damn it. I'd earned it. The bottle even had trickles of condensation running down the glass, just like in the commercials. I could almost *taste* it.

I'd left the bottle opener at my station. Popping out for a second to grab it wasn't a big deal, was it? I'd be quick. I crept to the saloon doors and cracked them open.

The pub was quiet except for Darius's clear voice. Every single Assholes Anonymous member sat facing the wall where Darius stood with a few papers in his hands. Clara waited beside him, nodding along as he spoke. Everyone listened intently like employees in a business meeting.

Actually, scratch that. The atmosphere was more like a task force being briefed on a recent crime. Way more serious than any employee meeting I'd ever attended.

Darius held the attention of the fifty or so people with flawless confidence. "The amendment to the regulations on GM accountability will require a few changes behind the scenes, but I don't expect it to affect our day-to-day workings. The MPD's document suggested strict enforcement, but—"

"But when has that ever stopped us?" someone called. Snickers sounded through the group.

"Dunno, boss." Aaron's familiar voice rang out, and I spotted the three guys at a table with a blue-haired girl. "Are you sure this won't change the first rule?"

"Don't hit first—" someone else began.

"*But always hit back!*" The shout rang from almost every voice in the building. Eyes wide, I stared incredulously as Darius smiled like a proud parent.

"The first rule will never change," he said. "After all, don't forget our second rule."

More laughter.

"Back to business. MPD has issued a few safety notices that—" His eyes turned and met mine.

I lurched backward, clutching my coke. As the doors swung into place again, his voice continued with barely a stutter, and no screech of chairs warned of a furious stampede to lynch me for eavesdropping. Retreating into the office, I sat my unopened coke on the desk.

Don't hit first, but always hit back. What kind of rule was that? If this really was an Assholes Anonymous support group, they were teaching all the wrong lessons. I bit my thumbnail. He'd talked about GM responsibilities and what sounded like a regulatory body of some kind—that MPD thing. Maybe this was related to businesses or restaurants or something.

I put it out of my mind. Whatever the meeting was for, it didn't matter because I wasn't coming back.

I waited out the rest of the hour playing a game on my phone, though I did take a couple minutes to text Justin more details about where I was, just in case he needed to identify my body later. Shortly after eight, Clara appeared in the doorway.

"How was your break?" she asked cheerily. "Ready to go again?"

"Yeah," I said heavily, not bothering to fake any enthusiasm.

Her forehead scrunched with what was either disappointment or worry, but before she could comment, I pulled myself together and smiled.

We returned to the front, and the atmosphere in the pub brought me to a halt just outside the saloon doors. Had Darius dosed everyone with laughing gas? Relaxed chatter filled the room, interspersed with joking tones and mirth. I blinked. Had to be drugs. No other explanation for the mood shift.

I got back to work, but it was a breeze compared to earlier. And though I would never call them friendly, the patrons' antagonism and impatience had subsided. Either that, or they were afraid I'd drench them if they were rude. Even the creepy old man was reasonably polite, so I poured him a real drink.

The next hour slipped by, and between customers, I assessed the bizarre gathering. An ancient Chinese couple was talking to a petite woman with a short bob that screamed attitude, her platinum hair streaked with pale pink. Beside her was a guy with dirty blond hair and thick glasses who looked like he'd gotten lost on his way to a tech convention.

Another table held a prim businesswoman with designer sunglasses perched on her head. Across from her was a young man with magnificent cheekbones and hair longer than mine done up in elaborate braids like an elfin cosplay. An old lady wearing a knit cap and turquoise-framed spectacles was showing off playing cards to a younger woman with teak-colored skin and wooden beads decorating her hair.

And, of course, the three Wonder Boys. Aaron the redhead joker, Kai the exotic smooth-talker, and the nameless third one. They lounged at a table with a pretty young woman, her wavy hair dyed bright blue. At least they were leaving me alone.

I ducked into the kitchen for more ice and found Ramsey perched on a stool, reading on his phone with a hairnet covering his goth locks. Filling my bucket, I hauled the ice back to the front—and groaned when I saw who was waiting for me.

"What now?" I asked Aaron testily.

He rolled his vibrant blue eyes. Kai and the other man flanked him, the former with his hands tucked in the pockets of his slim black jeans and the latter leaning casually against the bar.

"Well." Aaron cleared his throat. "Even though meeting nights are on the house, we went around and collected some tips for you."

I stared at him. "You … what?"

He pulled a wad of cash from his pocket and pushed it across the bar. "Don't play dumb. You earned it, new girl."

"My name is Tori," I snapped. I really wanted to snatch that pretty stack of bills, but I still had *some* pride.

A second passed, then I stuffed the money in my apron pocket. Who needs pride?

"Thanks," I added. "I appreciate it."

As though offended by my suggestion that he'd done something nice, Aaron shot his nameless friend a scowl. "It wasn't my idea … but yeah. I'm looking forward to hearing you insult Sylvia again."

"Are you looking forward to another margarita facial?" I retorted.

He flashed me a laughing grin that—to my horror—made my stomach flip. Just a little. Very minor. When he wasn't talking, the jerk was almost charming.

Aaron and Kai headed back to their table, but the third guy stayed put. "Could I trouble you for a coke?"

"Sure." I poured him one and slid it over. "Was it your idea to collect tips for me?"

"Mmm," he murmured vaguely. "Like Aaron said, you earned it. We aren't the easiest bunch to deal with."

I thought he meant Aaron and Kai, but then I realized he meant everyone—the whole weird lot of them. I glanced across the pub, then back to him. Even knowing it was there, the scar cutting across his features threw me off, but I didn't hesitate when I met his mismatched eyes.

He smiled—not Aaron's boisterous grin, but a quiet smile that exuded an infectious calm. And my stomach did another little somersault. Damn it.

"What's your name?" I blurted.

"Ezra." He offered his hand over the bar and I shook it. His grip was warm and strong, his palm calloused. "Thanks for putting up with us, Tori. I hope you'll stick around."

I pulled a face before I could stop myself.

"We're not that bad, I swear," he said with a laugh. "Anyone who can leave Aaron speechless will fit right in."

Carefully scooping up his drink like he might spill it—not that it was overly full or that my bar wasn't plenty spilled on already—he rejoined his friends. I watched him walk away, admiring the view. Three super-hot fit men, and *one* was actually nice. Not bad odds, I supposed.

The evening wound down over the next hour. Before I knew it, the pub had emptied, the patrons wandering out in twos and threes until it was just me, Clara, and Ramsey again. The quiet was almost deafening as I wiped tables and tucked in chairs. What a night. I was exhausted, and a heavy weight was growing in my stomach.

Time for another rejection.

I lifted my chin. Whatever. As much as I'd tried to control my temper, insulting rude customers, refusing to serve jerks, and standing up for myself while on the clock had been fun. I mean, most of the night had sucked balls, but throwing that margarita and shouting at Aaron had been satisfying as hell.

Sighing, I cleaned up the last few tables. As I returned to the bar, Clara burst through the saloon doors in the same haphazard rush as always. What could she possibly be hurrying over now?

"Tori! I was worried you'd left." She slumped against the bar, almost knocking the soda gun out of its holster. "What a night. My feet are killing me."

"Same."

Her eyebrows knitted together. "How did your night go? What did you think?"

"Me? Uh …" My brain fizzled. What kind of question was that after the way I'd behaved?

"I know they can be unpleasant," she said earnestly. "They're just very protective of—this is their safe place, you know? Anyone new is an unknown entity."

"Um … okay."

"You did a really good job—and you didn't ask me for help at all. Darius was impressed too."

I could have used help more than once, but Clara had been almost as slammed and—wait. Did she say the general manager was *impressed*? "You *were* watching, weren't you? Didn't Darius see me throw a drink on those guys?"

Clara laughed. "I didn't see it, but knowing Aaron, he had it coming. Kai and Ezra are almost as bad."

"You're not mad? You're not throwing me out?"

"Throwing you out?" Clara frowned at me. "Of course not. I want to hire you."

I braced a hand on the bar. "I'm sorry, but are you drunk?"

"Tori, you did an amazing job! I told you not to take any crap, and you didn't. The last five bartenders stuck around for all of a week, but I think you can handle it." She smiled encouragingly. "It gets better, I promise. Once they get used to you, you'll be a member of the gang in no time."

There was that word again. *Gang.* "Uh, Clara, don't take this the wrong way, but … is this place doing, you know, criminal stuff? Because I'm not into that kind of thing."

"Oh, no, no, we follow regulations, don't worry." She clasped her hands together. "What do you think, Tori? Will you give it a shot?"

What was this ironic twist of fate? A manager begging me to take the job instead of the other way around? "I'm not … sure."

Nasty people. Weird gang stuff. Alarming meeting mottos. Dangerous part of town. There weren't many pluses here.

"I'll start you at fifteen dollars an hour."

My eyes popped wide. Uh, okay, that was a plus.

"Your schedule will be Tuesdays to Saturdays from four to twelve," she continued. "Cooper covers the bar on Sundays and Mondays … though I may call you in if he's out for the day and you're available."

I pursed my lips. Four to twelve worked perfectly with my college schedule. Another plus.

"You can eat whatever you'd like while you're on shift and non-alcoholic drinks are free. As long as you keep it reasonable, you can have a few other drinks too."

Okay, now she was seriously tempting me. Great pay, great hours, and free food. "Will it be a problem if I'm, er, extra firm with difficult people when—"

"Oh, not at all," Clara said happily as though my question had been a hearty, "Ay, I'll take the job!" She dug into her pocket and pulled out a folded stack of bills. "Here's your pay for tonight. Can you work tomorrow? Sundays aren't normally your shift, but Cooper is sick and it'll be a quiet night for you to learn your way around and get more comfortable."

"Um." I blinked rapidly. "That sounds … good?"

"Wonderful! Can you come at three thirty? We can do up your paperwork so you'll be ready to go at four. And we can discuss your membership application then, if that's something you're interested in." She beamed and pulled me into an unexpected hug. "Welcome to the Crow and Hammer, Tori!"

I was still shell-shocked when she dashed off. I'd been prepared to walk out and never return. But ... I had the job? And I was getting paid *fifteen freaking bucks an hour*?

Tilting my head back, I squinted at the huge hammer hanging above the bar. My confused elation twisted into a prickling sensation that crept down my spine.

Just what had I gotten myself into?

5

I SAT at the peninsula in Justin's kitchen and eyed the neat stacks of bills laid out on the counter. The early afternoon sun streamed through the windows, warming my back. I pushed my loose curls, still damp from the shower, over my shoulders.

Lips pursed, I methodically counted the money for the third time.

By my best guess, Clara had paid me for a full eight-hour shift even though I'd worked less than six hours. And the rest … I hadn't stopped to count the tips Aaron, Kai, and Ezra had collected for me until I'd gotten home. If I'd realized how much had been in that wad of cash, I'd have been a *lot* nicer to Aaron.

Almost four hundred dollars. Four. *Hundred*. Dollars. They must have approached every single person in the pub and gotten them to cough up five or ten bucks. Times fifty people.

I bit my lower lip. Collecting tips had been Ezra's idea, but he seemed too quiet and soft-spoken for the job of getting money out of people. But Aaron and Kai … those two had likely done all the cajoling—or bullying.

Pushing away from the counter, I returned to the sofa and pulled my laptop onto my legs. The browser was still open to my earlier search. According to the internet, the Crow and Hammer had been in business for over fifty years, but its online presence was limited to a few restaurant review sites with no actual reviews, and one business listing.

No internet presence meant no desire to attract new customers. Clara had called it their "safe place" and mentioned something about a membership. I still couldn't figure out what would attract such an eclectic mix of people from all ages and walks of life to the same club, but maybe it was an invitation-only sort of deal. That would explain why they hadn't even bothered with a Facebook page.

But what if it was an illegal organization hiding behind a pub front? A criminal gang … with elderly members, businesswomen, girls my age, hot guys, goth cooks, and bubbly AGMs who gave new employees welcoming hugs.

Something didn't add up, but the big question wasn't what the Crow and Hammer really was.

The question was whether I wanted to work there.

My gaze slid to the pretty piles of money. I was still staring greedily when the front bolt turned and Justin limped inside, shoulders bowed and his police uniform smudged with dirt.

"Justin!" I tossed my laptop onto the sofa and ran down the hall. "Are you okay? What happened?"

"I'm fine," he assured me. "Tackled a guy, but I fell the wrong way and ended up in a ditch. All for nothing, too."

"All for nothing?" I ushered him down the hall to the kitchen where he sat on a stool. "But you caught the guy, didn't you?"

"I did, but I couldn't complete the arrest. All I could do was confiscate the cash he was carrying—thousands of dollars conned out of unsuspecting people. Filthy scam artist."

As he talked, I filled the kettle and plugged it in. For reasons I would never comprehend, Justin liked a cup of tea after a bad day. Me, I'd rather stomp around and shout at people until I felt better. Maybe he and I had gone into the wrong careers.

"I don't get it. You had him. Why couldn't you arrest him?"

Justin hesitated, then muttered, "Stupid politics, I guess. It was out of my hands."

"That's bullshit."

"I think so too." He tapped a finger on the counter. "Tori, I've got to ask. What's with the cash?"

I got out a mug, ignoring my stacks of money. "Rent payment."

"Is this all from that shift you picked up last night? Looks like you got good tips."

"*Really* good tips." I poured hot water over the teabag and slid the mug to him. "They offered me a full-time position. Tuesday to Saturday, four to midnight."

He didn't congratulate me, instead picking up the twenties from Clara and fanning them out. "Judging from your texts while you were on break, I got the impression it wasn't going well."

"Me neither, but ... I guess they want someone who's tougher? The clients are assholes, but"—I nodded at the money—"they tip well."

"What's this place called again? Where is it?"

I described my night, glossing over the weirder details because, I mean, how did I explain the motto chanting at the meeting?

"That's a rough area. It's not safe, especially for a woman by herself." He set the cash down. "And no offense, but it doesn't make sense that they'd hire you if you were throwing drinks and insulting people."

"Yeah, I agree it's weird, but maybe they're really desperate." I sat beside him. "It's a job, right? And I really need it. I can work there for now, and keep applying for something better."

"It's not worth the risk. I can help you out until you find a new job—a safe one. Who knows if this place will stiff you—or worse?"

"I can handle it." I wasn't letting Justin take care of me. He was already sharing his apartment. "It'll only be for a couple weeks."

"You can't walk home at midnight, not there."

"There's a bus stop a block away." When he gave me a hard look, I grumbled, "I'll take a cab home." That would eat into my earnings.

"It isn't worth it. Let that job go and keep searching." He pulled the money into a single pile and slid it toward me. "Hang on to this. I'll cover rent this month."

"No." I pushed it back toward him. "If I'm going to live here, I'm going to pay my fair share."

He narrowed his eyes and I glared back. Angrily gulping the rest of his tea, he stood. "Why won't you ever let me help you, Tori?"

Not waiting for a response, he headed into his bedroom. I watched him close the door, ignoring a trickle of guilt. I was keeping things even between us as best I could—paying rent, cleaning, keeping all my stuff confined to boxes.

I scooped up the money and stuffed it into Justin's mail organizer. Despite my terrible employment track record, I hadn't missed a rent payment yet and I wasn't going to. Even if that meant a stint as a bartender at the mysterious Crow and Hammer.

Let's hope the place was as law-abiding as Clara claimed, because if not ... ruining Justin's career on top of mine would just be the icing on this year's craptastic cake.

THE WALK from Justin's apartment to the Crow and Hammer took just over thirty minutes. This time, I wore sensible shoes with capris pants and a sleeveless emerald blouse. My red curls were tamed into a ponytail, my bangs swept to one side where they would hopefully stay. I was ready for another shift from hell.

If I was honest, the jittery anticipation pooling in my stomach was definitely more positive than negative. With an energetic bounce in my step, I inhaled the cool breeze, smelling of rain to come. I had a job, my wage had taken a *huge* jump, and management let me yell at customers. I really couldn't complain.

The bright colors and busy sidewalks of Gastown transformed into the barred windows and boarded-up doors of the Downtown Eastside, and within a few blocks, I was turning down a nondescript street. I stopped in front of a black door with peeling paint and faded lettering. Back again.

When I reached for the door, sickening repulsion swept away my excitement. Like yesterday, I had the overwhelming urge to run in the opposite direction. Teeth gritted, I shoved through the door.

The interior was quiet, but the rumble of voices drifted down the staircase in the corner. Only three customers were grouped around a table—a trio of familiar guys. Red hair, black hair, and brown curls were bent over a spread of paper.

As I approached, Ezra's head lifted. His mismatched eyes, one warm brown and one white, met mine. "She returns!"

Aaron straightened, his grin flashing. "Back for more punishment, new girl?"

"Don't worry, I'm well armed." I'd have my soda gun, after all.

As I breezed past their table, Clara zoomed out of the kitchen with a handful of papers.

"Tori!" She beamed at me. "I was afraid you might change your mind."

"Nope, not me." I slid onto a bar stool as she rifled through the papers. Aaron, Kai, and Ezra had turned their attention to a large map.

"I'm relieved." Clara pulled out a paper and slid it to me, then handed me a pen. "I'm so far behind. I have six months of paperwork I can finally catch up on now that I don't have to share bar shifts with Cooper. He'll be delighted to go back to his usual schedule too. Working hard isn't his forte."

I nodded absently as I frowned at the sheet. It didn't look like any employment paperwork I'd ever filled out before. A logo at the top of the page displayed the letters MPD—the same acronym Darius had mentioned during the meeting last night.

With a mental shrug, I started filling it out. All the usual info—name, birthdate, address, phone number, emergency contacts. A line near the top asked for a "MID Number" but I skipped it. Employee number, maybe? Clara could figure it out.

I finished that one and she slid over a perfectly normal tax form. A few tables away, Aaron's voice rose, irritation lining his words, but I stayed focused on the form. Last thing I needed was to screw it up and have the government subtract double taxes or something.

"I'll need to make a copy of your ID and your server certificate," Clara said, reading over the first form. "Oh, and you forgot your MID number."

I dug my wallet out of my purse and passed her my driver's license. "I forgot my what?"

She didn't hear me as she took my ID. "Oh, you're from Ontario? Do you drive? We have a parking lot."

"I drove in Ontario," I commented dryly. "But not here. Who needs a car?"

She laughed. "No one who lives downtown has a car—except that dummy." She called the last part at the three guys and Aaron flipped her the bird without pausing his annoyed tirade—something about being more cautious than a granny on an ice rink.

Clara snorted, amused by his response. Me, I wanted to smack him for being rude.

"Anyway," she said, pulling a second pen from her pocket. "I'll add your MID number while you …"

I looked up. She was squinting at my license with a deep furrow between her brows. Then she extended my card. "I need your real ID."

"Uh." I blinked. "That is a real ID."

"No, I mean, your *real* ID."

"Like … my passport?"

"No, your MID!" She waved my license in emphasis. "This doesn't have an MID number."

I leaned back, confused by her sudden agitation. "What's an MID number?"

"That's not funny." When I gazed vacantly at her, she visibly paled. "Tori, what's your class?"

"My class?"

She pressed her hands to the bar top, eyes wide. "Your class, what is it?"

"You mean at the community college? I'm taking—"

"No, your mythic class!" She shoved my card under my nose, even more frantic. "Why doesn't your license have a mythic identification number? You're *registered*, aren't you?"

"Registered for what? Clara, I don't have a clue what you're talking about."

Panic flashed in her eyes. "Oh my god. I don't believe it."

"Don't believe … what?"

"You're *human*."

I blinked again. Squinted. Rubbed one ear like I might have misheard. "Beg your pardon?"

Clara dropped my ID on the bar and hid her face behind her hands. "Darius is going to kill me. Why didn't I check your ID last night? I'm an idiot."

"Clara," I said, alarmed and confused in equal measure. "I swear it's a real ID. I'm twenty-one, old enough to bartend, and—"

"That's not the problem," she moaned. "How did you even find out about this place? About the job?" She whipped her hands down. "Do you have a mythic relative? Did they tip you off about the job? Please tell me you do."

"What's a mythic?"

"Oh god. I'm in so much trouble. I never should have—but you were *perfect*. You weren't scared of anyone—not even Aaron! I thought you were some badass mythic who wanted to bartend, but you—"

"Get over yourself, Aaron." Kai's angry voice rose over Clara's. "We're not doing this your way—not again. Your plans always end in fireballs and explosions."

Fireballs? *Explosions?* I glanced at them as Aaron snapped, "What's wrong with that?"

"Tori." Clara's panicked tone drew my attention back to her as Kai and Aaron continued to argue. "Last night, did you see anything?"

"Huh?"

"Did you see anything … *unusual?*"

"Did I see anything unusual?" I repeated. "Like what?"

"Say that again," Aaron shouted furiously, "and I'll toast your pale ass to a healthy crisp!"

His hand shot into the air—and fire burst from his fingers. The red flames danced across his skin, sparks raining down on the table. Curling his hand into a fist, he cocked his arm back, aiming for Kai.

"Aaron!" Clara shrieked. "Put your fire away!"

He froze in mid-motion, his fist still blazing. "Clara? What's wrong?"

"Put it out!" she yelled, her voice high with panic. "Now!"

He flicked his fingers open and the flames vanished. "Jeez, don't get your panties in a twist. I wasn't actually going to roast him."

"Just—just *shut up* for once in your life, Aaron!" Clara pressed her hands to her head like she was trying to squeeze her brain. "This is already bad enough."

"What's bad?" He pushed back from the table and strode over, Kai and Ezra on his heels. "What's going on?"

I didn't move, my eyes fixed on his hand—his hand that had been engulfed in flames. Did that count as *unusual*?

"I screwed up," Clara groaned, covering her face again like she couldn't stand to see me. "I didn't check her ID yesterday."

Aaron slid my driver's license off the bar top and read it. "*Victoria* Dawson? Your name is Victoria?"

I shook off my shock to scowl at his sniggering tone.

Kai plucked the card out of Aaron's hand. "There's no MID number."

"Is it a fake ID?" Aaron asked with amusement. "Did you hire a rogue, Clara?"

"Worse," Clara whispered. "She's *human*."

The three guys stared at me, and I stared back without the slightest idea what the hell anyone was talking about. But more important than the incomprehensible conversation was the fact Aaron's hand had been *on fire*, and I couldn't figure out how it could possibly have been a trick.

"No way," Aaron finally said. "What's your class, Tori?"

I pointed at his hand. "Was that real fire?"

"Oh, shit," Kai muttered. "How did she get past the repelling ward on the door?"

"How did she know about the *job posting*? She doesn't even know what the MPD is." Clara pulled a stool from the back corner behind the bar and dropped onto it. "Darius is definitely going to kill me."

"So …" I straightened on my seat. "You guys planning to explain what you're all going on about?"

"No," Clara said. "I'm sorry, Tori, but I can't hire you. You shouldn't even be here."

Sharp disappointment shot through me, followed by stinging rejection. Somehow, I wasn't surprised. This job was too good to be true.

Whatever they were talking about, I wouldn't beg for an explanation. If they didn't want me here, I was gone. I pulled my license out of Kai's hand and returned it to my wallet, then slung my purse over my shoulder. Clara didn't meet my eye as I got to my feet.

I was about to walk to the door with all the dignity I could muster, but a niggling curiosity stopped me. I swung back toward Aaron. "Hey, um, before I go, could I … see the fire thing again?"

Surprise flickered across his face, then he grinned.

Clara straightened sharply. "Aaron, don't—"

He extended his hand toward me, palm turned up. Sparks flashed over his fingers, then flames ignited on his palm, racing over his skin like he'd dipped his hand in oil. Warmth bathed my face. Holy shit, it was real fire.

Grin widening, he flexed his fingers. The fire burst outward, engulfing his hand, then raced up his arm and over his shoulder. I jerked back, the heat blasting my exposed skin. He relaxed his arm and the flames extinguished, leaving his skin and shirt unmarked.

"Whoa," I breathed. "That was cool."

"No, it was hot," Ezra corrected.

Clara growled. "Aaron, you are *breaking—the—law*. Stop showing off. She needs to leave."

"Oh, come on, Clara. She won't blab. Right, Tori?"

"Nope," I said with a pop on the P. Besides, who would I blab to? I looked at Kai and Ezra. "Can you two light yourselves on fire too?"

The corner of Kai's mouth lifted in an amused smirk. He clenched his hand and white electricity crackled up his arm.

"Fire is overrated," he said.

I turned eagerly to Ezra, but he sighed glumly. "My element isn't flashy. I'm just a boring aeromage."

"What's that?"

He waved his hand vaguely and a puff of wind spun around me, whipping my ponytail into my face. I shoved my hair back, goggle-eyed.

"If you three don't cut it out," Clara growled, "I'll report you to Tabitha."

Aaron flinched. "Don't do that. She's just itching to write me up."

"Tori, you need to leave now. Please."

"Hold on," Kai said. "It isn't illegal for humans to work for guilds."

"No, but there are a million regulations we can't meet." Clara shook her head. "That aside, it would never work. She'd get eaten alive."

"She seems tough enough," Ezra disagreed.

"She was tough yesterday because she didn't know she should be afraid!" Clara pointed at Aaron. "She doesn't know the Sinclair name. She threw a drink on you because she had no idea you could light her on fire in retaliation."

"She's hilarious." Aaron beamed like he treasured the memory of my margarita-throwing meltdown. "We should keep her."

"What?"

"You need a bartender," Kai pointed out. "Desperately. Give her a chance, see how she does."

"But …" Clara shook her head again. "No. It'll never work. She won't want to bartend for a guild anyway."

"A guild?" I echoed.

"See? She doesn't know *anything*. She—"

"Clara," Ramsey the cook hollered from the kitchen. "The repairmen are here!"

Clara looked wildly from me to the saloon doors. Ramsey stuck his head out, his dark hair swept over one side of his face.

"Repairmen," he repeated. "For the freezer? They're waiting for you at the back door."

As he vanished into the kitchen, Clara glowered at Aaron, Kai, and Ezra. "You three, keep your blabbermouths shut. Tori, I'm really sorry, but you need to go."

With a final warning glare at the four of us, she rushed into the kitchen. The saloon doors were still swinging when she popped out again, a finger pointed accusingly at the guys as though she'd expected to catch them in the act. "I mean it! I'll be back in a minute."

She disappeared. I waited to see if she was really gone this time, then glanced at the three guys. Three … mages.

With a sly smile, Aaron pulled his wallet from his back pocket, slid his driver's license out, and handed it to me. I blinked down at it. Beneath his photo, the logo from Clara's paperwork stood out boldly, a ten-digit number beside it.

"Oooh," I murmured. "So *that's* an MID number."

"Mythic identification number," Aaron said. "A mythic is anyone who can use magic, and we're all registered with the MPD, an international regulatory body."

"Will you get in trouble for telling me that?"

He shrugged and slipped the card back into his wallet. "I'm always in trouble."

That didn't surprise me. Clara's voice echoed from the kitchen, interspersed with the rumble of unfamiliar men. Since she seemed busy, I sidled closer to Aaron. "What's a guild?"

He spread his arms grandly, taking in the whole building. "This."

I pulled my face into a twist of annoyance at the unhelpful answer.

Laughing, he slouched against the bar. "It's kind of like a union for mythics. MPD requires all mythics be guilded, and the guilds ensure their members follow proper regulations."

"And the foremost regulation," Kai told me, "is keeping mythics out of the public eye. As far as the general populace is concerned, we don't exist."

But some people suspected they existed. Like my brother, a decent minority believed in the wild conspiracy theory that magic hid in plain sight among us and was overseen by a mysterious, government-like organization. I'd never given the tales any more credence than UFO landings or lizard men controlling the White House.

"Technically," Kai added, "we violated regulations by letting you in here, but you walked in on your own, so ..."

"How *did* you find out about this place?" Ezra asked curiously.

I dug into my purse and handed him the page with three job postings. He, Aaron, and Kai clustered together to read it.

"I found it in the street," I admitted. "I was having trouble getting work downtown, so I figured I'd give the bartending job a try."

"Good thing." Kai tapped the page. "Things wouldn't have gone well for you at that law office. Those guys are trouble."

The saloon doors flew outward. Spotting me, Clara stomped over. "What did you tell her?" she barked at Aaron. "I *told* you—"

"It's fiiiine," he drawled, waving a dismissive hand. "You should give Tori a chance, Clara. She can handle it."

Um. Could I? My head was spinning and I really wanted to sit down. Assuming this wasn't an elaborate prank or an unusually convincing hallucination, I'd stumbled into a magical guild populated by a fire mage, an electricity mage, an aeromage, and forty-something other "mythics." All those strange people from last night—young and old, normal and weird—were magic users.

Clara took my arm and guided me into motion. "I'm sorry, but—"

"Hold up." Aaron caught my other arm and spun me out of Clara's grip. His hand felt five degrees warmer than it should have. "Before you kick her out, let's ask Darius."

"I don't think—" Clara began fretfully.

Aaron didn't wait for her protest. He steered me toward the staircase in the corner, Kai and Ezra following. Clara rushed after us as we headed up the steps to the mysterious second level.

The landing revealed a huge room, as large as the pub and filled with worktables and mismatched chairs. A bank of computer desks ran along one wall, and whiteboards, cork boards, and a floor-to-ceiling map of the city covered the other walls. A flat-screen TV mounted in the corner had a scrolling list of text.

Half a dozen people, some I vaguely recognized, were working at the tables or hunched over the desks, but I barely caught a glimpse before Aaron directed me to the second flight of stairs across the landing. We zipped up to the third floor and into a hallway, where Aaron led me through an open door. The large room inside held three messy desks piled with papers, binders, and several monitors each.

"Hey guys," Aaron said breezily to the three people manning the desks. "Is Darius in?"

A woman, tall and thin with alabaster skin, jaw-length wispy brown hair, and sharp cheekbones, gave Aaron a stern stare. "You are not permitted on this level, Sinclair."

"But since Darius is on this level, here I am."

"Actually," the older of the two men said, "Darius isn't here. He left for the MPD conference this morning, which you'd know if you'd listened during the meeting last night."

Aaron grimaced over his shoulder. "Clara, why didn't you say he was gone?"

"I forgot," she muttered.

The third occupant of the room, a blond guy with a wiry frame and large glasses that I recognized from last night—I'd identified him as a tech refugee—walked around his desk. "What do you want to see Darius about?"

"Darius is the GM—the guild master," Aaron told me. "Clara is the assistant guild master. Her role is mainly administrative. These guys are the guild officers—kind of like shift supervisors. They're next in charge."

Not general manager. Guild master. Oops.

"Sinclair—" the woman began with a note of irritation.

"Clara, you're up," Aaron proclaimed.

She marched past him and turned. "Tori, please stay. Aaron, Kai, Ezra—out. Now."

"But—"

"Out!" the other woman barked.

Aaron and his friends retreated. Clara shut the door behind them and heaved an exasperated breath.

"So ..." the blond guy murmured. "What's going on, Clara?"

She pulled out an extra chair for me and I perched on the edge, evaluating the three officers. The older man, with shoulder-length salt-and-pepper hair, a thick beard, and a glorious mustache, would've looked dignified if not for the amused arch to his expressive eyebrows. The woman, maybe forty, was beautiful in a marble statue sort of way—flawless but without a hint of warmth. The blond guy was the youngest, probably in his thirties, and really seemed like he should be programming a robot or something.

"Tori, this is Girard, the first officer. Tabitha, the second officer. And Felix, the third officer. Since Darius isn't here ..." Clara pursed her lips unhappily. "I made a mistake last night. I didn't check Tori's ID, and it turns out she isn't registered."

"Is she a mythic?" Tabitha asked sharply.

"One hundred percent human."

"Then send her home."

Standing beside my chair, Clara shifted her weight. "She did very well yesterday, and I'm desperate to fill the bartender position so I can focus on my work again. We've never employed a human before, but—"

"Absolutely not," Tabitha interrupted.

Huh. Given Clara's protests downstairs, I hadn't expected her to vouch for me.

"The allowances for hiring non-mythics exist for guilds with public-facing businesses," Tabitha continued, "which does not apply to us. Humans have no place in or around the Crow and Hammer."

"If Tori can fulfill the role," Felix mused, "perhaps we should consider it. Clara has been stretched thin for too long."

"The girl did a fine job last night," Girard added, smiling through his beard. "She tamed our fiery beast with admirable efficiency."

Tabitha's face went even colder. "Regardless, the MPD will never approve her employment, and if we apply, we'll suffer significant fines for the regulations we've already broken."

"It may not be a long-term solution," Felix said, "but the paperwork will take a couple weeks to process. It would give Clara a break."

"What about the fines?"

Felix thought for a second. "Deduct them from Aaron's bonuses."

"Hey!" came a muffled protest from the other side of the door.

Growling, Clara turned on her heel and stalked into the hall, slamming the door behind her and leaving me alone with the guild officers.

"To be frank," Girard told me, "the chances of the MPD approving your employment are slim to none, but we can hire you until they give an official refusal. Are you interested in working here for a couple weeks?"

I honestly had no idea, but I've never been good at admitting uncertainty to strangers. "It seems like it'll be an interesting experience. I'm game."

"Your tenacity is admirable, but misplaced." Tabitha's dark eyes swept across the other two officers. "I won't support her working here, even temporarily. The Crow and Hammer is an exclusive collection of carefully vetted mythics committed to our mandate and loyal to our success. She's a human with no concept of guild loyalty."

Girard stroked his beard. "I always figured we were a ragtag band of misfits and rogues who don't fit anywhere else."

Tabitha glared at him. "Our members count on the skills and competence of their fellow mythics. She's a liability."

"She'll be tending the bar, Tabitha, not taking jobs."

"What of *her* safety, then? She was deliberately antagonistic yesterday. Not all our members have perfected their self-restraint, and if she continues that behavior, she could get hurt."

Girard and Felix regarded each other with furrowed brows, offering no counterargument. I shifted in my seat, wondering what the hell I'd gotten myself into. They didn't care about Tabitha's other arguments, but the question of my *safety* had stopped them cold. That did not bode well.

Girard straightened. "I know just the solution. Aaron!"

The door opened and Aaron stepped inside, Clara on his heels, red-faced and glowering.

"Yes, sir?" Aaron asked with a casual salute.

Girard steepled his fingers. "I'm assigning you as Tori's chaperone while she's on the premises. You'll be responsible for her safety whenever she's here."

"You're ... wait, what?"

"Girard—" Tabitha began in a catlike growl.

"It's perfect," Girard said. "Aaron is well equipped to keep any antagonism from other members in check, and—"

"Sinclair *inspires* more antagonism than—"

"*And* it's an excellent opportunity to evaluate Aaron's commitment to taking on more responsibility." Girard turned his amused brown eyes on the speechless fire mage. "An officer can't pick and choose his duties, Aaron. If you want to be considered for a future promotion, you need to prove you can approach dull jobs with the same dedication as exciting ones."

"But—but—why *me?*"

"You brought her up here," Felix pointed out. "If you didn't want to be involved, you should have kept your nose out of it."

Aaron spluttered. "But how will I get anything done? We're in the middle of the bounty for that rogue sorcerer, and—"

"If you need to delegate, you can ask Kai and Ezra to help you," Girard suggested. "Though if you plan to pass the job off to anyone else, be sure they're as capable and committed as you."

"But …"

Girard turned to his fellow officers. "Any objections?"

Felix shrugged. "Sounds good to me."

"I object to everything," Tabitha snapped.

Girard sat back in his chair. "We don't have the authority to override Clara's hiring decisions unless there's a threat to the guild. Tori isn't a threat, and Aaron's supervision will forestall any serious drama. I'm satisfied we've addressed the relevant concerns." A note of finality entered his voice. "The decision is up to Clara and Tori."

Tabitha's dark eyes, flashing with anger, slid to me. "Then I hope you'll make an intelligent decision, Tori."

I like to think I'm not susceptible to intimidation, but I'll admit my heartbeat stuttered just a little. Still, Tabitha had made a critical oversight. She didn't realize that contrariness was my favorite hobby. At her words, my doubts extinguished faster than Aaron's magical flames, replaced by stubborn determination.

"Like I said," I announced, casually folding my arms. "I'm game."

Girard and Felix smiled. Tabitha glared. Clara frowned.

Aaron groaned loudly. "Damn it, new girl. You've singlehandedly ruined my month."

I grinned. Even better.

6

MY DOUBTS returned once I was back on the main level. Clara had me finish the new-hire paperwork, then vanished into the kitchen to supervise the freezer repairs, leaving me to man the bar—along with my new chaperone.

Aaron slumped at a table, his head in his arms, while Kai and Ezra watched him sulk with the caring sympathy of close friends. Nah, just kidding. They looked entertained as hell, zero sympathy in their smirks.

"You realize this will completely screw our schedule, right?" Aaron complained, his voice muffled. "We have to be here, instead of working, for five days a *week*."

"*We* don't have to be anywhere," Kai said. "Just you."

Aaron groaned again. "Ezra, I'll trade you. You do the babysitting, and I'll go with Kai on jobs."

"No way."

"I'll give you half my bonuses for however long Tori is here."

I raised my eyebrows, busy wiping down my station while I listened in. Aaron must really want out of this assignment, but I didn't feel bad for him. I felt bad for *me* having to put up with him all shift, every shift.

"Eighty percent," Ezra countered.

"That's robbery!"

"Forget it then."

"Sixty percent."

"Eighty."

"Sixty-five."

"Eighty."

"Goddamn it!"

Hmm, too bad. I would've rather spent my shifts with Ezra than Aaron. I'd even take Kai as a second choice. I finished wiping the counters, eyed the empty pub, then headed for the guys' table. They watched me pull out a chair and sit.

"Are you *sure* you want this job?" Aaron asked plaintively. "You'll be out the door in a couple weeks once the paperwork goes through."

"I can earn a paycheck while I apply for a new position. It's great." I propped my chin on my hand. "Weren't you the one who said, 'Let's keep her!' less than an hour ago?"

"That was *before* I had to babysit you."

I shrugged one shoulder. "Not my problem."

He glared, a dangerous gleam in his eyes, and the air around him heated. "You've got a bad attitude, new g—"

"Don't be an asshole, Aaron," Ezra interrupted quietly. "Intimidating her is low."

I almost told them that I wasn't intimidated—a lie, but whatever—except I was too fascinated by the way Aaron's temper subsided at his friend's calm words. He slouched in his chair, saying nothing.

Yep, I'd definitely prefer Ezra as my chaperone over Aaron. Too bad Ezra was a tough negotiator.

It bothered me that I needed a chaperone at all, but I wasn't an idiot. I had no idea how far in over my head I was. With that in mind, I needed to find out what I'd signed up for—and if I didn't like what I heard, I just wouldn't return for my next shift. Problem solved.

Getting up, I poured four rum and cokes, then carried them back to the table and set them out for the guys. As I sat, Kai picked up Ezra's glass and put it on his other side.

"Thanks," Ezra murmured, picking it up with oddly careful movements.

I glanced questioningly between him and Kai.

"He would have spilled it all over our stuff." Kai gestured at the map spread over the table, then added, "He's blind in that eye."

"He … oh."

As I tried not to stare at the scar cutting down his face over his strangely pale eye, Ezra smiled ruefully. "My depth perception sucks. I have to be careful about knocking things over."

I hesitated, unsure if questions might offend him. I might be ruder than a pirate with a broken peg leg, but I wasn't a total jerk. "What happened?"

His expression sobered. "An accident. There was this ice cream truck—"

"Not *that* story again," Kai interrupted. "You need a better one."

"You don't like the shark attack one either."

"That scar looks nothing like a shark bite."

"Maybe it was a one-toothed shark," Ezra suggested seriously.

Aaron leaned toward me. "The actual story is that he was running with a pair of scissors and—"

"I hate that one," Ezra complained. "I sound like an idiot."

"And you *don't* sound like an idiot talking about an ice cream tr—"

"Okay, okay, forget I asked," I said, waving my hands. "What I really want to know is ..." I trailed off, unsure where to start.

"You want to know about mythics and guilds and how much of the conspiracy theory bullshit is real," Kai guessed.

"Yeah, pretty much."

"How do you even explain it from scratch?" Aaron took a gulp of his drink. "There's so much."

Kai rubbed his jaw. "*Should* we explain it? If this job is temporary, the less she knows, the better."

"Even with Aaron watching out for her, she needs to understand the basics," Ezra said. "Ignorance is dangerous. She should know about magic classes and their most common orders."

Oh, so that's why they'd kept asking me what my "class" was?

"The coolest and most powerful class is Elementaria," Aaron told me smugly. "It only has one order: mages."

"And you three are all mages," I observed. "Fire, air, and ... lightning?"

"Electramage." Kai cradled his drink in one hand. "Aaron is a pyromage. Ezra is an aeromage."

"Arcana is the commonest of the classes." Aaron pulled a face. "Boring as shit. Spellcasting is the most tedious magic you can imagine. All sorts of rules, you need to learn ancient languages and memorize runes, and their incantations sound ridiculous."

"Arcana requires a lot of study," Ezra told me. "But it can be very powerful."

"The other common one is Psychica." Aaron wrinkled his nose derisively. "You know, psychic powers and stuff. They can be useful, but most psychics are little more than charlatans with a minor gift."

Kai stirred his drink with his straw. "The last two classes are Spiritalis and Demonica, but we only have five witches and no—"

"Wait," I interrupted. "Demonica? As in *demons?*"

Kai and Aaron nodded.

"Demons are *real?* Like, 'sell me your soul,' devil-with-pointy-horns demons?"

"Not quite like that, but ..." Kai pressed his lips together. "Whatever you're picturing, a real demon is more terrifying."

I may have paled.

"We don't have any demon summoners *or* contractors in the Crow and Hammer," Aaron assured me. "No Demonica mythics at all."

"That's good," I said faintly. Maybe I should take notes. I already felt overwhelmed.

Ezra noticed my dazed look. "There's an easy acronym for the classes. SPADE—Spiritalis, Psychica, Arcana, Demonica, Elementaria."

I arched an eyebrow at Aaron. "If Elementaria is the best class, why is it last?"

"Because *ESPAD* sounds dumb."

"How do you keep all this hidden?" I asked. "Guys who can light themselves on fire—"

"That's not the only thing I can do."

"—or make gusts of wind or cast spells or whatever. Why is magic just a rumor people scoff at?"

"You can thank the MPD." Kai drummed his fingers on the table. "MPD stands for Magicae Politiae Denuntiatores and they—"

"Magi-what?" I interrupted, boggled by the dozen or more syllables of *whoa-shit-was-that-Latin?*

"Exactly," Aaron agreed with obvious amusement. "That's why we usually call them MagiPol. You know, like Interpol, except for magic shit instead of criminals. They're hella strict. *Everything* is regulated." He downed the last of his rum and coke in one gulp. "I need another drink before I even start on that."

With a brief smile, I returned to the bar, but before I could start another round of rum and cokes, a few people from the second floor came down searching for food and drinks. By the time I took their orders, made their drinks, rang them up, and called the order back to Ramsey, another group had wandered in through the main entrance.

As I made their drinks, I wondered what sort of mythics they were. Mages? Psychics? Arcana spellcasters? Hadn't Aaron mentioned witches too?

At least there were no demons among them. Everything else, sure, but I was not okay with literal hellions.

Then again, I wasn't sure I was okay with any of this. Guilds. Mythics. MagiPol. Strict rules and regulations. Nervousness fluttered through me but I squashed the feeling down. I could handle it. A couple weeks of work, then I'd be on my merry way to a nice, normal job where standing up for myself meant getting fired—not barbequed by a pyromage.

I glanced at Aaron, flanked by Kai and Ezra as they pored over their map. The pyromage was my guardian, but the fact I needed a protector was a big flashing danger sign I really shouldn't ignore.

I WOULD have loved to lounge around on Monday, enjoying my day off work, but I had classes. I was up by 9:30 and out the door by 9:45. And, since it took twenty minutes at a fast walk to reach the community college, that meant I was late for my ten-o'clock class.

Considering what I was paying per course, I should have been focused on every word coming out of the instructor's mouth, but my attention kept wandering. Tax law for small businesses wasn't quite as riveting as it had been on Friday— not compared to the hidden world of magic I'd discovered over the weekend.

I hadn't seen Justin yet and I had no idea what to tell him. He was already a magic conspiracy theorist, which I did not understand since policemen were supposed to be down to earth and all that, but sharing what I'd learned didn't seem smart. He'd either think I was crazy, or he'd think the job was way too dangerous. Or he'd think I was on drugs.

As the instructor flipped to the next slide in his presentation, I absently blew my bangs out of my face and squinted at the text. I needed to pay attention if I ever wanted to own a business.

Contrary to popular belief, I wasn't stupid. Impulsive and temperamental, but not stupid. I knew I had issues with regular employment. No matter how hard I tried, I always ran afoul of either customers or management, then poof! My job was gone. I hated the uncertainty of imminent termination hanging over my head.

I wanted a job where no one could fire me. I wanted a paycheck that couldn't be docked. I wanted to buy my own place where no one could kick me out. I wanted to work hard and earn a living and support myself, and I didn't want *anyone* to have the power to take that away from me.

In other words, stability. Seriously, was that so much to ask for?

That goal was the reason I was sitting in this classroom. Courses on small businesses—planning one, starting one, running one. Everything I needed to know to start up a business where I could be my own boss. As for what sort of business I wanted to run, I hadn't figured that out yet. The important part was me running it. Alone.

I tapped my pen against my lower lip. Maybe an online business. Then I'd have time to think about my response before telling customers I'd rather swallow a puffer fish whole than give them a refund.

My thoughts drifted back to the Crow and Hammer. Keeping half an eye on the instructor's presentation, I opened a private browser tab and squinted at the search bar. Hmm.

Five minutes of Googling illustrated this shit wasn't searchable. Any combination of the words mythic, guild, mage, arcana, and magic produced millions of hits—all books, games, movies, TV shows, and comic books. I'd have to sift through fan Wiki pages for hours to find a single real result, and even then, how would I separate fact from fiction?

I popped onto the Wikipedia page about magic conspiracy theories and read through all the sections. Most of it sounded as cuckoo as it had before I'd learned magic was real, but I noted a few tidbits about government surveillance and a powerful international organization suppressing all information about magic. The MPD—Magicae Politiae … something—was the easiest concept to grasp out of everything Aaron had explained. Discussing magic made my head spin, but red-tape bureaucracy was familiar to anyone who'd ever filed taxes.

Back to Google. My search of "MPD" produced a whole lot of boring businesses, but after scrolling through six pages of results, I found an ugly white website for a financial investment company—with a logo that matched the one on Clara's forms and Aaron's ID. The homepage was a login portal, waiting for a username and password. Well, that was a dead end.

I closed the tab and tried to focus on my lesson, but it was hard. Magic existed. Mages were real, and I'd met three. I'd trespassed in their forbidden world, and for a short time, I could be part of it.

The distraction was a small price to pay for the chance to explore a hidden society of magic and those who wielded it.

7

TUESDAY. Shift number three. I arrived ten minutes early—the community college was only fifteen minutes away—and started setting up. The place was empty. Ramsey wasn't in yet, and Aaron, Kai, and Ezra weren't around either.

On Sunday night, the guys had assured me I didn't have to tell anyone I was human—that it was better if I didn't. Let the guild members assume I was a mythic. The longer they went not knowing how "powerful" I might be, the less likely they'd be to throw a fit about my human-ness contaminating their precious headquarters.

But no sooner did I set up the bar than two guys came trotting down the stairs and made a beeline for me.

"Is it true?" the younger one asked eagerly. "Are you *human?*"

Why did they all say "human" like it was a contagious disease? I scanned him up and down, unimpressed. Short, wiry, with bleach-blond hair in a messy mop and odd round sunglasses perched on his nose despite the dim interior. A couple years younger than me by my best guess.

His pal was a bit older and average looking—nothing obviously weird about him. He wasn't anywhere near as fit as Aaron, Kai, and Ezra, but he wasn't flabby either. Brown hair and deep-set eyes with dark circles under them.

"Well?" the bottle-blond demanded. "Are you?"

Clearly, someone had spilled the beans. "Yeah. Who told you?"

"Everyone is talking about it." He stuck out his hand. "Name's Liam. Telekinetic."

"Tori." I shook his hand. "Telekinetic means … moving things with your mind?"

He flashed a smile. My spray bottle of cleaning solution lifted weightlessly into the air, and I couldn't hold back my shocked gasp. Whoa. It was just like film special effects, except for real. Concentration tightened his face, and a liquor bottle from my station floated upward too. The whiskey drifted over and settled gently on the counter in front of me.

I picked up the bottle, half convinced it was a prop. "That's gotta be handy."

"Pretty useful," he admitted, barely containing his glee at my reaction. "So how did *you* land this job?"

"Kind of by accident," I replied evasively. No need to get into the details, right? Liam's friend was watching me hopefully so I offered him my hand. "I'm Tori."

"Tom." He shook my hand, his grip limp.

"What's your … class?" I asked.

"Psychica. Clairaudience."

"What's that?"

"Super hearing," Liam answered before Tom could. "He can hear people talking within a certain vicinity."

"Neat," I said politely, even though that wasn't nearly as cool as telekinesis. "Can I get you guys drinks?"

They both placed their orders and I whipped up their drinks while Liam chatted about telekinesis—waxing technical about how his ability required intensive training to develop control, enhance strength, and stretch limitations. It got boring in about ten seconds.

"A telekinetic can only move objects with his mind that he can physically move with his body," he explained with the enthusiasm of a toddler talking about his toy firetruck. "So no throwing cars around like in the movies. Some telekinetics will—"

"Here you go!" I said brightly, cutting off the lecture. "Enjoy!"

To my irritation, Liam and Tom slid onto stools and nursed their drinks like old ladies with hot tea. I grabbed my cloth and started wiping, working my way toward the opposite end of the bar.

"So what do you do for fun, Tori?" Liam asked. "Are you a party girl? Got a boyfriend?"

I privately rolled my eyes as I scrubbed away a sticky spot. Great. Awkward flirting had commenced.

"Not really a party girl," I answered. Last time I'd gone clubbing, I'd clobbered a guy for feeling up my ass on the dance floor.

"What do you like to do? Seen any good movies lately?"

I moved farther down the bar, dutifully scrubbing the polished wood. "Not recently. Excuse me, guys. I've got work to do."

"Aw, take it easy, Tori," Liam said in a chipper tone. "You don't need to …"

I lost track of his voice as I walked into the kitchen and stopped in surprise. Ramsey the goth cook was absent from his stool, and in his place was a guy my age with stringy hair and the strong smell of cigarette smoke clinging to him.

"Oh, hey," he said. "You must be Tori. Clara told me she'd hired you as a temp."

"You must be Cooper." The other cook—the one who'd called in sick over the weekend.

He smiled wanly. "Clara didn't mention you were so pretty."

This time I rolled my eyes without hiding it. "Smooth. Very smooth."

"My friends tell me I'm slick as oil."

I snorted and swept past him. Grabbing a bottle of rum to restock my station, I returned to the bar to find the liquor well empty—and over twenty bottles lined up in front of Liam.

"What are you doing?" I snapped.

The rum was pulled from my grip as if by an invisible string. It zoomed down the bar and settled beside the other bottles. Liam smirked at me.

"Come work over here," he said. "It's hard to talk while you're rushing all over the place."

Gritting my teeth, I stalked over and snatched up an armful of bottles. "I have a job to do."

"We're your only customers."

My glare snapped from Liam to Tom, who winced guiltily, then back to Liam. Pivoting on my heel, I marched to my station and started replacing bottles—only for them to float away as soon as I set them down.

"Stop that!" I grabbed a bottle out of the air and put it back, but it rocketed upward again.

Liam laughed. "You can't win, Tori. Just come chat for a few minutes."

I clutched my remaining bottles to my chest, heart pounding. Anger wasn't quite winning the battle against the sinking cold in my stomach. Aaron had scoffed at Psychica mythics for being weak and useless, but with my arrival at the guild, Liam and his ilk were no longer at the bottom of the power totem pole. I was.

And the way he was smirking at me—he knew it. He felt powerful. He was in control.

Just as I was considering whether my soda gun line was long enough to spray down the asshole, Aaron strode through the front door, carrying a black zippered case over three feet long in one hand.

"Ah shit," he said breathlessly as he hurried up to the bar. "I knew those dicks would make me late. I told them—" He broke off, his blue eyes sweeping over my face then down to the bottles I was clutching like priceless collectibles. His attention snapped to Liam, the rest of my liquor lined up in front of him. "What the hell are you doing, Liam?"

Liam's eyes widened and he shifted nervously. "Nothing! Just—uh—harmless teasing and—"

"It's fine." The words came out more terse than I'd intended, but I was annoyed at how relieved I felt to see Aaron. I needed to handle this kind of shit myself. "Everything is fine."

Aaron gave me a sideways look as I dumped my bottles back where they belonged and marched over to the rest. The guys watched me replace each bottle, the silence painful. Tom had shrunk to half his normal size.

Setting his strange burden on the counter with a thud, Aaron muttered, "I'll be right back."

He strode the length of the pub. As the door banged shut behind him, the final bottle in my hand shot from my fingers and flew along the bar. It plopped down in front of Liam, and he chortled as he waited for me to come get it.

Apparently, because I'd snapped at Aaron, Liam was under the impression that I thought his little game was *fun*. I stomped over to him and wrapped my hand around the bottle's neck. Gripping it tightly, I got in his face.

"I am not your plaything," I hissed icily. "And if you ever want another drink from me, you'll start acting like a goddamn adult. My job *isn't* entertaining you."

Liam's eyebrows rose over the top of his stupid round sunglasses—then his gaze dropped below my eye level.

An invisible tug pulled at the front of my blouse. I jerked back and looked down. The top button of my shirt was undone, and Liam was grinning again.

"I don't know, Tori. I think you're lots of fun."

For a moment, I just stared. Then I slugged him in the face.

The impact jarred up my arm, pain flaring through my knuckles. His head snapped back and his sunglasses flew off, clattering across the floor. He pressed a hand to his cheek, his amusement gone and jaw clenched in fury. He lurched up, knocking his stool over backward. The bottle in front of me twitched.

A wave of heat rolled over my back, and Liam froze where he stood.

Aaron slung an arm around my shoulders, his skin almost hot enough to burn. "As much as I would *love* to see Tori beat your pathetic ass, Liam, the blood would upset Clara. So, how about you get the hell out?"

"I ... have work to do, and—"

"Get lost."

"You—you can't tell me what—"

Aaron smiled, his side pressing against mine. "I can, and I am."

Liam opened his mouth, then closed it. Pressing his lips together until they turned white, he spun around and stormed for the exit. His sunglasses flew off the floor and zoomed to his hand as he disappeared outside. Instead of following, Tom slunk to the farthest table and sat, clutching his drink.

Aaron slid his arm off my shoulders and stepped back. "Next time, go for his eyes. He needs to see to use his telekinesis."

I redid my top button. "Am I fired for punching him?"

He laughed, back to his usual relaxed self like he hadn't just terrified a telekinetic into fleeing the building. "Liam is a weasel. He deserved a good punch in the face."

That wasn't quite a "No, you're not fired."

Maybe sensing my doubt, he asked, "Do you know the first rule of the guild?"

I shook my head.

"It's 'Don't hit first, but always hit back.'"

"Oh. That." I frowned. "Didn't *I* hit first?"

"Liam didn't hit you, but you were defending yourself. With enthusiasm," he added amusedly. "Where'd you learn to punch like a pro?"

"I took a few years of taekwondo in high school." Justin had dragged me with him while he was training for the police academy, but I hadn't kept up with it. "If that's the guild's first rule, what's the second?"

"Rule number two is, 'Don't get caught.'"

"Don't get caught at what?"

"Anything." He smirked. "You can't get in trouble if you don't get caught."

My eyes narrowed. "Clara told me this guild is on the up-and-up."

"We are." He grabbed the laptop he must have gone outside to get before sneaking in through the kitchen. "Following the letter of the law and following the *spirit* of the law are two different things."

"And which one does the Crow and Hammer follow?"

"Whichever is most convenient at any given moment." He jumped over the bar and landed neatly on the other side. Setting his laptop down, he slid onto a stool. "I need something stronger than rum tonight."

"What would you like?"

"Surprise me."

While I poured him a double whiskey sour, he flipped open the laptop. I slid the drink over to him, then eyed the long, thin object he'd carried in, encased in heavy-duty black fabric.

"What's that?" I asked.

"Hmm? Oh, just my switch."

"Your ... what?"

He dragged his attention off his screen. "Oh right, sorry. Guess you wouldn't know." He pushed his laptop aside and drew the case closer. "A switch is a magical conduit. The real term is *caduceus*, but who wants to say that all the time?"

Unzipping it, he pulled the narrow bag open to show me what lay within. I looked from the glossy black sheath to the gleaming hilt, then back at him.

"That is a sword." A freakin' *sword*. Who walked around with a sword?

"Only useless mages train with wands. *We* train with weapons. If someone is trying to kill me, I'd rather have a sword than try to poke their eyes out with a piddly wand."

I grasped the leather-wrapped handle and lifted it a few inches, its weight surprising me. "Do people try to kill you often?"

"Not usually." He zipped the bag. "MagiPol doesn't have the manpower to track down every rogue mythic across the globe, so they post bounties instead. Guilds do the tag and bag, then hand the perp over to MagiPol for trial."

"Huh." I remembered a passing remark he'd made on Sunday. "And you, Kai, and Ezra are after a bounty for a rogue ... sorcerer?"

"Yep. Thought we had a solid lead this afternoon so I grabbed Sharpie, but the guy gave us the slip."

"Sharpie? You named your sword Sharpie?"

"We're supposed to be incognito, Tori. What if someone overheard me talking about my Fiery Deathbringer or Warblade of Murderous Doom?"

"They'd probably think you were talking about a video game." I poked the sword bag. "So how does it work? You can make flames without this."

"A switch is like a focus. It's easier to control the elements through a tool, and using a switch lets you create more specific and targeted effects." He shrugged. "I can light the room on fire easily enough, but if I want to create a concentrated band of flame, I need a switch."

"Any switch, or only Sharpie?"

"A sword similar in size and shape to Sharpie would be functional, but we work best with the switches we've trained on."

"Magic is complicated," I informed him dryly.

"Try talking to an Arcaner. *That's* complicated."

Lucky for me, Liam the telekinetic weasel was the worst part of my day. Sylvia, the older woman I'd called a hag during my first shift, was a close second, though. Realizing she'd been insulted by a measly human, her hag level had increased by ten. We had another friendly chat about how I wasn't serving her a damn thing until she proved she had manners.

Again, I was reluctantly relieved that Aaron was nearby, though he may have riled up Sylvia even more than I had.

Somehow, *everyone* knew I was human, but they didn't all see me as a weak runt of a bartender. A friendly young woman who identified herself as a witch spent a solid twenty minutes talking about yoga and invited me to join her and her also-a-witch boyfriend on their weekly nature walk. A sweet old lady with turquoise-framed glasses and a knit cap offered to do a tarot card reading for me. A fortyish-year-old man with dark bronze skin and a fantastic goatee chatted with me about local restaurants—many of which I'd attempted to work at.

When a man approached—built like a tank, shaved head, heavy brow that shadowed his dark eyes—I almost shrank behind the bar. He looked like a mobster, but Aaron murmured distractedly, "Hey, Lyndon."

"How's the hunt going?" Lyndon asked in a deep, gravelly voice.

"The bastard is a slippery one. If we don't hurry, someone else will nab him."

"Have you asked Taye to scout around?" He gestured at the bronze-skinned foodie I'd spoken to earlier.

"We need a confirmed starting point first," Aaron replied. "Kai will figure it out. He always does. Knowing him, he's already got a new lead and he's just letting me slave away here for nothing."

Lyndon chuckled, then turned and offered me his hand. "Lyndon McAllister. Arcana, sorcerer."

"Pleasure to meet you," I said. "Tori Dawson. Human, bartender. Can I get you a drink?"

"Bourbon on the rocks, please." He watched me pull out a glass. "How's it going so far? This can't be an easy adjustment."

"Not bad. Aaron is entertaining, at least."

The pyromage in question glanced up. "What does that mean?"

I smirked at him, just to be annoying, then said to Lyndon, "I admit I've been picturing sorcerers as old men with beards to their waists and giant spell books."

He chuckled as I set his drink down. "Let me guess. Aaron has been telling you how boring and stuffy we are, and how lame Arcana magic is."

"Hmm, yeah, pretty much."

"I never called it *lame*," Aaron muttered distractedly, eyes fixed on his screen.

Lyndon perched on the edge of a bar stool. "Sorcery is the most common Arcana order. I specialize in counter magic, meaning spells that affect other magic. I used to be a combat sorcerer but ... those days are behind me."

Curious, I asked, "Why the switch?"

He rubbed his jaw. "Counter magic is ... safer. In some guilds, the line between legal and illegal spells can get blurry, especially when it comes to offensive magic. After the MPD dissolved my last guild, I decided a change was in order."

They *dissolved* his guild? That sounded ominous. I decided to shift the topic away from his potentially sensitive history. "How long did it take you to learn counter magic?"

"A few years, but I was well past the apprenticeship stage by then." He smiled whimsically. "Most sorcerers spend at least twelve years in training. Alchemist and healers take even longer to complete their apprenticeships."

"Whoa."

"It isn't easy to learn, but it's the most versatile magic and, for experienced practitioners, it's the most powerful."

Aaron scoffed.

"We'll see who's laughing next time Girard puts you on your ass," Lyndon remarked cheerfully before tossing back the last of his bourbon. "I've got work to do. See you two later."

As I committed Lyndon's information about Arcana magic to memory, I entered his drink in the till. Each guild member had a running tab and hardly anyone paid cash, which didn't bode well for my poor, empty tip jar.

"Hey, Aaron," I said after a minute.

"Hmm?"

"You said you're hunting a rogue sorcerer, right?"

"Yeah."

"What if he's a really powerful one?"

He looked up from his laptop, an amused sparkle in his eyes. "Don't worry about me, new girl. Lyndon meant one on one, but a single Arcaner against me, Kai, and Ezra? Even an experienced combat sorcerer would have a hell of a time beating us, and this rogue is far from the best."

"Strength in numbers, huh?" I murmured. Not my thing. No one on the planet was as invested in saving my butt as I was, and I didn't like counting on someone else to be there when I needed them only to find myself alone.

Aaron didn't notice my doubtful expression as he focused on his laptop, strong fingers zipping over the keyboard. I glanced at his sword, hidden in its black case. For a supposedly easy opponent, he'd brought along an awfully big weapon.

Well, I wouldn't lose sleep over it. His ability to navigate dangerous situations inspired minimal confidence, but Kai oozed competence and I had yet to see Ezra appear anything less than utterly unfazed. If they wanted to chase down dangerous rogues with deadly magic, that was their business.

Me, I was just here to tend the bar—and I planned to keep my nose out of anything that wasn't a cocktail recipe book.

8

TO MY DISAPPOINTMENT, Kai and Ezra didn't make an appearance on Wednesday. My shift passed much like Tuesday's, with a few ugly encounters, a few pleasant ones, and a whole bunch of people who didn't care to speak to me beyond ordering a drink. Liam didn't return but Tom showed up for the better part of the evening, taking the same seat in the far corner and nursing drinks while he read a thick sci-fi paperback.

Sylvia came in and we had a slightly more polite snarling match. I made her a proper Manhattan, and she seemed pleased that I'd learned it for her. Not that I'd studied up for *her*—just so I didn't look stupid again.

I was getting an idea of the regulars and the less-regular regulars. Many members I'd glimpsed during the big meeting hadn't returned, but others showed up every day. They'd grab a few drinks and a meal, then head upstairs or downstairs depending on what they needed to do.

According to Aaron, the second level was for work—planning and executing jobs, completing paperwork, coordinating with team members, and research. Rogue hunting wasn't the only work mythics could take on to earn extra cash—or bonuses, as Aaron called them—but no one went into detail about it. Probably a not-for-human-ears topic.

The basement level was for training, both magical and physical. Aaron mentioned a gym, a sparring room, a bunker for practicing magic, and an alchemy lab. The third level, where I'd met the guild officers, was off-limits for most members—the territory of the guild master, assistant guild master, and officers.

Aaron was late again but I didn't give him too hard a time—he was clearly exhausted. He, Kai, and Ezra had pulled an all-nighter tracking the rogue sorcerer. Instead of working on his laptop, Aaron lined up a row of chairs along the wall and lied across the makeshift bed, covering his eyes with a borrowed dish towel. At least he didn't snore.

Clara checked on me each night around six or seven, praising my efforts and gushing about how much work she was getting done, before heading home for the night. Felix popped in once to see how Aaron was handling his new assignment—triggering a lecture about sleeping on the job—but I saw no sign of the other two officers.

Friday's shift went the same. I wouldn't admit it to anyone, especially Aaron … but getting the cold shoulder from most of my customers was wearing on me. They weren't rude enough to yell at, but neither were they friendly. Aaron napped through my shift again, even more tired than the day before.

For a magical guild, it wasn't all that fun, yet I could see glimpses of how it might have been if I were a mythic instead of an unwelcome human. I could hear laughter from other levels, and I got to watch the smiles fade off mythics' faces when they approached the bar. The sociable members were in the minority.

For my Saturday shift, I had high hopes the weekend would mean a busier night—and maybe friendlier faces. The afternoon weather was hot and balmy, so I picked out bright red shorts almost the same shade as my hair, a tank top with a strappy back, and cute white sandals. For a change, I wore my hair down, my usual wild waves straightened into sleek locks that fell almost to my elbows.

I was feeling good. Tips had been shit all week, but maybe I could charm some generosity out of my customers tonight.

Once again, Aaron was late, but I had no issues setting up. I was just laying out my freshly cut garnishes when he breezed in, a bounce in his step.

"We got him!" he announced before I could ask. "Tagged him in the marina, five minutes before he would've booked it straight for international waters."

"Nice!" I said, my earnest relief surprising me. Had I been worrying about the guys that much? "Glad it's over with."

"Same." He dropped onto his favorite stool just to the left of my station, the circles under his eyes offset by his grin. "Looking good today, Tori."

Huh. I'd expected him to be too oblivious to notice I'd put extra effort into my appearance. "Thanks."

He caught a lock of my hair and slid it through his fingers. I froze, my thoughts thrown completely off track.

"I kind of miss the crazy curls, though."

I arched my eyebrows. "What are you implying?"

"Nothing?" he said uncertainly. Aware enough to notice I'd dressed up, but oblivious of how he was treading on thin ice with that comment.

I decided to spare him a bout of female insecurity. "How are Ezra and Kai?"

"Kai is fine, as always. Ezra took a nasty hit, but he's just bruised. The sorcerer came out way worse."

I poured two rum and cokes and passed him one. "A toast to a successful job?"

"Damn right!" We clinked glasses and he took a long gulp. "After a tough job, we usually hit the bar for a few celebratory drinks, but Ezra wanted to take it easy and Kai has a date. So it's just me tonight."

"Well, you and me." I nudged his glass with mine. "I'll celebrate with you!"

His grin flashed again and I returned it, a flutter in my stomach.

He downed half his drink in a few swallows. "Man, I'm going to sleep like a rock tonight. I haven't had a good night's rest all week."

I finished straightening my garnishes. "How does Kai have the energy for a date?"

"He's been getting his sleep while I've been here," Aaron grumped. "Slacker."

"Does he have a girlfriend?" I asked curiously, trying to imagine what sort of girl Kai would go for. With his exotic looks and classy style—from what I'd seen, anyway—he could attract almost any woman.

"Girlfriend*s*," Aaron answered, emphasizing the S. "I don't know where he finds them, but he goes out with a new lady every damn week."

No way. Kai? A player? I hadn't pegged him as the womanizing type. "What about you?"

"Happily single."

Ramsey waltzed out of the kitchen, his unnaturally black hair extra spikey and his eyeliner drawn on with more finesse than I'd ever managed on my own face. "Aaron isn't mentioning his string of relationships that've failed spectacularly. We take bets on how long each girl will last."

Aaron scowled.

"The current average is four months," Ramsey added.

"Wait, wait," I cut in. "Aaron has located *multiple* women who were willing to tolerate him for four whole months?"

Ramsey laughed.

With a sulky glare at the two of us, Aaron hunched over his drink. "Like you can talk, Ramsey."

"I've been with my boyfriend for three years, thanks very much."

"That's my point. I'm way better with women than you."

Rolling my eyes, I poured Aaron another drink and slid it over. "I'm sure you'll find the right girl eventually."

"Real comforting, Tori."

Once Ramsey returned to the kitchen, I gentled my tone. "If it's any consolation, my track record is basically the same."

He glanced up. "Oh?"

"Are you surprised that I don't have a boyfriend, or surprised that I've ever had one?"

"Bit of both."

I shook my head, but I was more amused than anything else. "We gingers have it rough, huh?"

He laughed and raised his drink. "I'll toast to that."

The evening didn't stay quiet for long. People started filtering in around five, and by six I was too busy to keep Aaron company. He joined a table with Lyndon the sorcerer and two girls my age, animatedly describing his rogue sorcerer takedown while I zipped back and forth between the bar and kitchen. Ramsey and Cooper were both working and I found myself carrying way too many baskets of chicken wings for the number of people in the bar.

The lack of friendliness continued, but I ignored it, offering smiles and bright greetings to everyone. Eventually they'd warm up to me, right? A few more tips made their way into my jar than on other nights.

Around eight, excited voices cut through the rumble of conversation. Five people squeezed through the door, chatting and clapping each other on the back. At their appearance, most of the mythics in the pub cheered and whooped.

"Victory!" one of the new arrivals yelled, pumping a fist in the air. "A round on me!"

More cheers. I scrambled into position, my eyes widening. The five newcomers were wearing several cows' worth of black leather and had weapons strapped to their limbs or slung over their backs, along with thick belts carrying fat pouches. They looked like a cross between special ops soldiers and vampire slayers.

"How did it go, Andrew?" someone called.

"Kicked ass," a fifty-something guy answered. Despite his Blade-style outfit, he had a fatherly air that made me think he should be coaching a kid's soccer team. "Bagged four and scattered the remainder of the nest."

"And did some damage to the escapees, too," a petite woman added, running a gloved hand over her pixie-short blond hair streaked with pink. The top of a monster-sized weapon jutted above her shoulder. "And get this. Right when we were packing up, the—"

"The Odin's Eye guild showed up, ready to clean house," the tallest guy boasted, the one who'd proclaimed a round of drinks on the way in. "They were *pissed*."

Laughter rang through the room as the group reached the bar. The petite woman and older guy broke off to join Aaron's table, while the other three stopped in front of me. The tallest guy, with a narrow face and patchy beard, might not have looked impressive on any other day, but his gear was doing him all kinds of favors.

"Congrats," I said, though I had no idea what for. "What do you want to do for the round?"

His excitement faded as he assessed me. "Whiskey shots. *No*, not that one. The good stuff."

I halted my reach for the whiskey in my well as he pointed imperiously at a bottle on the shelf behind me.

"Hurry it up," the other guy said—a big dude with lots of muscle who would've been intimidating even without the leather duster. "We're trying to celebrate here."

I bit back a retort and reached for the bottle. How was I supposed to know the drill if no one had explained it? Jeez. I swiftly lined up shot glasses and poured, spilling in my rush. The third mythic of the team, a girl around my age with sleek blond hair tied into a ponytail, watched me with her nose scrunched like she'd stepped in dog shit.

Everyone in the pub crowded around the bar to partake in the shots. I did a rapid count and added another six glasses. The triumphant team passed them around, and Ramsey and Cooper popped out of the kitchen to grab shots too. The older leader, Andrew, lifted his into the air.

"To another—"

"Hold up," Aaron interrupted, his shot in hand. "Tori, pour yourself one."

Everyone looked at me and most of the stares were unfriendly.

"Um." I shifted awkwardly. "That's okay, go ahead."

"It's tradition. Everyone does a shot when a team makes a clean sweep on a job."

"Every *hammer* takes a shot," someone corrected. "She's not guilded."

"She's part of the group. Pour a shot, Tori."

"Shove it, Aaron," the tall guy snapped. "You're killing the mood."

Aaron's usual good humor was gone without a trace. He held his shot out to me. "Take mine, then, Tori."

"That—that's okay," I mumbled. Damn it, Aaron. Stop making them hate me!

To my shock, Andrew, the team leader, gave me a smile. "Pour another one."

"Go on, Tori," Lyndon added, pushing in beside Aaron.

The petite blonde with the giant bad-guy-smasher on her back reached across the bar and gave me a friendly slap on the shoulder. "Everyone celebrates a victory. Do it!"

The silence thundered as I pulled out another shot glass and splashed whiskey into it. Most of the mythics were glaring at me, from the victorious team to the two girls Aaron had been chatting with.

Once I had my shot in hand, Andrew lifted his glass. "When you're a hammer," he shouted.

"Everything's a nail!" the mythics shouted in turn, the ebullient atmosphere bursting through the room again as everyone laughed and downed their shots.

Aaron met my eyes, grinned, and tossed his whiskey back. I tipped my head, dumping the liquid into my mouth. It burned all the way down and I wheezed.

The petite blonde clapped me on the shoulder again. "Good stuff, right?"

"Yeah," I gasped.

"I'm Zora," she added. "This is Andrew." She waved at the team leader. "Cameron." The tall jerk. "Darren." The muscly jerk. "And Cearra." The female jerk.

"Pleasure to meet you." I directed the words at Zora only, otherwise I would've been lying. "Congratulations on the victory. What was the job?"

"Exterminating a vampire nest." She said it the same way I might remark on squishing a spider in the bathroom. "It'll be a big payday this month."

"Wow," I said faintly. My guess about their outfits had been spot on.

"Oooh." Aaron leaned on the bar. "I hadn't mentioned vampires yet, had I?"

"No …"

"What about werewolves? Did I mention those?"

"Also a no."

Zora laughed. "Don't worry. Vampires and shifters are hardly the scariest things out there."

"You don't say," I muttered, feeling queasy. How was that supposed to make me worry *less*? I hoped they were just messing with me, but I doubted it.

"Looking pale there," Cearra commented snidely, sweeping her ponytail over her shoulder. "Don't faint. You might hurt yourself."

"I bet she'd do better than you did on your first vamp sighting," Zora shot back before I could respond. "Didn't you piss yourself?"

Cearra went red. "I fell in a puddle!"

"Sure you did," Aaron agreed mockingly.

Cearra slammed her shot glass down on the counter and stalked away. The two younger guys followed her.

"Those kids," Zora remarked. With a friendly wave at me and Aaron, she joined another group clustered around a table, where Andrew had launched into a detailed rendition of their adventure.

The evening flew by and I was busy for all of it. Around eleven, the place started to empty. The vampire hunters left first—probably overheating in their leather gear—and others trickled out until it was just Aaron in conversation with Lyndon the sorcerer, Tom the shy psychic reading in the corner, the two girls who'd chitchatted with Aaron earlier, and a handful of others whose names I didn't know.

At eleven thirty, Ramsey stuck his head out to let me know Cooper had left and he was heading out now too. I wished him a good night, then announced last call to the remaining mythics.

Rising from their table, the two girls came up—both my age, one with her hair dyed a shocking teal-blue and the other with dusky skin, a wild mop of dark curls, and large eyes. Blue-hair carried an armload of what appeared to be perfume bottles filled with brightly colored liquids.

"Can I get … hmm …" Calculation lurked behind her gaze as she set the perfume bottles on the bar top. "Actually, just a coke."

I forced a smile, but it wasn't as convincing as earlier in the evening. "And you?" I asked the other girl.

"Water."

As I got out two glasses, Blue-hair gathered up her perfume bottles. Her fingers clumsily bumped a bright green one and it toppled over, rolling across the counter. I lunged to catch it as her hand shot out—but instead of grabbing it, she smacked it off the bar.

It hit the floor and shattered. A poof of green mist exploded outward, dousing everything within six feet—including me.

"Whoa!" Aaron exclaimed, leaping up from his chair. "What happened? What is that?"

I backed up a few steps, my short apron coated in shimmering green. The floors, the counter, my station, the shelves of liquor bottles—all stained with the liquid.

"Oh no," Blue-hair said with unconvincing dismay. "My dye! Well, that's a shame." She picked up the remaining bottles. "You know, I think I'll head out now."

"Head out?" Aaron repeated angrily. "It's your shit and you knocked it over. You can help her clean it up."

"No, Sinclair." The cold voice drifted from the corner of the room. A woman descended the staircase and paused a few steps from the bottom. Tabitha, the second guild officer. "It's Miss Dawson's responsibility."

Her dark eyes turned my way and I suddenly had a real good idea who had leaked the truth about my human status to the entire guild. The only ones who'd known beside Aaron, Kai, and Ezra were Clara and the three officers.

Aaron stepped toward me. "I'll help you, then."

"Set foot behind the bar and I'll write you up for insubordination, Sinclair. You know the kitchen area is staff only." Tabitha smiled coolly at Blue-hair and her friend. "Have a good night, ladies."

Oozing smugness, the girls strolled out the door. Aaron looked between me and Tabitha, then started around the bar to join me.

"Sinclair," Tabitha warned.

"Go ahead and write me up."

"You'll lose your bonuses for the month."

"Fine."

I raced to the edge of the bar before Aaron could step onto forbidden ground. "It's okay," I said quietly, blocking his path. "I'll take care of it."

His eyes blazed with anger. "I don't care about the damn bonus. I'll help you."

"It's just a bit of cleaning. I can handle it." I wasn't letting him lose the money he'd gone all week without sleep to earn. I lowered my voice more. "If you help me, she wins."

Jaw flexing, he reluctantly stepped back. Tabitha's expression didn't change, but I could sense her smugness. She won whether Aaron helped me or not. Ignoring her, I strode into the back to get cleaning supplies.

Whatever the hell the dye was made of, it was impossible to clean. The oily texture smeared over everything no matter how hard I scrubbed it, and after turning four dish rags completely green, I switched to paper towels.

Midnight came and went as I wiped and scoured and rinsed and washed everything the oily mist had touched. Tabitha returned every ten minutes to check on my progress and ensure

Aaron remained in his chair, seething as he waited. The last few members made their way out, no one speaking.

Finally, I threw the last of the green paper towel into the overflowing garbage bin and straightened my aching back. All the dye was gone except for what was liberally splattered over me. I hurried into the staff bathroom and groaned when I saw my reflection in the mirror. My apron hadn't saved my clothes—my red shorts and white top were ruined. Green smeared my skin and coated the ends of my hair on one side.

Ditching my apron, I washed my hands, arms, face, and legs. The substance came off my skin with soap, but no amount of soap, water, or scrubbing would dim the green in my hair.

I bit hard on my lip, blinking furiously. Be mean, be rude, insult me, wreck my workspace, stain my clothes. Fine, whatever. But I loved my hair and now the bottom six inches on one side were dyed a hideous green. Would I have to cut it off?

With angry movements, I finished washing up, collected my purse and umbrella, and circled back to the front. When I came through the saloon doors, Aaron was waiting. He took in my stained clothes and wet, green hair.

"It didn't wash out?" he asked gruffly. "I'll call Katherine tomorrow and have her come in to figure it out."

"Figure out what?" I asked tiredly as I pulled out my cell phone.

"That dye is an alchemic potion. Katherine is our master alchemist. She'll know how to get it out of your hair, I promise."

I nodded, trying not to get my hopes up. As I walked to the pub door, Aaron at my side, I dialed the cab company. The phone buzzed a busy signal.

"Saturday night," I muttered. It was late—pushing almost two. The cab companies would be swamped with late-night clubbers. I called again and got another busy signal. My back ached and my legs throbbed from crouching for two hours. I just wanted to go home, shower, and curl up with a blanket and a cup of tea. Maybe Justin's tea fetish wasn't so strange after all.

I called one more time and got the busy signal. Screw it. "Guess I'll go on foot."

"I'll walk you home," Aaron said.

"That's fine," I assured him. "I'm over in Coal Harbor off West Georgia Street and—"

"Tori." His stern growl made me freeze. "I'm walking you home."

I measured his uncompromising expression, then surrendered. "Okay. Thank you."

He pushed the door open and I walked out. Conveniently, I didn't need to lock up. There was always at least one officer at the guild headquarters, so they never locked the doors. Tabitha, obviously, was tonight's on-duty officer.

My blood boiled at the thought of her, and I wondered again if she was the one who'd leaked that I was human. She didn't want me at the guild, and since her fellow officers wouldn't ban me, the easiest way to get rid of me was to make me quit. How much of the antagonism I'd experienced over the past week had she quietly encouraged?

Side by side, Aaron and I ambled past barred windows and boarded-up doors, and despite the warm night, I shivered. The disreputable street was quiet but not deserted. A handful of men walked quickly through the darkness, while others, tucked into nooks or sitting beside shopping carts covered in ratty tarps, watched us with empty stares.

I didn't want to admit it, but walking alone would've been stupid. I was glad Aaron was with me.

"Thanks," I said again as Victorian-style buildings and respectable shops replaced the graffiti-tagged walls. "I appreciate it."

"No problem." He glanced at me out of the corner of his eye. "I'm sorry about earlier."

"It wasn't your fault."

"Yeah, but …" He raked a hand through his rust-orange hair. "It always takes time for the gang to warm up to a new member, but I've never seen them this … I wasn't expecting it."

"It's because I'm not a member. I'm just a … liability." Tabitha's word.

"You're a good bartender. What else do you need to be?"

I huffed, pleased by the compliment even though I knew it wasn't true. "Okay, first off, I'm not that good at bartending. If anything, I'm an amateur. Admit it."

"You're doing a great job."

Smiling, I patted his arm, surprised again by the warmth of his skin. "You'll make a good officer someday, Aaron."

His hand brushed my arm, slid down, and caught my fingers. "I don't want to see you go, but if you've had enough of those assholes, I get it."

I resisted the urge to peek at my hand enveloped in his warm grip, my heart beating faster than our brisk pace warranted. "I can manage for another week before the MPD gives the official no."

"Ah, about that." He casually slid his hand free from mine, and I hid my disappointment. "I asked Clara yesterday where your paperwork was at, and it turns out Darius needs to sign off on it before she can submit it. He won't be back for another week or more, so the official 'no' won't come for another couple weeks after that."

"Oh." I bit my lip. One more week of cranky jerks I could deal with, but *three*? Was I that masochistic or was it time to call it quits?

His gaze darted over my face, reading my reaction. We crossed the redbrick intersection where I'd found the guild job printout and headed down Water Street, passing cute shops, restaurants, and cafés, all closed now. A few people strolled by, on their way home after a night out.

"How long have you been a member of the guild?" I asked.

"Six years." He smiled as though recalling a fond memory. "Me and Kai joined the day I turned eighteen—the minimum age to join a guild."

"There are other guilds, right? What made you choose the Crow and Hammer?"

"Honestly? I picked C&H to tick off my parents. They wanted me to join their guild, but there I would've always been the GM's spoiled son, constantly having to prove my worth while everyone questioned whether my parents had handed me my success on a silver platter."

"So you picked a guild where you could earn your place?"

"I could have done that at almost any guild. I picked C&H because it's the opposite of my parents' guild. They can't stand C&H's reputation." He laced his hands behind his head as he walked. "The Crow and Hammer has been collecting misfits for decades—mythics who don't fit in, people who have skills to offer but can't get on at another guild, rogues who need a second chance. The only respectable thing about us is that when we take a job, we get it done. Always."

"Hmm. That explains a few things."

He laughed. "Most guilds are boring—they specialize too much. All mages or all sorcerers, or they only do specific work. Ever heard of Smoke & Mirrors?"

"Yeah, isn't that the company that does practical effects for all the big movies—wait. Are you suggesting what I think you are?"

"They're a guild. Sorcerers, alchemists, a few mages, and a load of telekinetics. They do all their filming on closed sets, and people think it's to protect their trade secrets, but it's more than that."

"Holy shit."

"Right? They were my second choice for a guild, but I wanted to catch bad guys. Smoke & Mirrors doesn't do any bounty work."

We crossed another brick intersection, passing the famous Gastown steam clock, its face indicating 2:10 A.M. The breeze was warm, with that nighttime freshness I loved. I breathed deeply as we continued down the street.

"You said Kai joined on the same day as you," I murmured. "What brought him to the Crow and Hammer?"

"He followed me. He didn't care what guild he joined, and his time was almost up." He noticed my askance look. "Guilding is a requirement once a mythic turns eighteen. Unless you want to be unguilded, but that's like being on parole—a million restrictions, mandatory check-ins, random inspections."

"That sucks." I scrunched my face. "Why is it so strict? I mean, don't some mythics want to live normal lives and not battle vampires on weekends?"

"Most mythics want to live like humans. There are lots of guilds to choose from—over a dozen in the downtown core alone. Some are businesses in their own right, and being a member is like working a regular job. Others, you pay a monthly or yearly membership fee and carry on with your mundane life like any other person."

He gestured widely, encompassing the city. "The whole point is regulation and enforcement. Mythics pay their guilds, the guilds pay MagiPol, and MagiPol uses that money to keep the world sane. Guilds collect some of that money back as bonuses and bounties for helping MagiPol enforce their laws. The restrictions on unguilded mythics are so harsh because it means someone has to monitor those people. Guilds are responsible for their members' behavior."

"I see. It's like ... mutually assured obedience."

"Exactly. If I break a minor rule, MagiPol will fine me *and* my guild. If I really screw up, MagiPol can arrest me and levy large fines and other punishments against my guild. Screw up enough, and they'll dissolve a guild that fails to manage and control its members."

"And if that happened, they would offer bounties to other guilds to ensure you disband?"

"You got it. The system is built on self-regulation. The guilds enforce their members' adherence to the rules, and MagiPol enforces the guilds' adherence. It's the reason we can keep all this hidden from the public. Otherwise, MagiPol would need to be as large as any government."

A system built entirely on the guild structure, hidden in plain sight—part of human society while also separate. I mulled it over as we strolled into the nest of skyscrapers that marked the center of the downtown area.

"What about you, Tori?" Aaron asked after a few minutes. "Your driver's license is from Ontario. When did you come out to the west coast?"

"Eight—almost nine—months ago. I needed a fresh start and my brother lives here."

"Find your own place yet?"

"No," I grumped. "Still sleeping on his couch."

He chuckled knowingly. "It takes around a year for most newcomers to find a place of their own. The rental market is insane."

"That's an understatement."

"Why did you need a fresh start?"

His tone was curious but not insistent, and I considered whether to answer.

"I was living with relatives, but my father started butting into my life. I didn't want to deal with that, so I packed my bags and moved away." I shrugged. "Plus, a new job market was helpful. I was running out of options back home."

"You mentioned you were having trouble finding a job here too?"

I swept my green-tinted hair over my shoulders. "Yeah, well, most places do fire you for throwing drinks on customers or punching creeps in the face."

"That's shitty." His grin returned. "No one at the Crow and Hammer would reprimand you for defending yourself."

"I wasn't defending myself when I threw a drink on you."

I expected him to laugh, but his expression sobered. "I was being an ass, and I deserved it. I'm no better than the others. Razzing new people is a habit that's hard to shake."

"You were annoying but not cruel." I plucked at my stained shirt. "*This* is crossing a line, though. Honestly, I'm not sure how much longer I can stay."

"If I could make them understand how awesome you are, I would," he murmured. "They don't know what they're missing out on."

To my dismay, my cheeks flushed hot. I was *not* a blusher. I could count past occasions without using all my fingers.

"I'm not that great," I muttered, ducking my head. "You barely know me."

"I can tell," he said confidently. "And even if *I* wasn't sure about you, Ezra likes you."

"He seems like the sort of nice guy who likes everyone."

"He's nice to everyone—too nice, if you ask me—but he doesn't go out of his way for strangers." He tilted his face skyward as though remembering something. "By the way, don't ask Ezra why he joined the guild."

"Uh … okay."

"And best not to ask about his family either."

I nodded. I could understand someone not wanting past ghosts stirred awake by nosy questions, though I was dying of curiosity now, of course. "Anything else I shouldn't ask him?"

"Hmm … maybe don't ask him out either."

I blinked. "Did it seem like I was planning to?"

"No, but Ezra doesn't date so he'd turn you down and things would get all awkward." He slanted a glance at me. "Plus, I'm planning to ask you out, so I don't want that messed up."

My heart gave a small flutter and I sternly told it to quit that bullshit. Still, I had to fight back a grin. "You are, are you?"

"Damn right."

"And when were you intending to carry out that plan?"

"If you're going to say yes, then ..." He squinted around. "How much farther to your place?"

"Four blocks."

"In four blocks, then."

I laughed. "What if I'm going to say no?"

"Then I'll wait until I can butter you up first." He canted his head. "Do I get a hint about your answer?"

"Hmm." I sauntered along, hands folded behind my back and purse bumping my side, my oversized umbrella hanging from the strap. "Do you need a hint?"

"I mean this in the best way possible, but you're a difficult woman to predict, Tori."

I gave him my best mysterious smile. "Three blocks now."

He grumbled. We walked in companionable silence for another two blocks, and my nerves jumped in anticipation. Was he planning to merely ask me on a date, or did he have something more in mind?

High-rise apartment buildings closed in on all sides, a few windows still alight. As we reached the next intersection, he looped an arm around my waist and pulled me around the corner.

"Uh, Aaron, this is the wrong way."

"I know," he said in a low voice, his grim tone surprising me. "It's just that I'm pretty sure the two guys back there are following us. We might be in trouble."

9

MY HEART jumped, and not in a good way. "Following us?"

"I noticed them after we left Water Street," Aaron muttered. "It could be a coincidence, but I doubt it. Keep your eyes forward. I'll check if they keep tailing us."

Adrenaline surged through my veins. I hooked my arm through his and we power-walked to the next intersection and turned right again. Resisting the urge to look back, I kept my focus on the sidewalk ahead, well lit by streetlamps, traffic lights, and the occasional flare of headlights as a car passed.

We made another right turn and came out on our original street. We'd made a pointless one-block circle that no one in their right mind would walk unless they were lost.

"Shit," Aaron hissed. "They're still on our tail, and they know we've spotted them."

He extended his stride until I had to jog every third step. I risked a glance back and spotted a pair of men in dark clothes a block away. They appeared normal enough but that didn't mean anything.

"How far is your apartment?" Aaron asked tersely.

"Turn right at the next corner. It's the third building."

"Good. Okay." He pulled me along with him, head tilted to keep our pursuers in view. "When we get close, run to your door and get inside. I'll wait until you're in, then draw them away."

"What?" I yelped. "No way. Come inside with me."

"Too risky." His eyes kept moving, scanning every shadow before returning to our stalkers. "They're after me, not you. I'm not leading them to your apartment."

"I won't leave you to—"

"They're mythics, Tori. You can't help." His arm heated under my hand. "I can take care of myself."

He said that now, but at the pub when he'd talked about his odds against powerful mythics, he'd included Kai and Ezra as his teammates. His mage friends weren't here to back him up. Could he take on two mythics alone?

"This isn't a good plan," I whispered as we rounded the corner and Justin's building came into view. "Let's figure out something else."

"It'll be fine," he said. "Tori, I fight with fire. I need you safe first so I can defend myself without hurting you."

"But you don't have Sharpie," I protested desperately.

Shaking off my arm, he stopped at the broad sidewalk that crossed a manicured lawn to the front of the towering high-rise. His head turned as he watched our stalkers. "Run inside. Go!"

My hands clenched. With a furious hiss, I turned and bolted across the lawn. I shoved through the main doors into the vestibule but didn't unlock the security door. Spinning around, I squinted through the glass.

Aaron turned on his heel and strode into the street, heading for the alleyway on the other side—getting out of sight so he could use his magic. His two pursuers broke into a jog, chasing after him.

Then, farther up the street, two more men in black clothes ran toward the alley.

Four? There were *four*?

Gasping through my panic, I pulled my phone out—but could I call the police? Aaron and the mystery men were mythics. I was almost positive the police would make this worse. If Justin had been home, I would've called him and taken my chances, but he had a shift tonight. Swiping my thumb across the screen, I pulled up Clara's number and called it. It went straight to voicemail. She was probably sleeping.

Cursing, I ran outside. Aaron couldn't take on four mythics at once, could he? I might be a useless, magic-less human, but I wasn't abandoning him to an unfair fight.

Slowing as I reached the head of the alleyway, I crept into the darkness between hulking skyscrapers. Aaron hadn't gone far. He stood in the middle of the alley, illuminated by the flames dancing across his upraised palm. Shadowy figures had formed a loose circle around him, and as I slunk behind a dumpster and peeked out, I counted them. Then counted again.

Not two. Not four. *Six*.

"Come quietly and we won't hurt you," a black-clad man said in a raspy voice. "Our orders are to bring you in alive, but they said nothing about unharmed."

The flames on Aaron's palm flared, gleaming across the switchblade in his other hand. "How about you get lost, and then I won't have to hurt *you*?"

The man smiled. From beneath his coat, he pulled a long dagger with a glowing inscription on the steel. Crouched behind the dumpster, I clutched my purse like a shield. Oh god. This couldn't be happening.

Aaron flicked his hand—hurling fire into the face of a man on his left—then launched toward the guy with the dagger. The man swung his weapon in a sideways arc and a sparkling white wave swirled around it. Aaron slashed with his switchblade, a trail of flames whipping out, and the two forces collided.

Orange sparks and white glitter exploded into hissing steam that engulfed the two men. Ice, I realized. The sparkling white power was ice.

Fire rippled out from the steam cloud, and as Aaron reappeared, two men attacked him from behind.

He spun, fire spiraling out of his switchblade, and the other men launched flashes of light from small objects I couldn't make out in the darkness. Aaron dodged them, pivoted again, and cast a crackling fireball at Ice Guy, who countered with a burst of white that exploded into snowflakes.

Aaron jumped back, fire racing up his arms and over his shoulders. He thrust his switchblade in a strange pattern and the steel glowed red. A wall of flame erupted from the weapon and surged toward Ice Guy.

Another enemy jumped to Ice Guy's side, something small in his hand.

"*Ori repercutio*," he declared.

The air rippled like a shock wave and when Aaron's fiery attack hit it, the blaze snapped in the opposite direction. The red-hot flames sloughed off Aaron's body, his clothes singed but his skin unharmed. Teeth bared, he raised his switchblade again.

Behind him, light flashed painfully bright. I flinched, blinded. A shout, a crunching sound, a clatter of something metal skittering across asphalt, then another flare of light. Eyes watering, I peered through the mist.

The six men had converged in the center of the alley, and I couldn't see Aaron's red hair among them. Then, as a man crouched, I spotted Aaron—on the ground, Ice Guy kneeling on his back, one hand gripping his dagger and the other pressed to Aaron's shirt, frost spreading from his fingers. Snow fluttered around them, the air sparkling with ice crystals, and Aaron's harsh breaths puffed white.

Another man stepped on the back of Aaron's neck, pinning him in place, and pulled a small vial from his pocket, its contents sickly yellow. He unscrewed the top.

I dropped my purse, grabbed my umbrella, and charged out from behind the dumpster.

No one saw me coming until I was winding my umbrella up like a baseball bat. I swung it full force into the guy's face, knocking him and his creepy vial off Aaron. Skidding on the ice-coated ground, I whammed my umbrella into Ice Guy's face too. It cracked against his nose and he recoiled with a shout.

As I swung the umbrella for strike number three, someone caught it and wrenched it out of my hands. I turned in time to catch a fist to the face. My head snapped back, my skull splitting open along my eye socket—or that's what it felt like. As I went down, my near-forgotten taekwondo training kicked in and I caught myself without scraping my elbows open to the bone.

Rolling over, I shot to my feet. A couple yards away, a guy went flying in a spiral of flame as Aaron launched upright. I was diving for cover when the same asshole who'd punched me grabbed my hair and yanked me back. Balling my hand into a fist, I jammed it into his stomach.

He doubled over with a wheeze and I rammed my knee between his legs. As he toppled, something small fluttered from his hand. I snatched it off the ground—a Queen of Spades playing card, worn and yellowed like it was fifty years old.

My attacker straightened with a hiss, his teeth bared. "Give that back."

I flipped the card so the queen was facing him. "Why would I do that?"

As fire exploded on my right and someone screamed, the guy stuck his hand in his pocket and yanked out a new magic toy—another playing card.

"*Impello!*" he yelled.

"*Orepecutio!*" I shouted.

A ripple of air—and an invisible force slammed into my chest like a battering ram. I flew backward and hit the ground hard. This time I couldn't save my elbows, but I stopped my head from smacking the pavement.

"It's *ori repercutio*, idiot girl," he snarled, advancing on me. "What kind of sorcerer are you?"

Who said I was a sorcerer? Nice of him to correct my pronunciation, though.

He swapped to the second card in his hand—an Ace of Hearts with a twisty rune in the center. "*Ori impello potissime!*"

I thrust the Queen of Spades at him. "*Ori repercutio!*"

The air rippled and a massive force struck the man. He was hurled almost straight up, crashed into a wall, then tumbled to the ground in a heap. I glanced in awe at the Queen of Spades. Wow.

Grabbing my umbrella from a puddle, the magic card in my other hand, I scrambled up. Two other men were down, but Ice Guy and the last pair had Aaron surrounded. Flames blazed over his limbs and sparks swirled around him. The ground was on fire and steam billowed, tinted orange by the inferno.

Ice Guy faced him from within a cloud of white, frost clinging to his clothes and lining his dagger. Where the fiery aura around Aaron met the dense cold around Ice Guy, the air sizzled and steamed.

Aaron punched his hand out, his weapon gone but his flames undiminished. A fireball exploded from his fist and flew at Ice Guy. The other two men attacked Aaron from behind with small items like my new playing card, shouting incantations.

As Aaron whirled on them, I ran toward the battle, my sandals splashing through ice-cold puddles. I jumped behind Aaron and pointed my card at Ice Guy.

"*Ori repercutio!*"

Nothing happened.

Ice Guy slashed his dagger at me. I whipped my umbrella up and the blade hit it, snapping the metal rod. As the umbrella folded in half, the dagger caught in the layers of nylon fabric and I wrenched it sideways. The dagger tore out of Ice Guy's grip, and I flung both items away.

Unfortunately for me, Ice Guy didn't miss a beat. He grabbed me by the throat, fingers squeezing. Agonizing cold flashed over my skin.

Heat washed across my back, then Ice Guy threw me aside as Aaron charged in, fire rippling over his arms. He tackled Ice

Guy and they went down in a cloud of hissing steam. I clambered up, my throat throbbing.

Ice Guy broke free and scrambled backward, and my neck immediately felt better when I saw the blistering burns on his arms and face. Ha, take that!

Aaron rolled to his feet, still on fire like it was no big deal, and I sidestepped closer, the heat blasting me like I was standing next to a bonfire. I clutched my unpredictable Queen of Spades card, afraid to rely on it but with no other weapons.

The man beside Ice Guy stuck his hand into the back of his coat—but the weapon he withdrew wasn't a dagger or a spell or even a playing card.

He swung the black pistol up, and before I could move, he pulled the trigger.

10

THE SHOT didn't ring out, blasting our eardrums into dust. Instead, it popped like a toy gun—and something bright flashed toward us.

Aaron jerked away, hideous yellow liquid splattered across his bare arm and sizzling from the heat of his skin. Not a pistol with bullets—a paintball gun. But that yellow liquid wasn't paint.

He swayed. Lurching for balance, he grabbed my arm. His hand burned and I gasped as his legs gave out. He dragged me down, hitting the pavement on his knees, and both his arms clamped around me.

The air heated, crackled, burned.

Fire exploded out from Aaron, turning the alleyway into a wall of flame. Only the tight circle within his arms was spared the fire, but the *heat*—I couldn't breathe. My head spun, my skin screaming, my clothes scorching.

The flames died, revealing the blackened alley. Ice Guy was gone, as were his companions. The downed attackers were far enough away that the lethal inferno had missed them. I glanced at my hands, relieved they weren't blistering—just pink, like I'd turned the shower too hot.

Aaron's skin cooled and his arms loosened, then he tipped over, catching himself on one elbow.

"Shit," he rasped.

I gripped his arm. "Are you okay?"

"Poisoned. No idea what it does." His arms trembled as he pushed himself up. "We have to get out of here."

"What—" I broke off as, in the distance, police sirens echoed through the streets. Oh crap. I did not want to get caught in an alleyway with several weapons, three unconscious men, a poisoned pyromage, and a lot of fire damage.

"Okay," I gasped, struggling to think straight. "Let's go. Come on, Aaron."

Shoving the Queen of Spades into my back pocket, I heaved on his arm. He staggered upright and sagged against me, almost toppling us both. My legs quivered as I supported his weight.

"My apartment is across the street," I panted, dragging him past the dumpster. "Crap, my purse."

I helped him lean against the dumpster, grabbed my purse, then pulled his arm over my shoulders again. We hobbled out of the alley and across the street. Kicking the building's main door open, I dug one-handed in my purse for my key fob. I slapped it against the panel to unlock the security doors, then wrangled them open and limped into the lobby.

A middle-aged woman, waiting at the elevator with a wheeled suitcase, watched us approach with eyes that grew wider and wider the closer we got.

I forced a smile, trying not to crumple under Aaron's weight. "He had too much to drink."

Her bug-eyed stare shifted from him to me. "Good god, girl. What did he do to your face?"

Oh damn. So I wasn't imagining that my eye felt hot and puffy. "Wasn't him."

Her look screamed skepticism, but then the elevator dinged and the doors slid open. I heaved Aaron inside and he slumped against the wall, groaning. His eyes were squeezed shut, his face white and shining with perspiration. If he'd been drunk and not poisoned, I would've been searching for a bucket for him to puke in.

The woman must have thought the same, because she backed up. "I'll take the next one."

Relieved, I jammed the button for the ninth floor three times. The door slid shut and the elevator glided upward.

"Hang on, Aaron," I whispered, rubbing his shoulder. Flakes of his crisped shirt fluttered to the floor. "Almost there."

He didn't answer, his concentration consumed by the battle to stay upright.

The elevator dinged open to reveal a quiet, carpeted hall. I pulled him past the rows of doors to Justin's apartment, fumbling with my keys. Unlocking the door, I dragged Aaron inside. He was staggering badly, his weight too much for me. We stumbled down the short hall into the living room and I pushed him toward the sofa. He fell, landing half on the cushions, yellow potion smearing over the blue fabric.

I rushed back to shut and bolt the door, then quickly checked myself for any poison. None of it had gotten on me, so that was one problem I didn't have to worry about.

Returning to Aaron, I fought back a wave of panic. His clothes were charred, his elbows scraped and the knee of his jeans torn out from a fall. A long slice down his forearm leaked blood, and scary white patches on his skin warned of frostbite from Ice Guy's power. His cheek was scraped to hell from that dickwad stepping on him and pushing his face into the gravelly pavement.

"Aaron?"

His face was slack. He'd lost consciousness.

Panicked buzzing filled my head. Aaron had been poisoned by who knew what sort of nasty magic potion. He was unconscious, possibly dying. What was I supposed to do? Hyperventilating, I dug out my phone and called Clara. It went straight to voicemail, but I called again. And again.

Giving up on Clara, I stared at my phone, my finger trembling over the 9. Did I call 9-1-1? Could human emergency services save him? What should I do?

I squeezed my eyes shut, commanding myself to focus, then threw my phone aside. Kneeling beside the sofa, I patted down Aaron's front pockets, then wiggled my hand under his ass to check the back ones. My searching fingers found the hard rectangle of his phone. I pulled it out and swiped the screen. Locked.

Grabbing his poison-free hand, I pushed his limp forefinger against the fingerprint reader. The screen flashed awake. Thank goodness for hackable technology.

I opened his contacts and speed-scrolled past a zillion names to the Es—but Ezra's name wasn't there. Swearing, I zoomed down to Kai's number and called it. The phone rang, rang, rang, then clicked to voicemail.

"No!" I yelled at the phone. "Why won't you answer?"

On a date. Aaron had said Kai was out on a date tonight, but Ezra had stayed home. I checked his contacts again, but Ezra's name wasn't there. With trembling hands, I opened his most recent apps, found his messenger, and pulled it up. A conversation with Kai, and—

"Cyclops?" I hissed. "You put him in your contacts under Cyclops?"

I dialed Ezra's number and held the phone to my ear. It rang … rang … rang—

"Hello?"

Ezra's groggy voice was the most beautiful sound I'd ever heard. I opened my mouth but only a whimper came out.

"Aaron?" Ezra asked, alertness sharpening his tone.

"Ezra!" I burst out, my quavering voice on the edge of tears. "Aaron needs help!"

"Tori?" His drowsiness vanished. "What—"

"We were attacked walking home," I blurted. "There was a guy with ice magic and sorcerers—I think they were sorcerers—and one of them shot Aaron with this yellow stuff and Aaron said it was poison but now he's unconscious and I don't—"

"Tori, calm down." Ezra's level voice, meltingly smooth, soothed my panic. "Take a deep breath."

I sucked in air.

"Is Aaron breathing?"

"Yes."

"Is he bleeding?"

"A little."

"Where are you?"

"At my apartment." I rattled off the address.

"I'm coming to you. I'll be there in ten minutes, okay? Call Kai and tell him to find an alchemist and meet us at your place."

"I already called him. No answer."

"Keep calling. He'll pick up. I'll be there soon."

"Okay," I whispered.

As soon as the call disconnected, my panic started to climb again. Inhaling deeply, I crouched beside Aaron to watch his chest—making sure he continued to breathe—and called Kai. The phone rang until it went to voicemail. I called again. It rang twice, then the line clicked.

"Yes?" No drowsiness from Kai—just an irritated snap.

"Kai? This is Tori."

"Tori?" His sharp tone transformed into concern. "Why do you have Aaron's phone?"

"He was attacked walking me home," I said. "Ezra is on his way here, and he said you need to bring an alchemist."

"Where are you?"

I gave him my address. "Hurry, please."

"I'm leaving right now. Are you safe there?" As I confirmed our relative safety, his phone picked up the sound of a door slamming and footsteps thudding on a hard floor. "Tori, if Ezra arrives before me, have him wait outside until I get there."

"What? Why?"

"He doesn't handle it well when his friends get hurt." Another door banged open. "Trust me on this. I'll be there as soon as I can. Just hang tight."

He ended the call and I lowered the phone. Don't let Ezra inside the apartment? Ezra, Mr. Calm and Collected?

I set Aaron's phone on the end table and shifted closer to him. His breathing was even but slow, his face still slack. I twisted my hands together, wishing there was something I could do besides wait.

After a minute, I wobbled into the bathroom to pull the first aid kit from under the sink. Back at Aaron's side, I opened an alcohol swab and gently cleaned the slice on his arm, but blood was leaking out as fast as I was wiping it away. Whimpering, I grabbed a fat roll of gauze and wound half of it around his arm. Red soaked through it almost instantly and I whimpered again, sternly telling myself that he wouldn't bleed to death from the shallow cut.

Under normal circumstances, I'm pretty damn levelheaded—I like to think so, anyway—but this … this had shaken me bad. Not only the ambush, but the violence of it. The fire, the ice, the magic. Guns and bullets might have been deadlier, but at least they were familiar.

Aaron's phone erupted in a video game tune, scaring me out of my skin. I leaped to grab it and swiped the screen to answer.

"Hello?"

"I'm here," Ezra said. "Can you let me in?"

I hesitated. Kai had been clear, but … Ezra sounded as unruffled as always. Not only would I feel stupid leaving him down in the lobby, but I didn't want to be alone.

"Dial 1187 on the number pad and I'll buzz you through. My unit is 909."

I disconnected, and a second later, my phone rang. I pressed 9 to unlock the lobby's security entrance, then unbolted the apartment door. Kneeling beside Aaron again, I waited, my stomach twisting.

Ezra was on his way up, and I really hoped Kai was just paranoid.

II

WITH A QUICK RAP on the door, Ezra pulled it open. His dark brown curls were tousled from sleep, his black t-shirt wrinkled like he'd put on the first clothing article he'd spotted. I got up from the floor, but he didn't pause as he strode straight to Aaron. I wasn't sure he even saw me.

He crouched beside the sofa, his back to me as he surveyed his friend. My nerves prickled, my heart rate increasing. Gooseflesh rose on my arms and legs and I shivered. Was it just me or was it cold in here?

I exhaled and the air puffed white. Holy shit, it was *freezing*.

My gaze snapped to the doorway, searching for Ice Guy, but there was no one in sight. It was just me, Aaron, and … Ezra. My breath turned to white mist as the temperature kept dropping.

"Ezra?" I whispered.

His head twitched in my direction, and the lamp on the end table brightened, flooding the room with light. I frowned. When had it gone so dim?

The inexplicable chill lessened, and Ezra rose, facing me. For a moment, he looked normal—quietly unfazed, his brown eye warm and his colorless iris as unnerving as usual. Then his mismatched eyes widened in horror.

"Tori!" he gasped, reaching for me. "What happened to you?"

I blinked in confusion as his hands, hot compared to the chilly air in the apartment, gently took my wrist and lifted my arm. I blinked again when I saw the blood streaking my forearm, having run from the nasty road rash that had taken the skin off my elbow.

"Ow," I said in surprise.

Ezra's hands tightened painfully around my wrist, then gentled again. "Have you looked in a mirror?" he asked with forced amusement. "Your eye will swell shut soon."

I gingerly pressed my fingers to my cheek. Damn, it throbbed. If my injuries were that spectacular, I wondered why he was only just noticing—but as he searched my face, I understood. I'd been standing on his left when he came in, and he was blind in that eye.

He turned my arm over to check for more scrapes. "Are you hurt anywhere else?"

"Um. Face. Elbows." I glanced down, bemused to see my knees were mincemeat too. Why didn't it hurt more? Adrenaline was a hell of a drug. "Knees. I think that's it." Well, that and the bruises and soreness that would set in soon.

"I didn't realize they had attacked you too," he muttered. "If they were after Aaron, they had no reason to hurt you."

"Well, maybe not, but they didn't like it when I started beating them with my umbrella."

"When you … what? Didn't Aaron tell you to run?"

"Of course he did," I growled. "But I followed him because there were *six* of them, and when the ice guy got Aaron on the ground, I couldn't just stand there and watch while they …"

I trailed off as Ezra's face went eerily blank. The temperature plummeted again, the air chilling like the dead of winter. The lamp dimmed until only a faint glow leaked from the bulb, shadows deepening throughout the room.

My heart pounded and I wanted to pull my wrist from his hands, but I didn't dare move.

Then the front door banged as Kai swept in.

"Ezra." His voice cracked through the room. "Walk. Now."

Light bloomed as the lamp recovered. Ezra's expression didn't change as he released my arm, strode right past Kai and the woman who'd come in behind him, and vanished out the door. I inhaled unsteadily as warmth returned to the room, then peered at Kai's guest.

My hackles rose. It was none other than Blue-hair, the girl who'd "accidentally" spilled green dye all over my bar.

"What are you doing here?" I snarled.

She pressed her lips together, clutching a wooden case with a carry handle.

"Sin is an alchemist." Kai leaned down to check on Aaron. "I picked her up on my way. She'll sort out this poison."

"Apprentice alchemist," Sin corrected, brushing past me to join Kai. "Let me see what we've got."

As she knelt beside Aaron, Kai's dark eyes flashed over me from head to toe, and his all-business attitude faltered. "Why are you covered in green? Is that an alchemic potion?"

I shot a glare at Sin.

"That's my fault," she muttered, her shoulders hunching guiltily. "I spilled some dye earlier."

Kai's eyes narrowed. Without comment, he pulled a stool out from the kitchen peninsula and guided me to it. "Tell me what happened."

While explaining how Aaron had walked me home and the resultant stalkers, I watched Sin open her case. It unfolded into an intricate construction of small shelves and cubbies, all filled with vials, pouches, cloths, papers, and other tools. She swabbed Aaron's yellow-stained arm and dropped the cotton into a clean vial.

"Then the ice guy and Aaron started fighting, and it was … ugly," I told Kai. "He had a big dagger thing … that would make him a mage, right? Since he was using a switch?"

"A kryomage, yes," Kai said tersely.

And the others had been sorcerers—their incantations were a big giveaway.

"What happened next?" he prompted.

As best I could recall, I described the initial fight until Aaron went down. At that point I had to pause and breathe, adrenaline whipping through me at the intensity of the memory—the terror I'd felt for Aaron.

"That kryomage must have been very powerful," Sin murmured as she poured a few drops of liquid into the vial with the yellowed cotton. "A pyromage like Aaron should've been able to take him out easily."

Kai folded his arms. "Depends on the circumstances. The kryomage had a proper switch, and Aaron had five others to defend against."

I nodded. "Six against one was completely unfair. I wasn't much help, but I bashed the potion guy with my umbrella, and I gave the ice mage a good whack too, but—"

"Wait." Kai spun to face me. "You fought them?"

"What, do you think I got this banged up from running away?"

"But you … never mind. Please continue."

I finished the tale, but even though I glossed over my role, Sin stopped working to gawk at me. Kai's expression hardened, and I stuttered as I got to Aaron's explosive wall of fire. "I helped him get up here and he passed out. Then I called Ezra with his phone."

Kai gave a slow nod, then rubbed both hands over his face like he was trying to wake up. "Well?" he asked Sin.

She held up her vial. The yellow cotton had turned purple. "Looks like a basic sleeping tincture—a powerful one. The only reason he didn't immediately pass out was his fire evaporated most of it, and the smaller dose was slow to take effect."

"Do you have a counter?"

"I do, but it's safer to let it wear off naturally. I'll clean him up so his skin doesn't absorb any more."

"So he's going to be okay?" I asked, an edge of anxiety in my voice. "It's not a poison?"

"Any potion with a harmful effect is considered a poison," Sin said. "But yes, he'll be fine. He should wake up in a few hours. Do you have a spare towel so I can clean him up?"

I pointed her toward the linen closet. As she wet a cloth in the kitchen sink, Kai picked up the first aid kit from the floor. "Come on, Tori."

"Huh?"

"To the bathroom. Your injuries need attention."

"I'm fine. I can—"

"Now."

No arguing with *that* tone. Scowling, I headed for the bathroom and sat on the edge of the tub. He crouched in front of me, pulled out a chemical ice pack, and gave it a hard smack to trigger the cold reaction.

"Put that over your eye." He passed it to me, then ripped open an alcohol swab. I bit my lip as he scrubbed the dirt from my scraped knee with a lot more confidence than my attempted ministering of Aaron's injuries. Fresh blood ran down my leg. Owww. Kai bandaged it up, then cleaned my other knee and my elbows. Not fun.

When I was all band-aided, he set the kit on the counter. "You probably saved Aaron's life. Thank you."

I hunched, embarrassed. "I did what anyone would've done."

"No, you did what one in a million people would do."

He offered his hand. I clasped it and he pulled me up. Back in the main room, Sin had finished cleaning the sleep potion off Aaron and was tending to his cut arm with supplies from her alchemy tickle trunk.

"Where is Ezra?" I asked Kai in a low voice.

"Out in the hall, most likely." He pressed his lips together. "I warned you not to let him in."

The temperature was back to normal, but I couldn't forget the sudden, bone-deep chill. "Isn't he an air mage? How did he make the room so cold?"

"Most mages have one primary element, but also develop a secondary element. Air and water can be combined to produce ice."

"Oh," I muttered. "What about the light?"

"The light?"

"He made the room go dark."

Kai glanced at the lamp. "That must have been because of the cold."

"Kai, can you help me?" Sin asked, gauze in her hand.

As Kai knelt beside her, I crossed the apartment and slipped out the open door. In the hallway, Ezra leaned against the wall, hands in his pockets and head tilted back. Since I was on his blind side again, I opened my mouth to alert him to my presence, but he looked up first. As usual, he seemed downright tranquil, and the temperature was perfectly normal.

"Hey," I said, keeping my voice low so it didn't carry into the neighbors' units.

His gaze swept over me, and despite the colorless iris, his blind eye appeared deceptively functional. "How are you?"

"The adrenaline is wearing off. Everything hurts."

"You should take painkillers now, before it gets bad."

"Yeah." I slouched against the wall beside him and pressed the ice pack to my throbbing face. As half my vision disappeared, I felt a surge of sympathy for his impairment. "Aaron will be fine. Sin is taking care of him."

"Yeah, I heard you three talking." He stared at the wall across from us. "Sorry I didn't hold it together so well there."

"It's fine. I understand." I let my head thump gently against the wall. "You may have noticed I don't control my temper all that well either."

"Mm," he murmured vaguely.

"Are you okay?"

He looked away from me, and I took that as a "no." The fact he *seemed* so calm, yet apparently wasn't, disturbed me more than if he'd been shouting curses or throwing punches. When

I was in a temper, everyone knew it, but Ezra's silent, undetectable fury unnerved me.

I knew the kind of helpless fury that could drive a person half out of their mind. I wished I could help him rebalance. Only one thing had ever worked for me, but …

Gulping down my hesitation, I stepped away from the wall and faced him. "Would you … like a hug?"

His gaze flashed to me. "A hug?"

Already regretting the offer, I shrugged self-consciously. He hesitated, then lifted one arm in invitation.

Surprised, I stepped over to him and put my arms around his shoulders. His hands settled lightly on my waist, almost like he wanted the option to push me away. I rested my head on his shoulder, my face turned away from his. My attention settled on the warm contact of another person—the rise and fall of his chest, the sound of his heart beating under my ear, his hands on my waist.

The final jitters left my muscles and I relaxed. Hugs could work miracles, at least for me. When I was a ragey teenager hating all the adults in my life, Justin used to hug me until I calmed down, even if it took half an hour.

As I closed my eyes, Ezra relaxed too, the tension sliding from his muscles. He slipped his arms around my waist, holding me more naturally—pulling me closer.

Raising my head, I gave his shoulder a friendly pat and stepped back. "Better?" I asked in a chipper tone.

"Yeah." He gave me a faint smile. "Thanks."

I slapped the ice pack over my face again. "Let's go inside, shall we?"

Marching to the door, I cursed my stupid brain. Or stupid hormones. Or whatever. I hadn't meant to end our calming hug so abruptly, but when he'd finally relaxed, I'd done the opposite. All of a sudden I'd noticed I was pressed against a well-muscled chest, his broad shoulders under my hands, his warmth soaking into me, and dear god he smelled mouthwatering. Did he bathe in ambrosia or something?

Sweeping into the apartment, I found Kai sitting on the arm of the sofa beside an unconscious Aaron while Sin repacked her alchemy supplies. Kai gave Ezra a searching look.

"So," I announced. "Can we talk about the elephant in the room?"

"Which elephant is that?" Kai asked.

"The 'why did six mythic goons attempt to kidnap Aaron' one. I'd kind of like to know, seeing as I owe one of them a good punch to the face."

"It's not really a mystery" Kai replied tiredly. "Since they were trying to take him alive, it was probably another ransom kidnapping."

"Another … ransom … kidnapping." I repeated each word, boggled by the casual way he had strung them together.

"Among mythics, Aaron's family is famous," Sin said, latching her case. "They're extremely wealthy."

"And Aaron is the sole heir to that fortune," Kai finished. "It isn't the first time greedy fools have targeted him, though it's the closest anyone has come to succeeding."

I looked from him to Sin to Ezra. "So, what, this happens all the time?"

"More so when he was living at home." Kai glanced at Ezra. "I can only recall one other attempt since we moved here."

"I don't recall any attempts. Must've been before I joined the guild."

"Either way, the Sinclair family will deal with it. Frankly, I'm surprised anyone would risk getting on their bad side." Kai stood. "Aaron can sleep off the potion at home. Ezra, help me carry him."

I got out of the way as Kai and Ezra lifted Aaron between them and carried him out. Grabbing my keys, I hurried after them, and Sin followed. The wait for the elevator was fantastically strange—two mages supporting the third, an alchemist with blue hair and a potion kit, and then me—black eye, bandaged limbs, and green dye splattered all over my clothes.

Outside the apartment tower, two vehicles waited—an older red sports car parked on the curb with its hazard lights flashing, and a sleek black motorcycle abandoned on the lawn, two helmets hanging off the back. The guys loaded Aaron in the passenger seat of the car, then Ezra pulled out keys and offered them to Sin.

"Do you mind driving? Aaron will kill me if I smash up his baby."

She took the keys. "Didn't you drive over here?"

"Yeah, but it was an emergency." He noticed my confusion and smiled sheepishly, tapping the scar that ran down his face. "I don't have a license. No depth perception."

"Oh."

He tilted the driver's seat forward and climbed into the back. As Kai rolled the motorcycle onto the sidewalk, Sin cleared her throat.

"Here." She pulled two vials from her pocket, one with a thick pale substance and one half full of clear liquid. "Put the white cream on your injuries. It'll speed the healing process. And this one ... mix a few drops with water and it'll wash the dye out of your hair and clothes. It'll clean the stain off your sofa too."

As I took the vials, my expression must have been more suspicious than grateful, because she winced.

"I'm sorry. I … misjudged you. Thank you for helping Aaron."

I didn't know what to say, so I said nothing. She climbed into the red car and started the engine.

"Tori, will you be okay?" Straddling his bike with a helmet under his arm, Kai held the second one out to me. "You can come back to our place if you want."

The overwhelming urge to take the helmet and jump on the motorcycle with Kai swept through me. I didn't want to sit by myself in the apartment, listening at the door for signs of Ice Guy returning for revenge. Kai's aura of competence didn't allow stupid fears to exist in his vicinity.

But every bone in my body hurt, and I really needed a hot bath, my favorite pillow, and a bottle of painkillers.

"Thanks, but I'm good."

He nodded. "Call me if you need anything."

Sliding his helmet on, he started the bike and zoomed onto the road. The red car pulled away a moment later, following the bike's taillight. I watched the vehicles speed off, then peeked at the dark alley where Aaron and I had fought Ice Guy and his cronies. Fear zinged through me and I hastened back into the building.

It was only when I walked into the apartment and noticed Aaron's forgotten phone on the end table that I realized I couldn't call Kai if I needed anything. I didn't have his number, and without Aaron, I couldn't unlock the phone.

12

AN ELECTRONIC TUNE blared, startling me from sleep.

I tried to spring onto my feet but ended up spasming in place, groaning as every muscle in my body violently protested. Painfully rolling over, I grabbed my phone and squinted at the display, but it was blank. The ringing continued.

Fumbling for the end table, I snatched Aaron's phone and swiped the call button to answer. "Hello?"

"Morning, sleeping beauty," Aaron's cheerful voice declared. "I see you have my phone."

"You can't see anything," I mumbled, burrowing into my pillow. "Why are you calling me so early?"

"I know I said 'morning' but it's actually twelve thirty."

I groaned and flipped onto my face, dislodging half my blankets off the sofa onto the floor.

"Uh, hello?"

"Tori isn't here right now. Please call back when she's had more sleep."

He chuckled. "I'll keep it quick. I just wanted to make sure you're okay."

"I'm fine." I squinted my eyes open, blinded by the sunlight. "Are *you* okay?"

"Yep." A pause. "Entirely thanks to you."

"It was no big deal." I yawned, almost cracking my jaw. "You owe me a new umbrella, though."

"Consider it done. Can I swing by later today to get my phone?"

I nodded before remembering he couldn't see it. "Sure. Any time after … three."

"You're going to sleep *that* long?"

No, but it would take a very long, very hot shower before I was anything close to mobile. "I'll see you then."

"Later, Tori."

I tossed his phone onto the table and pulled the blankets around myself. Everything hurt and I wasn't even going to *think* about getting up for at least an hour.

PERCHED ON A STOOL at the kitchen counter a few hours later, I turned the Queen of Spades over, examining it from every angle. It looked like a regular, if ancient, playing card. The hand-painted queen wore a black dress with a cowl over her hair and held a spiky scepter that resembled a weapon more than a decoration. Her faint smile was enigmatic and commanding.

I'd forgotten the card was in my pocket until I prepped my shorts to wash with Sin's anti-dye potion. It had worked like literal magic, lifting the stains from my hair and clothes with a quick scrub.

I flipped the card over again, silently repeating the incantation: *ori repercutio*. From what I could tell, the spell reflected magical attacks, but not reliably. Still, it was cool. Would its previous owner miss it? I grinned evilly at the card. Finders, keepers.

Sticking it in the pocket of my comfy yoga shorts, I arched my back, grimacing at the painful ache. Nothing like a few hard falls to make all your muscles hate you. My bandaged elbows and knees stung but were easy to ignore. My black eye, not so much. It wasn't completely swollen shut, but close. I'd reapplied Sin's healing cream this morning, but it did nothing to hide the spectacular purple bruise.

Justin, dressed in thin sweats and a t-shirt, stepped out of the bathroom, releasing a wave of steam into the hallway. He'd arrived home from his shift an hour ago and his next stop was bed—already delayed by an extended interrogation about the state of my face before he'd gone to shower.

"How are you doing?" he asked. "Do you need anything?"

"I'm fine, Justin. It's just a bruise." I tried to roll my eyes but it hurt too much. "Seriously, I'm good. Get some sleep."

"You should quit that job before you get hurt again."

I shouldn't have told him I'd been injured in a bar fight at work, but it was the first lie that had popped into my mind. "It was an accident. Could've happened anywhere."

"You didn't come home with a black eye from any of your other jobs."

Grumbling, I started to rise when my phone rang. The caller ID flashed "Door," meaning Aaron was here to retrieve his cell. I hit 9 to unlock the security entrance.

"I'm meeting someone," I said. "Why don't you go to bed?"

"Meeting who?"

"A new friend from work. I accidentally took his phone last night." I stood up and stretched more stiff muscles. "It'll just take a minute."

I could feel Justin's eyes on me as I padded down the hall. A long minute passed, then someone knocked. With a warning glare at Justin, I opened the door. Aaron stood in the hallway, scratches marring his cheek and gauze taped over his arm, but otherwise as casually sexy as always in a maroon t-shirt and well-worn blue jeans.

Then I spotted the oversized purple gift bag hanging from his hand, a hot-pink umbrella hooked over the edge. "What is *that*?"

"*That* is the result of a bet," he said shamelessly. "I'd better win this one, Tori. I mean it."

"What bet?"

He peered over my head into the apartment. "Am I allowed in?"

"My brother is home."

"Ah. In that case—"

I sensed Justin approaching from behind.

"Don't be rude," Justin said, all sorts of territorial undertones in the simple words. "Invite him in."

Ugh. "Nah. He can just take his phone and—"

Aaron stepped forward, forcing me to back up. The three of us jammed into the cramped entryway. Aaron pulled the door shut, then offered his hand to Justin.

"Aaron Sinclair."

"Justin Dawson."

They shook hands and I swore their knuckles turned white. I really wished I could roll my eyes without hurting myself.

"Okay, okay, quit it." I grabbed Justin's shoulder and steered him down the hall ahead of me. "I guess you can come in, Aaron."

"I'm already in." He followed me into the main room, and as I plopped onto my stool, he leaned against the counter. "Nice place, man."

"Thanks," Justin said, slouching against the wall. "What happened to your face? And your arm?"

"I told you there was a bar fight," I jumped in. "Aaron is a regular. He broke it up."

"It was no biggie," Aaron said modestly. "Just a few scrapes."

"How did Tori get a black eye?"

Shit, Justin was cross-examining the witness to see if I was fibbing. "Justin, we're not suspects in a crime. Could you please lay off?"

He didn't look away from Aaron. "I don't like it when my little sister gets hurt."

Oh, screw this. I headed for the door.

"Tori," Justin called. "Where are you going?"

"Somewhere else. See you later."

"Wait." He pushed away from the wall. "I'm going to bed. You don't have to leave."

I paused, waiting skeptically. With a stern glance at Aaron, Justin went into his room and closed the door.

Reluctantly returning to my stool, I hissed, "You couldn't have just stayed in the hall, could you?"

Aaron grinned, unrepentant. "Then I wouldn't have found out if I won the bet."

"What bet?" I demanded.

"Do you like your new umbrella?" He unhooked the pink monstrosity and handed it to me. "I can't wait to see you hit someone with it."

I set it aside and gave him a hard stare. "The bet?"

"Sin started it." Laying the gift bag on the counter, he gestured grandly. "She said I should give you a thank-you gift for saving my ass—"

"I don't need a *gift*—"

"—but me, Kai, and Ezra disagreed on what to give you." He nudged the bag toward me. "Open it and take a look."

I almost told him to shove it. I hadn't expected thanks for helping him last night, let alone *gifts*, like I was some kind of high-maintenance princess girl. But my curiosity was too strong.

Grudgingly, I opened the bag and pulled out the first item— a huge bouquet of pink lilies and orange roses. The second gift was a box of chocolate and a bottle of wine, tied together with a red ribbon. I dug my hand into the bag and withdrew the last item: a fluffy white blanket with a pattern of colorful owls.

"So?" Aaron prompted. "Which one do you like most?"

"That's the bet? Which gift I'll like?"

"Yep."

"Did it occur to any of you that I might find this offensive?"

He dropped onto the stool beside me, unexpectedly somber. "I know we didn't need to get you anything, but … you've got to be hurting today. We can't fix that, but we wanted to give you something that would bring you some comfort."

Biting my lip, I looked again at the gifts. Explained like that, my annoyance melted away. "The flowers are from Kai."

Aaron blinked. "How'd you know?"

Kai was—reputedly—a playboy. Made sense he'd go for the traditional woman-charming gift. "You picked the wine and chocolate."

Aaron squinted at the items like they might have nametags. "Yeah …"

I touched the silky fluff of the blanket, tied into a bundle with a blue string. That meant the blanket was from Ezra. Had he made the logical leap from hugs to cuddly things, or was it a coincidence? Lost in thought, I picked up the flowers and circled the peninsula to the sink.

"Flowers? That's your favorite?"

"No." As far as I knew, Justin didn't own a vase, so I grabbed a tall beer glass and filled it with water. "I like all three."

"No, you have to pick one."

"Nope. I like them all." When he groaned, I arched an eyebrow. "Sore loser, huh?"

"I don't believe it," Aaron muttered. "I owe Kai fifty bucks."

I paused in the middle of arranging the flowers. "Huh?"

"He bet you wouldn't pick one."

Finished with the flowers, I absently opened the chocolates. Popping one into my mouth, I glanced at Justin's door then shifted closer to Aaron.

"I forgot to ask," I began in a whisper. "What happened to the guys in the alley? When we took off, the police were coming this way." Even out of sight in an alley, we'd caused more than enough commotion to draw attention from the surrounding condo buildings.

"Unless they dragged their sorry asses out of there in time, they were either questioned by the cops and released immediately, or they were arrested and released later."

"How do you know they were released?"

Aaron helped himself to a chocolate. "Our existence isn't public knowledge, but it isn't a complete secret either. Certain people at various levels of government and law enforcement know about mythics and keep in contact with MagiPol. Police are trained not to arrest anyone with the MPD logo on their IDs. Instead, they take down our info and submit it to MagiPol, and *they* go after the culprit."

"Seriously? Do the cops have any idea why they aren't allowed to arrest certain people?"

"No idea how it's explained to them, but they don't normally know about mythics. It's safer that way." Aaron selected another chocolate. "Think about it. If human cops tried to arrest a rogue mage, the mage could seriously hurt them or worse. Better if they stay out of it. Even if we get arrested, guilded mythics know better than to cause a fuss. MagiPol will step in and we'll be released within a few days."

"Huh."

"That doesn't mean those guys who attacked us get off scot-free. I already reported them to MagiPol. Normally, I'd have you file a report too, but then we'd have to explain why you were with me and that might bring up awkward questions about why you're working at my guild."

"Yeah, let's not do that." I picked out a second chocolate. "I'm glad you're okay."

"Me too." His hand closed around mine, the caramel-filled goodie between my fingertips. "Thanks for coming back for me, Tori."

Our eyes met, his blue stare so intense that my heart skittered wildly behind my ribs. Then he drew my hand up to his mouth and stole the chocolate from my fingers, his lips brushing my skin.

"Hey!"

"Mm," he said around the stolen mouthful of delicious caramel I'd been about to eat. "Good choice."

"That was mine!" I yanked the box away from him. "They're all mine. Last time I share with you."

He grinned and stood up. "I'd better go before I eat the whole box."

"You wouldn't dare." I followed him to the door, and as he stepped into the hall, I handed him his phone. "Don't forget it again."

"It would give me an excuse to come back."

"And risk another staring contest with my brother? Nuh-uh. I'll see you at work on Tuesday. Oh, but first." I pulled my phone from my pocket. "Can I get your number? And Kai's and Ezra's too?"

His initial smile faded at the mention of his friends. "A gorgeous girl asking for my number is less exciting when she asks for three numbers at once."

I snorted. "I need emergency contacts."

"I know." He took my phone and entered the three numbers. "There you go. One of us is always available, even if you have to call a few times."

"You didn't put Ezra under 'Cyclops,' did you?"

He laughed. "No, I just did that on my phone to annoy him."

I hesitated, then plunged in. "Does Ezra normally get a bit … strange in those sorts of situations?"

"He's protective of his friends," Aaron said with an airy shrug. "Who isn't? Take it easy until Tuesday, 'kay? And if you don't feel up to your shift, let Clara know."

"I'll be fine."

Once he was safely in the elevator, I returned to my apartment and surveyed the assortment of gifts. Humming thoughtfully, I carried the beer-glass vase to the end table, then unbundled the lightweight blanket and curled up on the sofa with it, the box of chocolates on my lap.

Snuggling into the blanket, I popped another chocolate in my mouth, feeling spoiled as hell. I'd never admit it to Aaron, but I did have a favorite gift—and I didn't plan to tell a soul which one I preferred.

13

BEYOND the unnecessary gifts the guys had lavished on me, my Saturday-night adventure produced an added bonus. When I arrived at the Crow and Hammer on Tuesday for my shift, my entrance was met with cheers. Before I knew what was happening, a dozen semi-familiar faces surrounded me, offering congratulations on kicking mythic ass and asking how I was doing. My black eye had faded to yellow-green, but it was still too hideous to hide.

I eventually made it into the kitchen, blinking stupidly. Ramsey looked up from the counter where he was slicing tomatoes.

"How are you doing?" he asked. "Heard about your escapade over the weekend."

"How does everyone know *already*?" I grumbled, stashing my purse and new hot-pink umbrella in the office. "You guys gossip like seniors at a bingo hall."

Ramsey flicked his dark hair out of his eyes. "News travels fast. Sin told the other alchemists, who told the sorcerers, who told everyone else."

"Sin?" I repeated warily. "What exactly did she say?"

"The story I heard is that Aaron was ambushed and outmanned when you saved his butt with nothing more than an umbrella and a stolen artifact." Faint skepticism crossed his features. "Did you really attack six mythics on your own?"

I twisted my mouth, embarrassed by all the attention. "I suppose, but what else was I supposed to do? Let them drag him off?"

"You're one tough cookie, Tori." His expression grew oddly intense. "What artifact did you steal?"

"Huh? Oh, you mean the card." I finished tying my apron, then pulled the Queen of Spades out of my pocket. "I snatched it from a sorcerer. He used it to shoot Aaron's fire back at him."

Abandoning the tomatoes and stripping off his latex gloves, Ramsey took the card and examined it. "A reflector spell?" He whistled. "That's rare stuff. What's the incantation?"

"Uh. *Ori repercutio.*"

"Wow. Crazy." His eyes brightened. "I specialize in this kind of Arcana—weapons to counter other magic—and this thing is throwing off arcane vibes like you wouldn't believe. It's no minor trinket."

Frowning, I slid the card from his hands. "Throwing off arcane vibes? It feels like a regular card to me."

"It's safe to say you have no latent arcane talent, then, but anyone can use an artifact like this. You don't need magical ability."

"It's not very reliable. It only worked once when I tried it."

"Different spells work in different ways." Leaning against the counter, he gestured at my card. "Arcana harnesses the energies of the natural world and gives them shape and purpose. Building spells can take hours, weeks, months, or even years, depending on the complexity of the result."

Huh. How long had the Queen of Spades spell taken to make? "That doesn't sound practical."

"It isn't, which is why combat sorcerers rely on specific tools, the most common being hexes and artifacts. A hex is a cantrip that—sorry, let me back up. A cantrip is a single-rune spell that can be cast with a brief incantation. Here, I'll show you."

He stepped into the office, grabbed a sticky note and a pen, and drew a strange symbol on the paper. Returning to the kitchen, he held the sticky note over the sink.

"*Igniaris.*"

The paper burst into fire, the hungry flames way bigger than the little paper should have produced. Ramsey snatched his hand away as the burning note fell into the sink.

"So, that's a cantrip. A hex is a pre-prepared one that can be reused instead of drawing it each time. If it isn't drawn perfectly, it won't work, so it's not something you want to do on the fly." He pulled a small object from his pocket and held it out—an oversized coin with a symbol etched in the center. "This is guaranteed to work every time. Hexes are the fastest magic a sorcerer can produce, but they lack power."

That fire spell had seemed powerful to *me*, but maybe that was because my standard for magical power was "zilch."

"An artifact is an enchanted object that contains a complex spell. Days or weeks of work goes into creating it, and it's far more powerful than a hex. Multi-use artifacts are the most valuable, but they can't be triggered over and over like shooting a gun. They passively gather energy to fuel the spell, and once you use it, you need to wait for the spell to recharge."

"Ooh, that explains why it didn't work every time. How long does recharging take?"

"Depends on the spell. For some, a minute or two. For others, days or weeks."

The sorcerer had used the Queen of Spades, then I had used it, but I wasn't sure how much time had passed. More than two minutes, less than seven, I was guessing.

Ramsey tapped the card. "All artifact incantations begin with '*ori,*' which awakens the spell. Then you speak the command word or phrase. '*Repercutio*' means to rebound or strike back."

"Hmm. So I just need to point this card at an incoming magical attack and speak the incantation, and it'll reflect it no matter what?"

"It'll reflect incoming magic up to a point. That spell has limits, though there's no easy way to determine how much it can handle. Still." He straightened. "It's valuable. If you want to sell it, let me know."

"You want to buy it?"

"I couldn't afford it, but I could find a buyer for you. Like I said, I collect this kind of stuff, so I know people."

"What's it worth?"

"I bet you could get twenty-five, maybe thirty for it."

I pulled a face. How broke was he that he couldn't afford thirty bucks? "I think we define 'valuable' differently."

"You don't think thirty thousand dollars is valuable?"

"Eh? I thought you meant—uh, yeah, that's a lot of money. I'll let you know if I decide to sell it." Controlling my shock, I stuck the dark queen back in my pocket. Note to self: do not lose card.

"Oh, and Tori? Keep that to yourself." He turned to the sink to wash his hands. "Humans aren't allowed to own artifacts. Most mythics would be delighted to take it off your hands whether you wanted to give it up or not."

Well, didn't that sound awesome. Was he including his fellow guild members as mythics I needed to watch out for?

Back at the bar, Aaron and Kai had appeared, sitting on stools with their heads bent over a laptop. I offered a quick greeting as I prepped my station and served drinks to the dozen patrons waiting for service—and waiting to hear more about the goon squad attack on the weekend.

By the time I had a breather, Sin had joined Aaron and Kai, her blue hair gleaming in the dim lights. She offered me a cautious smile when I approached, which I returned with equal wariness.

"How are your injuries?" she asked.

"Healing fast. That cream you gave me is amazing stuff." As I slid a rum and coke each to Aaron and Kai, I asked her, "Do you want anything?"

"Not right now, thanks."

I craned my neck to peek at the laptop screen. "Whatchya working on?"

Aaron leaned back. "I called my parents, but their sources can't find anything on a group of mythics aiming to exploit the family."

"I'm wondering if it might be related to the rogue sorcerer we took out on Saturday," Kai said, tapping away at the keyboard. "It seems too fast though."

"What about the attackers?" I asked. "Can't someone question them?"

"They all escaped before the cops showed up. We don't know who they are or where they came from." Kai glanced up, a darkly amused gleam in his eyes. "So Aaron is babysitting you, and I'm babysitting Aaron until we figure out who's after him."

Aaron gave a long-suffering sigh. "I don't need babysitting *here*. No one would be stupid enough to waltz into guild headquarters."

"True." Kai pulled the laptop closer. "But I need to get some work done anyway."

The evening passed quickly. Clara stopped to fuss over my eye and thank me for helping Aaron. I got more congratulations—according to mythics, a black eye was cause for celebration?—but what surprised me most was that Aaron didn't downplay how dire the situation had been. And if I answered questions too modestly, he would correct me— making it clear that if I hadn't jumped in to help, he wouldn't be here. I'd expected a guy with as much ego as him to hate admitting something like that.

When Sin came upstairs to the pub—she was working in the alchemy lab in the basement tonight—to get a soda, Aaron was in the middle of retelling the story to Lyndon the sorcerer.

"Doesn't it bother him?" I muttered as I passed her a coke. "Telling everyone how he needed help?"

As she slid onto a stool, Sin shrugged. "Mages are always tough, and Aaron is one of our best. Admitting he needed help only shows how powerful and capable his opponents were. We all know he isn't weak or stupid."

"Huh." I poured myself a coke. "What about Kai and Ezra?"

"Kai doesn't have as much brute power as Aaron, but he was well trained and disciplined even before joining the guild. I wouldn't want him as my enemy, that's for sure." She stirred her glass with the straw. "As for Ezra … he makes good use of the magic he has, but he isn't in Aaron and Kai's league. A lot of it is genetics. Some bloodlines are extremely gifted, others aren't."

Aaron and Kai didn't give off the impression that Ezra was a lesser mage, but when they captured that rogue sorcerer, Ezra was the only one who'd been hurt in the fight.

Taking a gulp of my coke, I remembered Ezra's invisible rage, the way the room had gone ice-cold and the lights had dimmed. That didn't seem like something a weak mage could do just out of temper, but what did I know?

"They seem like really good friends," I murmured.

"Best friends," Sin agreed, resting her chin on her hand. "Aaron and Kai have been as close as brothers since they were teenagers, and they joined the guild together. Ezra showed up a year or two after and applied to join, and Aaron and Kai took him under their wing—at least that's what I heard. They've been inseparable since the day I met them."

The last bit came out kind of grumpy and I raised my eyebrows questioningly. Sin checked no one was listening in, then bent closer.

"I've never met three guys who are this ridiculously hot but so *undateable*," she whispered vehemently. "Kai is always seeing like five women at the same time, Aaron only dates girls he thinks his parents will loathe, and Ezra practically runs and hides if you flirt with him. It's not fair."

Rant over, she primly sipped her drink.

I stared at her. "Aaron only dates girls his parents will hate?"

"Maybe not on purpose, but the pattern is obvious." She flapped her hand. "Anyway, sorry to derail. What were we talking about?"

"Um." I wasn't sure anymore. Aaron wanted to ask me out, though the ambush had delayed his plans. Did he see me as a girl his parents would hate? I smiled to myself. Upsetting parents—I was good at that.

Sin fiddled with her straw. "Honestly, Tori, I'm surprised you showed up today."

"You are?"

"I expected you to ghost us. It's not like we've been welcoming." Guilt flickered across her features. "Then being followed home, seeing Aaron attacked out of nowhere, fighting rogues and getting beat up. Dealing with mythics comes with risks, especially when you don't have magic to defend yourself, and the Crow and Hammer isn't a safe, easy guild. I figured you'd walk away and never look back."

She gazed at me expectantly, waiting for a response, but I said nothing, my thoughts scrambled. Now that she'd spelled it out, ditching the guild would have been the smart reaction to a near-deadly assault by criminal mythics, but I hadn't given the idea any serious consideration. Was there something wrong with me? Did I enjoy danger?

A strange feeling prickled in my stomach. Maybe it wasn't that I enjoyed danger but that I hated boredom. This place, these people—they weren't and never would be boring.

At the end of the night, Aaron drove me home in his old red sports car, Kai crammed in the back so I could ride in the passenger seat. We saw no signs of stalkers or would-be abductors.

The rest of the week passed in a comfortable routine. College in the morning, walking to the Crow and Hammer after class, hanging with Aaron—accompanied by Kai or Ezra—and visiting with Sin whenever she came up from the basement lab for a drink or snack. Now that she wasn't sabotaging my bar, she was fun to talk to. Her apology had been genuine and I'd decided to forgive her ... especially since I suspected Tabitha had been the whispering devil on her shoulder.

The biggest difference between my first week and my second, however, was the atmosphere. Putting my life on the line to protect a guild member had triggered a major shift in attitude. I wasn't living in a magical fairytale where everyone now adored me, but the overall response to my presence was improving.

More members smiled and made small talk. More friendly greetings. More tips. The cheer didn't vanish off their faces when they got near me. I'd thought weeknights were slow, but now I suspected members had been avoiding the pub. It was busier, livelier, and way more fun. Laughter, jokes, lots of banter. Drunken goofing off, mythic style.

Some people still despised me, but the number was shrinking. Any night Tabitha was on duty promised to suck. She always showed up at the worst moments, and though her cool remarks were never overtly antagonistic, by the time she vanished back upstairs, I'd be mired in bitter anger. Her subtle ability to make me feel unwelcome and unappreciated was as impressive as it was disheartening.

Sylvia the hag and I had reached a cold truce. Liam the weaselly telepathic had apologized and hadn't tried anything creepy since. Tom, the bookworm psychic, came in every night for a few drinks and quality reading time in his favorite corner. Alyssa, a girl with banana-blond hair, was so aloof I was surprised she hadn't injured herself walking around with her nose in the air, but whatever.

The jerk trio of vampire hunters, Cearra, Darren, and Cameron, had developed a real talent for insulting me whenever no one was listening, but I was coping. On the last occasion when Darren had deliberately spilled a freshly made Long Island Iced Tea across the bar, I'd spun around in the middle of pouring a drink and sprayed him in the face with my soda gun. Whoopsies.

It was getting better. It was getting fun. I was learning who was always up for good-natured banter and who was never in a good mood. Who liked to chat, who hated small talk, who was fun and who was trouble.

And through it all, Aaron was there with either Kai or Ezra, keeping me company and backing me up when someone was an asshole. For the first time in a long time, I found myself eager to go to work.

It was a good week, and by the time Saturday rolled around again, I was in the groove. Aaron and Ezra were parked at the far end of the bar, Aaron playing a video game while Ezra cheered him on. The pub was hopping and I zoomed in and out of the kitchen, taking orders and making drinks.

As the dinner rush died down, I carried a plate between tables. I didn't normally deliver food, letting patrons wait at the bar for their meal, but the girl who'd ordered was sitting at a table with cards spread across the surface in a strange pattern.

I nudged the plate onto the only free corner. "Need anything else?"

"This is fine. Thank you so much." She gave me a distracted smile and offered her hand. "I'm Sabrina, by the way."

"Tori. Nice to meet you."

Sabrina shifted in her seat, her large brown eyes emphasized with heavy makeup and fake eyelashes. "You spend a lot of time with Aaron and Kai, right?"

"At work," I confirmed. "Yeah."

"Do you have their numbers? I lost them and haven't had a chance to ask again."

Something about her innocent tone made me suspicious. "Sorry, can't help you there."

"Oh," she said glumly, adjusting her salon-perfect blond bob.

"Why don't you just ask? Aaron's right there."

When I turned to get his attention, she waved urgently. "No, no, that's fine. I'll ask later."

"Uh-huh."

Sweeping all the cards together, she beamed as though hoping to distract me. "Would you like a reading?"

The cards she was stacking into a neat pile had black backs with a gold sun and moon forming an ornate yin-yang, while the fronts featured ink drawings. Tarot cards. I'd normally scoff at that kind of stuff, but I was standing in a magic guild, so … yeah.

"You just used your cards, Sabrina." An old woman flounced over to the table, glaring through her turquoise-framed glasses. "You must *cleanse* your deck before performing another reading."

"I know how to use my cards." Sabrina straightened the deck with more violence than necessary. "Butt out, Rose."

Glare vanishing, Rose bestowed a gentle smile on me, her wispy white hair sticking out from beneath her knitted cap. "I'd be happy to do a reading for you, dear. Sabrina is a young diviner still learning her craft. I have many years of experience with which to—"

"Butt *out*, Rose!" Sabrina growled. "Tori, take a seat."

"Uh …" I looked from Rose's smug face to Sabrina's pleading stare and reluctantly sat. "I've never, um, had a reading … before."

"If a real diviner didn't do it, then it would have been useless anyway," Sabrina said cheerfully, shuffling her deck with mesmerizing speed. "A reading doesn't predict the future like those charlatans claim, but it shines light on the forces moving around you and it can reveal the path—or one of many paths— that lies before you."

Rose tittered. "Without cleansing her deck, Sabrina's reading will be tainted with the energies of her previous reading. And doing a reading here, in all this noise and activity? Useless."

"It's *fine*," Sabrina snapped. "I know my cards, Rose."

The old lady scoffed.

Sabrina set the deck in front of me. "First, shuffle the cards to imbue them with your energy."

I eyed them warily. "Um, will this take long? I can't be away from the bar for—"

"Only a few minutes, don't worry. Go ahead, shuffle them. While you do, think about the question you most want answered."

I picked up the worn cards, still warm from Sabrina's hands. As I clumsily shuffled them, I tried to think of something. A question immediately bloomed in my mind: *What next?*

It felt like I was settling in here … like I was *fitting* in. I enjoyed it. I could relax instead of dance across thin ice each shift, waiting for the guillotine to drop and my job to get cut out from under me. But it was only temporary. Once Darius got back from his conference thing, he'd sign off on my paperwork and MagiPol would give me the boot back into the human world.

Even if they didn't boot me, I'd already faced more danger at this job than at any other. Aaron's attackers were on the loose, their identities unknown. On top of that, Tabitha hated my guts—and she wasn't the only one.

What was I supposed to do? What came next?

"That should be enough," Sabrina told me. "Now cut the deck."

I cut it and passed it to her. She stroked the top card, her eyes losing focus. "Very good. Your energy has suffused the cards."

With dreamy movements, she pulled the top card and laid it face down on the table, then drew a second. One after another, she laid seven cards on the table in a V shape.

Rose sniffed. "I would have done a Celtic Cross spread for a more in-depth—"

"Shut up, Rose! This is the spread the cards want." Sabrina settled in her chair and placed her fingers on the first card. "This one represents your past."

She turned it over, revealing a painting of jeweled goblets. It faced me, making it upside-down for Sabrina.

"The Six of Cups, reversed. That suggests your past is holding sway over your future." She turned over the next card, revealing a tumbling building. "Your present, the Tower. Sudden, dramatic change has toppled your stable patterns."

Sudden, dramatic change? Oh, definitely. This job had thrown everything in my life out of whack. I wasn't complaining, though.

Sabrina turned the third card, revealing an array of blades. "The Seven of Swords. Hmm."

"What does it mean?" I asked.

"The third card in the spread represents hidden influences in your life, and the Seven of Swords suggests ... deception. Someone is misleading you."

Rose scoffed and Sabrina shot her a glare before touching the next card.

"This one represents your self." She flipped it. "The Hermit."

I wrinkled my nose at the artistic rendering of a bearded old man. "That's flattering."

"The Hermit is a card of wisdom and proud independence. But it's reversed." Sabrina pointed and I realized the card was facing me, not her. "The reversal warns that the strengths of the Hermit may also be weaknesses."

A chill ran down my spine. Okay, I was getting creeped out. "What's the next card?"

"The fifth card represents the people in your life." She turned it over to reveal an armored man with a sword. "The Knight of Swords. Loyalty, determination, courage. This is what surrounds you. Ah, but ..." She turned over the next card. "Eight of Swords. You fear commitment. You're holding back."

I sucked in a deep breath to calm my racing heart. "And the last card?"

"The last card is the outcome—the end of this path. Keep your question in mind, now." Sabrina touched the card, her eyes distant, then flipped it over. "Oh."

Rose gasped.

I stared, feeling cold all over. A lovingly detailed grim reaper with a bloody scythe graced the card. "Uh ... is that what I think it is?"

Sabrina coughed delicately. "This is the Death card, but it doesn't mean you're going to die. It's the card of transformation—of endings *and* beginnings."

Yeah, not particularly comforting.

Hovering her hands over the tarot spread, Sabrina sat quietly, her vacant stare moving from card to card. "Conflict surrounds you. You're caught in the midst of a violent change, and deception lurks in the shadows, calling the conflict ever closer. Your past stands in the way of your future, but though you've walked this far alone, others are waiting to join you. Even greater change awaits you, but its form"—she lightly touched the Eight of Swords—"will be shaped by the fear that rules your heart."

Ominous silence fell over the table. My focus shifted from the crumbling tower to the chilling specter of death to the armored knight with his sword raised, then darted to Aaron and Ezra, shoulder to shoulder as they battled aliens on the laptop.

"Conflict, yes, but the Swords deliver a different message," Rose declared. She tapped the Six of Swords, the Knight, then the Eight of Swords. "Secrets. Truth. Risk. Dangerous secrets will challenge the loyalty of your strongest allies, and if you seek the truth"—her gaze dropped to the Death card—"it will not be your fate alone bared to the reaper's blade."

Sabrina slapped Rose's hand away, huffing furiously. "You can't read another diviner's cards properly. Even an amateur knows *that*." She gathered up the seven cards and returned them to the deck. "Tori, what question did you ask the cards?"

I swallowed hard. "What comes next for me."

Sabrina and Rose exchanged a long, mysterious look that made me even more nervous.

"Ah," Sabrina muttered. "Um, well, you should know the cards don't determine the future. They reveal the path you're currently following, but you have the power to shift your destiny. Change your heart and you will change your path."

"Right." I forced a smile. "My question wasn't very specific anyway. The thing coming next for me is a shopping trip on Robson Street tomorrow. Maybe someone will try to rip me off."

Sabrina laughed. "I doubt the cards can predict something like that, but you're right. No need to worry. Just keep the reading in mind."

"She should take *my* warning seriously," Rose insisted. "That reading was fraught with conflict and danger. Life and death are bound to a secret she must uncover before—"

"Where are you planning to shop?" Sabrina asked loudly, drowning out Rose. "My favorite store is down by Burrard Street."

Grinning, I launched into a description of my favorite shops. Rose stalked off, shooting flinty stares at her young divination rival the whole way. I chatted with Sabrina for a few minutes, then got back to work, trying not to dwell on her reading—but the ominous words kept repeating in my head.

I would've loved to discount it as complete bullshit, but I'd seen too much magic in the last couple weeks to ignore the reading, no matter how unsettling it might be.

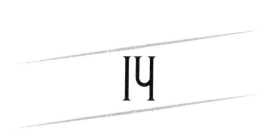

I **WASN'T BROKE** anymore, and it was time to splurge—just a bit. Friday had been payday, and thanks to my new-and-improved hourly wage, I had some cash flow. Rent for the month was paid, my bank account was comfortably outside the danger zone, and I was buying one brand-new top.

The limit on my purchasing power didn't bother me since I enjoyed the process of shopping a lot more than spending money. Yeah, I know, shopping is a girly activity, but I'm allowed to like *one* of those, right?

I strolled down Robson Street, moving with the flow of foot traffic. The sun beamed down and the air smelled of salty ocean water. I'd tempted fate by leaving my umbrella at home, but so far, so good. Not a single cloud marred the vivid blue sky, and half the city was outside enjoying the warm Sunday afternoon before the weekend tragically perished from a terminal case of Monday.

My phone chimed. Slipping it from my pocket, I quickly replied to Sin's text. We'd chatted this morning, and she was meeting me for lunch and a movie. I loved spontaneous plans, and I was long overdue for girl time. Making new friends was a skill I hadn't practiced since elementary school, and the coworkers I'd gotten friendly with at previous jobs had dropped me like moldy bread once I was fired.

Picking up my pace, I zipped through packs of tourists with cameras hanging around their necks and power-shopping prima donnas with six bags on each arm—or on the arms of her unlucky male partner. Flip-flops slapping on the sidewalk and oversized sunglasses perched on my nose, I headed for my favorite clothing shop.

Its doors were propped open and an assortment of tired boyfriends stood like sentinels on either side. Why they didn't wait in the air-conditioned interior, I had no idea. Maybe they were afraid they'd catch shopping cooties or something.

Breezing past a guy clad in head-to-toe black with a ball cap and sunglasses, I swooped toward the first sale rack and sorted through the tank tops. Picking out a blue one with fancy straps, I held it up to my chest, checking how it went with my cutoff jean shorts. Once, they had been my favorite pair of jeans. Now they were my favorite pair of shorts, and I would wear them until they unraveled around my ass.

I spent fifteen minutes loading up on discount tops, gradually making my way toward the changerooms at the back. My phone chimed again—Sin, checking in. I texted that I was almost done and would meet her at the café in twenty minutes. As I shoved my phone back in my pocket, I spotted Mr. All-in-Black leaning against a pillar, all alone, his sunglasses pointed at his phone. His unlucky girlfriend must've been avoiding association with him in public. Couldn't blame her.

Skipping to the changerooms, I locked the door and stripped off my flower-patterned tank top, then tried on the blue one. Not bad, except with my red hair I looked like Mystique. Maybe not.

I tried on a few more shirts, separating them into "probably not" and "what the hell was I thinking when I picked this up?" piles. As I pulled on a deep purple top with a neckline that plunged way deeper than expected, the changeroom door rattled.

"Occupied," I called as I squinted at my girls on full display, the edges of my red bra peeking out. Probably not a work-appropriate top. I bet Aaron would like it, though.

The door rattled again—then burst open. I yelped, jumping back before it hit me. "I said occu—"

Mr. All-in-Black shoved into the changeroom and grabbed me by the throat.

Choking, I clutched his wrist as he elbowed the door shut and locked it again. He pressed me into the wall, knocking hangers onto the floor, then lifted his sunglasses up.

"Remember me?" he growled.

Oh shit. It was the sorcerer guy—the Queen of Spades' original owner.

Fingers squeezing my throat, he pinned me against the wall with his body so I couldn't kick him. "I'd like my artifact back, girl."

I raked my fingers over his wrist, scoring bloody tracks. He hissed, then stuck his hand into his pocket. I felt him press a card against my stomach.

"*Ori torqueo male.*"

Heat flashed through my body—then agonizing pain raked across my nerves, lighting my bones on fire. I convulsed, his grip on my throat choking off my scream.

"That doesn't feel good, does it?" He loosened his hold and I sucked in a trembling gasp. "Where's my artifact?"

I stared at him, unable to respond, my vision blurred and my body shaking from the aftershock of the torment. I felt freezing cold all over.

"Where is my artifact?" he snarled, squeezing my throat again.

Jaw clenching, I tipped my head toward my purse. As soon as he turned, I flung my fist up and punched him in the ear. He grunted in pain and shoved me into the wall, but I rammed both arms down on his wrist, breaking his weakened grip on my throat. Air rushed into my lungs and a violent coughing fit racked my body.

He shoved me onto the floor. Silver flashed in his hand—a medieval-looking dagger, the blade pointed at my face.

Someone rapped on the changeroom door. "Everything okay in there, miss?"

I didn't dare look away from the sorcerer. He flicked his gaze to the unseen woman, then brought the dagger closer to my face. The warning was clear—if I said the wrong thing, he'd shove the blade into my eye socket.

"Fine," I rasped. "I just dropped my bag."

"Let me know if you need anything," the saleslady replied, her tone unconvinced.

Neither me nor the sorcerer moved, waiting to see if she said anything else. The normal bustle of the shop went on uninterrupted, our life and death scuffle unnoticed.

The sorcerer lowered the tip of his knife until it hovered just below my eye. "*Ori calefacio*."

The blade glowed cherry red, the heat scorching my cheek. "Where is it?"

Pressing into the floor to get away from the hot steel, I whispered, "My purse."

His lips pulled back in a malicious grin and his arm tensed, the dagger's point dipping toward my throat.

My phone chimed loudly.

He started, his head snapping toward the sound. I shoved his wrist upward, pushing the lethal blade away from my skin. My other hand slapped his hip—right over his pocket of card artifacts.

"*Ori torqueo male*," I gasped.

A strangled cry erupted from him, his muscles spasming from the pain spell. He crumpled on top of me, the dagger clattering to the floor. With a surge of panic-heightened strength, I shoved him off and scrambled up. He grabbed me and we toppled into the door.

The door gave way, dumping us onto the hard floor tiles. Shoppers cried out in shock. Flailing wildly, I tore free. As I shoved backward on my ass, he lunged into the changeroom. Someone yelled to call the police.

The sorcerer reappeared with my purse under his arm, his dagger in one hand and a playing card in his other. His lips moved in a near-silent incantation and the air rippled. Invisible force hit me like a football tackle, and the spell hurled me into a rack of plus-size bras.

As the bras and I crashed to the floor in a tangle of pink and white lace, the sorcerer bolted for the door. Panting, I burst out of the mess and charged after him. He could take his stupid card back if he wanted it that bad, but he was *not* stealing my purse!

The sorcerer raced out the open doors and bowled through the afternoon foot traffic. As unfortunate tourists went flying, I tackled the sorcerer from behind. He went down with a furious shout. Before I could pin him, he slammed me onto the sidewalk. Screaming people fled as he raised his dagger. He slashed the blade at my stomach.

A foot in a pink sandal swung out of nowhere and kicked his hand. The knife caught my shirt with a loud tearing sound.

Rearing back, the sorcerer pulled out a new playing card. "*Ori—*"

His shout cut off and his face went slack. He tipped over backward, head smacking the pavement.

I blinked dazedly at the pink sandals that had saved me. My stare rose up the woman's legs, over a cute sundress, and found Sin's blue hair. She stood with her hand extended over the sorcerer, a vial held upside-down over his unconscious form.

The vial disappeared into her purse as she crouched beside me. "Are you okay?"

"Um." I pulled a jumbo bra off my wrist and tossed it away. "Now I'm okay."

A crowd gathered around us, and three saleswomen from the store hung out the door, their faces ghostly white.

"We called the police," a woman said. "They're on the way. Do you need an ambulance?"

"I'm fine." My voice sounded like crunching gravel and I massaged my sore throat.

Sin pulled me up, her arm around my shoulders. Someone handed me my purse and I clutched it to my chest. *My* purse. No one was allowed to steal my purse. It had my wallet in it.

"We need to leave before the police arrive," Sin whispered in my ear.

"But I haven't paid for this top."

"I don't think they care. The shirt is trash."

Okay, that was mean. It wasn't the most tasteful shirt, but my boobs looked fantastic.

Sin pulled me into motion. "She needs to sit down," she announced. "There's a bench this way. Come on."

People moved aside for us, then closed the gap again, imprisoning the sorcerer behind a wall of captivated bystanders. Sin steered me away from the commotion, her pace increasing the farther we got. I stumbled along, my knees trembling.

Two blocks away, she pushed me onto a bench and dug out her phone. As she dialed a number, I hugged my purse and squinted at the bright street, trying to pull myself together.

"Hurry," Sin was saying into her phone. "I think she's in shock … I don't know yet! Just hurry!"

She stuffed her phone back in her purse and crouched in front of me. "Tori, what happened?"

"That jackass ambushed me in the changeroom. He wanted his card back."

"His what?"

"The artifact I stole when I helped Aaron."

Her eyes widened. "He was one of the rogues from last weekend?"

"Yeah. He kept demanding his artifact back." I frowned. "Where did you come from, anyway? Weren't you meeting me at the café?"

"The bus drives right by the store, so I got off early. I thought we could walk to the restaurant together." She tugged on my purse. "Let me see your stomach."

"What's wrong with my stomach?"

She pulled my purse away, and I saw what was wrong. The sorcerer's dagger hadn't caught only my shirt. Blood stained the fabric around the tear, but when Sin lifted the hem, we found a shallow scratch that had barely broken my skin. Well, this explained why she'd called my shirt trash—it was literally destined for the garbage.

"Okay, that's just a minor cut. Good." Sin tugged my shirt down. "Are you hurt anywhere else?"

"No, I'm just ..." I took a shaky breath. "He used a spell ... *ori torqueo* something ... and it ... really hurt."

"Oh," Sin murmured. "I'm sorry, Tori. That's an illegal spell. He shouldn't have had something like that."

"Well, it's not like he's a law-abiding citizen."

She sat beside me, patting my shoulder while I practiced slow, even breathing. In the frenzied panic of the fight, I hadn't realized how shaky and dazed that pain spell had left me. The dizzy out-of-body feeling lingered stubbornly.

A revving engine rose above the other sounds, then the squeal of brakes. A car lurched as a black motorcycle cut it off and veered toward the sidewalk. It jumped the curb and slid to a stop, forcing pedestrians to scatter. The leather-clad driver flipped his tinted visor up.

"Kai?" I blinked at him. Whoa. How had I not noticed how badass he was before now?

Sin dragged me to the bike and pushed me onto the seat behind him. The leather vibrated alarmingly under my butt.

Unhooking a spare helmet from the back, Sin handed it to me. "Put that on."

As I attempted to jam the helmet over my ponytail, she spoke quietly to Kai. I had to pull the tie out of my hair, freeing my curls from their ponytail, before I could get the helmet on. Sin stuffed my purse into the saddlebag behind my thigh, then squeezed my arm.

"Kai will get you out of here," she assured me. "Just hold on tight, okay?"

I obediently wrapped my arms around Kai's waist. "What about you?"

"I'm going to see what I can find out about that sorcerer before the police cart him off. I'll check in with you later." She nodded at Kai, then marched back to the scene of the crime.

"Pick your feet up, Tori," Kai instructed, pulling his visor down.

"I've never ridden a motorcycle before," I told him, reluctantly lifting my sandals off the ground and half expecting the bike to tip over, but Kai kept it steady.

"All you have to do is hold on." He craned his neck to look back at me. "Use the footrests."

Pulling my feet up higher, I found sturdy metal pegs to prop them on. Okay, this wasn't so bad.

The engine growled and the motorcycle jumped into traffic. I clung tightly to Kai, wide-eyed behind my helmet visor. The busy street was bumper to bumper, but Kai zoomed between cars and down the center line with no regard for traffic laws. He cut off Robson Street and wound through a maze of side roads, heading east toward the edge of downtown.

As we left the skyscrapers behind, I expected him to turn north toward the Crow and Hammer, but he took a right instead. Small, quaint shops with colorful awnings and outdoor markets replaced the downtown buildings. We passed the edge of Chinatown, then he turned onto a residential street lined with mature trees and cute little houses.

The motorcycle rolled to a stop in front of a beige house with blue trim, the tiny front yard enclosed by a wooden fence with a trellis arch over the front walk. As Kai cut the engine, I took in the adorable cottage-style house, then carefully swung off and wobbled a step away.

Kai jumped off the bike, set the kickstand, then pulled me into his arms.

I squawked in surprise. "I can walk!"

He ignored my protest and carried me under the trellis as Aaron rushed out of the house to meet us, his expression grim.

"How is she?" he demanded.

"Sin said no serious injuries, but he hit her with a torque spell."

Aaron hissed. Spinning on his heel, he backtracked up the stairs to the front stoop. "Ezra is on his way. He'll be here in a couple minutes."

"Guys, really, I'm fine."

The way my voice croaked from my bruised throat wasn't convincing, and unsurprisingly, they ignored me. Inside, Kai carried me past a landing with stairs up to the second floor. The living room featured big bow windows and French doors leading into a dining room. A large sofa and reclining chair filled the space, and a huge flat-screen TV took up the opposite wall, several game systems arrayed on a low stand beneath it.

Sweeping into the dining room, Kai deposited me on the table. I pulled my helmet off, glaring at them. "I said I was fine."

"I know what you said." Aaron took my wrist, his fingers pressed to my pulse. "But I don't believe you. Torque spells can send the body into neurogenic shock."

"Into ... what?"

Kai dropped his helmet on the table, knocking a stack of old flyers onto the hardwood floor. "Do you feel dizzy? Disoriented? Weak? Clammy?"

"No," I said indignantly, then hesitated. "Not anymore."

Aaron and Kai exchanged knowing looks.

"There's blood on her shirt," Kai said.

I swatted Aaron's hands away before he could lift my shirt, then pulled up the hem to display the shallow scratch. "It's nothing."

"I'll get the kit." Kai walked out, and his footsteps sounded on the stairs.

"Any other injuries?" Aaron asked.

"*No.* You guys are completely overreacting."

Aaron's eyebrows shot up. "Maybe it hasn't sunk in yet that a rogue mythic hunted you down and almost killed you. Personally, I don't think we're overreacting."

My stomach turned as belated fear shivered through me. When he put it that way …

Kai reappeared with a first aid kit so large it could store an entire paramedic team. "Tell us what happened. Every detail you can remember."

Holding up my shirt, I recounted the tale while Kai cleaned the scrape on my stomach. Since it had already stopped bleeding, he didn't bandage it. Dropping my shirt down again, I concluded with Sin's rescue.

"He was *waiting* for you?" Aaron growled. "How the hell did he know you'd be there?"

"No clue. I told Sin this morning where I was heading, but that's it. My brother knew I was going shopping, but not where."

"Then how could he have—" Aaron broke off as the front door banged.

Ezra strode into the room, dressed in running gear with his brown curls windswept. "Is she hurt? How bad is it?"

"She's okay," Kai said. "Just a scratch on her stomach."

Ezra stopped in front of me, his worried eyes sweeping down to check I still had all my limbs. As his gaze came back up, it stuttered to a stop a good bit lower than my face.

Huh, well. I'd wondered if Ezra didn't date because he wasn't interested in women, but my impressively displayed cleavage had just proved otherwise.

Aaron put his hands on his hips and gave me a once-over as though Ezra's ogling had given him permission to look too. "I've gotta say, Tori, that's a daring shirt."

"I shoplifted it."

The three guys gave me the same incredulous stare.

"I didn't mean to," I added glumly. "Sin rushed me away before I could pay for it." I tugged the neckline up, but it slid back down until my bra was peeking out again. "I didn't even want it."

"Uh." Aaron struggled to focus. "Would you like to borrow a shirt?"

"That's okay. I can change at home."

"Er, about that." He leaned against the table beside me. "I think you should hang out here for a few days."

"Huh?"

"If that sorcerer found you," Kai said, "other rogues involved in the ambush last week could find you too. They probably think you're a guild member—a mythic. They may come after you for that artifact, or use you to get to Aaron."

Alarm flashed through me, but I shook my head. "I'll be fine. I live with a cop, you know."

"You do?"

"Didn't I mention my brother is a police officer? Well, he is. I'm perfectly safe at home."

"You'll be safer with us." Ezra's smooth, soothing voice washed over me. "We'd worry about you by yourself."

Damn it. Why did he have to play the "we'll worry" card?

"It's only a few days," Kai added. "Since you and Sin took out the sorcerer, we have a place to start. We'll figure out where he came from, who he's working with, and most importantly, who he's working *for*."

My mouth twisted. I didn't want to freeload off the guys any more than I wanted three overprotective bodyguards shadowing my every move, but ... I thought of that sorcerer and his glowing dagger, and I imagined him stalking through my apartment. Justin might be a cop, but he stood no chance against mythics he didn't know existed.

Suppressing an anxious shiver, I reluctantly nodded. "For a few days, I guess."

"Great!" Aaron said brightly. "You can sleep in my room. I'll take the sofa."

Kai pulled a face. "You're a slob. She won't want to sleep in your room."

"Oh, are you offering yours? She'll love *that*."

"At least my room is clean."

"Mine's clean. Just a bit ... cluttered. *You* have weapons everywhere. She's liable to trip on a sword and impale herself."

As they argued, Ezra glanced between them, then walked away. Easing off the table, I followed him. Aaron and Kai continued to bicker, not noticing our departure.

At the top of the stairs was a small landing with three doors, one open. I stepped into the threshold as Ezra pulled folded sheets from the closet. The small bedroom, with one slanted wall where the roof cut into the space, was simple and tidy. A double bed with a gray patchwork blanket, a hand-me-down dresser with chips in the wood, and a bookshelf loaded with paperbacks and movies. An acoustic guitar on a stand sat in the corner.

The art on the walls surprised me the most: four large prints of mountain landscapes, one for each season. I studied them, finding an unexpected resonance between the peaceful scenery and Ezra's meltingly smooth voice that calmed me so easily.

"I'm good with the sofa," I told him. "I've been sleeping on one for nine months."

"You'll have more privacy here. I don't mind." He stripped the bed down to the mattress, then remade it with clean sheets. Flipping the comforter back over the bed, he turned, his gaze searching mine. "Are you okay, Tori?"

I threw my hands up. "How many times do I have to say I'm fine?"

"I just wanted to be sure." He tilted his head in question. "Do you want a hug?"

My exasperation evaporated—along with my forced nonchalance about the sorcerer's attack.

"Okay." The word came out in an embarrassingly childish whisper.

He stepped close and wrapped his warm arms around me. As I buried my face in his chest, my breath released in a shuddering exhale and I had to fight back the sting of tears. Helping Aaron had been one thing—I'd run headfirst into that fight. But being ambushed, getting strangled, having a lethal blade almost shoved in my guts ... even I couldn't shrug that off like it was nothing.

In Ezra's arms, I felt safe and protected. Part of me wanted to melt against him and cry like a baby. Another part of me hated this false feeling of safety that would only last for as long as he was around. Sooner or later, I'd be on my own again.

He held me as I steadied my breathing. With a quiet sniff— I was *not* crying, damn it—I raised my head.

Aaron and Kai stood in the doorway, watching. My face flushed, but they didn't seem shocked by my girly emotions, nor were they gleeful at catching me in their friend's arms. Concern was all I saw in their eyes.

Ezra stepped away, one hand on the small of my back. "I'm starving. Why don't we order pizza?"

"I don't know," Kai said. "That'll depend on Tori."

"Me?" I asked blankly.

"If you want pizza with pineapple on it, we'll have to throw you out."

I blinked, not entirely sure if he was joking, but Aaron laughed. "If she wants pineapple, she can have it. You don't have to eat it."

"Its existence alone is an insult to all pizza."

With a snort, Aaron scooped me to his side. He grinned, his confidence banishing the last shiver of my fear. I smiled back as he pulled me to the stairs. Ezra and Kai followed, the latter still explaining why pineapple on pizza was unforgivable blasphemy.

Halfway down, Aaron stopped. "Um, Tori."

"Yeah?"

"Are you cold?"

Did his fiery magic make him impervious to outside temperatures? The house was as hot as an oven. "No."

He glanced at the ceiling like it held the answers to all life's mysteries. "Are you sure you don't want to borrow a shirt?"

I looked down. My boobs stared back at me. "Fine. I'll borrow a shirt."

All three of them sighed, but I wasn't sure if it was from disappointment or relief. Huffing, I stepped out from under Aaron's arm and marched down the stairs alone. Men.

15

IT HAD BEEN MONTHS since I'd slept in a proper bed, but for some dumb reason, I couldn't sleep. Snuggled into a pillow that smelled of fresh laundry detergent and a hint of whatever nectar-of-the-gods soap Ezra used, I should have been floating on blissful clouds of slumber. But despite the exhaustion leading my eyelids, I couldn't keep them closed. With no distractions, worries occupied my thoughts—mainly, what would happen next.

Sin had called while we were waiting for pizza to arrive. She'd gotten the name of the sorcerer, and tomorrow the guys would do more research into who he was. The police had taken him away, but as Aaron had explained, he wouldn't remain in custody for long. Mythics weren't held in human jails. He'd be let go, and if he didn't turn himself in to MagiPol, they would put out a bounty for him.

I wasn't naïve enough to expect the sorcerer to turn himself in, which meant he'd be on the loose again tomorrow. We had no idea how he'd set up an ambush outside my favorite store—and no idea how to prevent him from stalking me.

Rolling over, I absently scratched at my neck. The shirt Aaron had lent me featured a horrifically itchy tag, and as I contorted my arm to adjust it, fabric rubbed against the cut on my stomach. My throat still ached from the sorcerer strangling me, and in the silent, dark bedroom, the array of pain and discomfort was difficult to ignore.

I hadn't been able to dwell on anything earlier in the night. After pizza, Aaron parked himself in front of the huge TV, picked up a video game controller, and challenged me to a go-kart race. I sucked at it, driving off cliffs and spinning out on banana peels, but trash-talking Aaron while he drove laps around me was fun. When Ezra joined us after showering, the game got even more fun—instead of me losing fantastically to Aaron, Aaron and I both lost to Ezra. I didn't mind, because watching Aaron curse Ezra out every time he plowed Aaron off the track was hilarious.

Kai eventually took up the fourth controller, and we raced the evening away, complete with popcorn and beer. I threw in the proverbial flag at midnight and watched the guys duke it out one more time on the most difficult track. Ezra won, again.

"I thought you couldn't drive," I told him as we high-fived.

"I can *drive* just fine." He grinned. "I just can't tell how far away the other cars are. Not a problem in a video game—especially when I'm in the lead."

I'd fallen into bed shortly after that.

Rolling over again, I squinted at the ceiling. Even with the window open, the room was stuffy and my sore throat was parched. Untangling from the blankets, I climbed out of bed. My borrowed t-shirt fell below my butt, and for comfort's sake, I'd ditched my shorts and bra. I scratched the back of my neck again. Damn tag.

My gaze drifted to Ezra's dresser. Would he mind if I borrowed a different shirt?

I cracked the top drawer open and peeked inside. Socks, folded in pairs, and boxer briefs, unfolded. Not wanting to dig through his underclothes, I went straight for the bottom drawer. Aha, t-shirts!

I dug into the tidy stack, searching for one without a tag. As I wiggled my fingers into the fabric, my nails caught on paper. Lifting the shirts up, I found a worn folder with a thin stack of paper in it. The edge of a photograph stuck out from the pile.

Sometimes I'm a bad person. With a guilty glance at the closed bedroom door, I slid the photo out.

A boy and a girl around fifteen stood with their arms around each other—a typical first-high-school-relationship photo. The girl had plain blond hair that looked like it had been trimmed with kitchen scissors, but her broad smile was beautiful in its unrestrained joy.

The boy, a few inches taller, had dark hair cut short and warm brown eyes in a handsome, olive-skinned face. Ezra, before he was scarred and blinded. Behind him and the girl, an expanse of mountains spread in a breathtaking view.

It was a happy photo full of youthful exuberance, but heavy sorrow infused me as I studied it. Despite the bright colors and the young smiling couple, the photo's location at the bottom of a drawer in an old folder told a different story. Ezra didn't want to throw the photo away, but he didn't want to be reminded of it all the time either.

I slid it back into its spot in the folder, leaving one corner sticking out the way I'd found it. I rearranged the stack of shirts, closed the drawer, and stood up. Pulling off Aaron's shirt, I turned it inside out and slid it back on.

Itching from guilt instead of a scratchy tag, I cracked the bedroom door open. The other two doors were closed, no lights glowing from beneath them. Aaron and Kai were asleep. I tiptoed down the stairs to the landing by the front door and headed for the kitchen, passing the living room.

On the sofa, Ezra was sprawled on his back, one arm hanging off the cushions. His ability to turn rooms ice-cold didn't appear to help him with the heat—his lightweight blanket was mostly on the floor, exposing his chest and the waistband of his dark boxer briefs.

I froze in place, staring. Illuminated by the dim glow of a streetlamp outside the window, his physique alone would've been enough to stop me—hot damn, the man was movie-star fit—but that wasn't what halted me in my tracks.

Long, thick scars raked across his side.

Scarcely believing my eyes, I stepped into the living room, my body cold all over. When I'd asked Ezra how he'd gotten the scar on his face, the guys had joked about a shark attack, but if they'd told me *these* scars had been inflicted by a nightmarish monster, I wouldn't have doubted them. The white lines started by his right hip and swept diagonally up his abs, stopping just shy of his sternum. The wounds ran parallel as though giant claws had ripped up his side.

Like the scar on his face, the edges were jagged and showed no sign of having been stitched closed. But cuts deep enough to leave scars like that should have required hundreds of stitches, right?

Moving closer, I picked out fainter lines on his bronze skin. None were as terrible as the three long scars on his side, but he'd suffered other injuries. What the hell had happened to him? I didn't know what life was like for a typical mythic, but *this* couldn't possibly be normal.

Don't ask Ezra why he joined the guild. Aaron's warning. He'd told me not to ask about Ezra's family either. Could those things be related to his scars, to his blinded eye? Were they related to the photo hidden in his bottom dresser drawer?

Ezra's head turned and I froze all over again when his eyes opened. He glanced across me like he wasn't the least bit surprised to see me standing there, then scanned the room behind me. I tensed, expecting him to demand why I was standing over him in the dead of night.

Instead, he gestured for me to come closer. Confused, I took two more steps. He grabbed my wrist and pulled me down, still surveying the room. I dropped into a crouch beside him.

"Someone is in the house," he breathed. "They just went up the stairs."

"What?" I whispered, fear rippling through me. "How do you know?"

"Air currents." He pushed up on one elbow, all those lovely muscles of his tensing and the exposed scars pulling taut. "When people move, the air shifts."

Whoa. I'd had no clue being an aeromage gave him that kind of extrasensory perception. No wonder it was so difficult to sneak up on him. He rolled off the sofa and onto his feet without making a sound. His head turned, his pale eye looking at me without seeing me.

"Tori, will you watch my blind side?"

Caught off guard, I whispered a hesitant affirmation. He started toward the stairs and I followed right behind him, scrutinizing everything on our left. Stopping beside the landing, he angled his head upward.

"He just came out of my room." Ezra raised one hand and made a small gesture.

Wind whipped down the stairs with howling force. Frenzied scuffling erupted, like someone trying to catch their balance, then came the crashing sound of a falling body. *Thump, crash, thump, BAM.* A man landed at the bottom of the stairs in a crumpled heap.

As Ezra lunged for him, the intruder lurched up, his face covered by a ski mask—real inconspicuous in this heat—but I could identify him by the bone-chilling cold and sparkling mist surrounding him. Ice Guy.

Arm snapping back, Ezra threw a lightning-fast punch. Ice Guy ducked and Ezra's fist went right through the drywall. The mage cast a wave of glittering ice chips but a swirl of wind deflected them. Spinning, Ezra decked the guy in the jaw. They grappled in the tiny landing, and I hung back helplessly. How was I supposed to watch Ezra's blind side while he was pummeling someone?

Gleaming steel flashed and Ezra leaped clear in another freakishly rapid movement. Ice Guy brandished his dagger, then thrust it. Foot-long shards of ice formed out of the snowy cloud clinging to the mage and the sparkling projectiles shot for Ezra.

He cast his arms wide and a gust of wind flung the shards away from him. Lunging in, he slammed into the mage, his physical fighting style a stark contrast to Aaron's fire-wielding approach—and Ice Guy wasn't prepared for it. His head smacked into the wall, and he whipped his dagger out, using the deadly edge to force Ezra to retreat. Teeth bared, the mage conjured another array of ice shards—but this time, they didn't shoot at Ezra.

They shot at me.

Ezra whirled around and flung a hand toward me. Wind hit me as it rushed toward the shards, countering their momentum. They tumbled out of the air, but now Ezra's back was to the other mage—and ice sprouted from his dagger, tripling its length as he swung it at Ezra's unprotected spine.

Ezra ducked and the ice blade swept over his head. Pivoting, he planted his feet, balled his hand, and hammered his fist into Ice Guy's stomach. Air boomed and the mage sailed the length of the entryway before ripping the screen door off its hinges. He tumbled right out of the house.

As Ezra shot after Ice Guy, I followed on his heels, resuming my blind-spot-watching duty. Ezra reached the threshold, then skidded to a stop. I ran into him. He spun, grabbed me, and threw us both to the floor.

An instant later, a barrage of glowing darts flashed through the air. The orange spikes peppered the walls at chest height, flashing with sparks before dissolving into nothing. Outside, an engine revved and tires squealed on the pavement. The roar of the escaping car shattered the quiet night and the tires screeched again as the vehicle took a corner on two wheels.

Ezra sat up, kneeling over my legs. I lay where I'd fallen, blinking dazedly but unharmed. In the instant before we hit the floor, the air had thickened under me like an invisible balloon, cushioning our fall.

"They got away, huh?"

Aaron stood halfway up the stairs, as casual as could be for having woken up to the sounds of battle. Kai waited a few steps above him.

Gulping, I whipped my gaze away. Yeah, so, Aaron and Kai were in their boxers too, and they were as deliciously toned as Ezra. Speaking of Ezra, guess where my stare ended up? Yeah, the hot aeromage sitting on my knees, shirtless and covered in a fine layer of moisture from Ice Guy's snowy aura.

Goddamn it. There was nowhere safe to look.

Aaron trotted down the stairs and hopped over the broken screen door onto the porch. Finally getting off my legs, Ezra offered me a hand up. My borrowed t-shirt was bunched at my waist and I hurriedly pulled it over my butt, but not before Aaron waltzed back inside. Fair's fair, I supposed. I'd seen their undies, and now they'd seen mine.

"They're gone," Aaron confirmed as he shut the heavy front door and locked the bolt, not showing the slightest concern for their demolished screen door.

"That was Ice Guy," I said. "The mage who attacked you last weekend."

"That was my guess too." Aaron rubbed his scruffy jaw. "Seems like these assholes aren't ready to quit."

"The big question," Kai murmured, descending to the bottom step, "is who they came for? You—or Tori?"

Aaron frowned, contemplating me like he couldn't imagine why someone would hunt me down. Then his frown deepened and his gaze jumped to Ezra. "Actually, I think the big question is ... what were you two doing down here *together*?"

"I came down to get a glass of water," I answered promptly. "Then I planned to jump Ezra's bones while he was sleeping."

Ezra blinked repeatedly. Aaron glanced rapidly between us like he was trying to catch me in a lie, but Kai smirked. At least one of them was awake enough to recognize a joke when he heard it.

"Back to bed, then?" he suggested.

"That's it?" I demanded incredulously. "A mythic home invader and a deathmatch in the entryway, and you're just going back to bed?"

Kai looked at Ezra. "You good?"

Ezra held out his hands and I was surprised to see his knuckles undamaged despite punching a hole in the wall. "I'm good."

"'Kay. Night." Kai ascended the stairs and, a moment later, a door clacked shut.

"He doesn't like his beauty sleep disturbed," Aaron remarked. "Tori, you all right?"

"Yeah," I muttered. "I'm going to get that glass of water."

When I returned from the kitchen with my water in hand, Ezra was sitting on the sofa and Aaron was scrolling through movie listings on the TV. "Since we're wide awake, we're going to watch something. Want to join us?"

I could have kissed them both from relief. I'd already been having trouble sleeping, and going back to the quiet bedroom would've meant spending the rest of the night straining my ears for sounds of a second invasion.

As Aaron curled up in the armchair, I plopped on the sofa beside Ezra and pulled his discarded blanket over my legs. Opening credits began to play, but I had no idea what movie Aaron had picked and I never found out. The moment I nestled into the cushions, with Ezra and Aaron nearby and the quiet sound of the TV filling the silence, I fell asleep.

16

STIFLING A YAWN, I slid my laptop into my purse—oversized purses are a lifesaver—and shoved a notebook and pen in after it. I'd had to get up earlier than usual so we could swing by my apartment and pick up my school stuff—plus a change of clothes—before class, and I was painfully exhausted. Easing out from behind the long table, I followed my fellow Small Business students out of the classroom.

Hot irritation spiraled through me as chattering people clogged the doorway. My temper wasn't the best on a good day, and I was way too many hours short of a full night's sleep. I shoved my way through, elbowing a girl in the back.

As students streamed down the wide halls, I headed for a study nook with two sofas and a few chairs arranged around a low table. Approaching cautiously, I eyed its occupants. Kai had his boots propped on the table, his laptop resting on his legs, and a black motorcycle helmet sat near his feet—my helmet, since I'd accidentally worn it inside.

When I'd left him a few hours ago, the study nook had been empty. Now it was full of women. Two had crammed themselves onto the sofa with him, and five more were arranged across the remaining seats.

My eyebrows climbed toward my hairline. Ah. Kai's playboy status had baffled me—he wasn't outgoing or even flirtatious—but now I got it. He attracted women with the oldest trick in the book: disinterest. He was hot, and he was ignoring them. That combination seemed to trigger some bizarre mate-hunting instinct in women, driving them to throw themselves at the man until he acknowledged them.

At least, that was my working theory as I stopped by the table and received no less than three icy warning glares.

"Hey," I said. "Ready to go?"

He snapped his laptop shut and rose, grabbing the sleek black helmet. As he joined me, passing over the helmet, I counted the disappointed sighs. We walked away side by side, and feeling the belligerent stares on my back, I gave in to my evil urges and slid an arm around his waist.

His arm wrapped around me in response, but his look was questioning.

I nodded at his fan club. "I couldn't resist crushing their souls."

Amusement flashed in his dark eyes and he pulled me closer. I could almost hear the dismayed growls echoing from the study nook. Swinging the helmet in my free hand, I grinned the whole way through the building.

"How many phone numbers did those girls offer you while you waited?" I asked teasingly as we exited the building, an unpleasantly muggy breeze greeting us. A solid blanket of gray clouds loomed above the skyscrapers.

"Five," he replied seriously.

I almost missed a step. I'd been kidding … "Planning to call any?"

"Maybe one. She was cute."

"What about the others?"

"Not my type."

"What's your type?" I asked as we stopped beside his motorcycle.

"Well." He pondered the question as he stashed his laptop in the saddlebag and unhooked his helmet. "I don't know."

I caught his arm before he could put on his helmet. "You were going to say something there. What was it?"

He grimaced. "The other four handed me their numbers like I should be flattered."

"Yuck." I pulled a face. "Yeah, don't call them."

His expression vanished behind his helmet's visor. "Happens a lot."

We climbed onto his bike and once my arms were safely locked around his waist, he took off, speeding into the beginnings of the Monday evening rush hour. At a red light, I leaned into his back so he could hear me over the bike's engine.

"I've heard you date a lot of women," I said baldly. "Are you waiting to find the right girl, or just not into long-term relationships?"

"Bit of both."

An illuminating response. Most people would have quit prying, but the mystery he presented had me intrigued. "What do you do when you're not on dates?"

His head turned as he tried to see my face—not that he could see anything through my helmet's visor. "Why do you ask?"

"Just curious."

"Do you date much, Tori?"

"Nuh-uh. I'm asking the questions. We can talk about my non-love life later."

The light turned green and the bike zoomed into motion. Unlucky for me, we got all greens the rest of the way to the Crow and Hammer. Kai pulled the bike into the back parking lot. Hopping to the pavement, I pulled off my helmet.

"So?" I prompted. "Interests? Hobbies? Pastimes?"

Swinging off the bike, he removed his helmet and gave me a sidelong glance. "You're not planning to set me up with your friends, are you?"

I snorted. "What friends?"

His hands paused in the middle of unzipping a saddlebag.

"Ah," I muttered awkwardly. "That came out way more pathetic sounding than I intended. It's been hard making friends in a new city, that's all."

Nodding, he tucked his laptop under his arm. "Aaron was the first friend I made here. Well, 'friend' is a stretch. We hated each other at first. We were thirteen and insanely competitive."

"How did you meet?" I asked as we circled around the building to the guild's front door.

"I enrolled in the Sinclair Academy. Aaron and I were in the same year so we went through all our training together."

"Whoa, hold up." I pushed the door open, ignoring the surge of panicky revulsion the entrance triggered—what I now knew was a spell to repel humans. "The Sinclair *Academy*?"

"Aaron's family runs the most exclusive mage-training academy on the West coast." He led the way across the pub, to where Cooper the sometimes-cook was manning the bar. "It's both a school and a guild, and they're extremely selective about who they admit. Underage mythics train there starting at thirteen, and when they turn eighteen, they can join the guild and continue training."

But he and Aaron hadn't joined the Sinclair guild. They'd left a fancy private academy to join the disreputable Crow and Hammer instead.

"Hey Tori," Cooper called, giving me a sloppy grin. "Looking smokin' as usual. Visiting on your night off?"

"Are you drunk?" I asked.

"Nooo. Definitely not."

I followed Kai to the stairs in the corner. "Dunk your head in the ice machine before Clara catches you."

Kai headed up the staircase. Was I allowed up there? I hesitated, then hastened after him. Guild rule number two: Don't get caught. Can't get in trouble if you don't get caught.

The second level, which I'd only glimpsed once, was a combination of study hall, library, and computer lab. Whiteboards, corkboards, and a city map with pins and sticky notes marking different locations filled the walls. A dozen guild members were scattered around, some at the computers, some browsing the bookshelves at the back, some sitting at the worktables.

At the farthest table, Aaron was bent over a laptop and Ezra was perusing a stack of printed papers. Kai sat beside Ezra and I dropped into the seat beside Aaron.

"How was class?" Aaron asked.

"Success," I declared. "Kai broke at least eight hearts without speaking a single word."

Ignoring that, Kai asked, "Find anything?"

"Dirk Peters, the sorcerer, was easy since we had his name," Aaron told us. "As for the kryomage …"

He clicked a tab open and turned his laptop toward me. A photo popped up—a man in his thirties with buzzed hair and a narrow face dominated by a square jaw. A name was displayed underneath: Sergei Durov.

"Looks like Ice Guy," I confirmed.

"I thought so too." He spun the laptop to show Kai. "Good news is we've identified them. Bad news is they're both rogue. Since they aren't working alone, I'd say they're part of the same guild, but figuring out which one will be tricky."

Kai studied the kryomage's profile, then flipped his own laptop open. "I'll see what I can find."

Aaron slouched back in his chair and laced his hands behind his head. "Excellent. I can relax now."

"Lazy ass," Kai commented, his attention fixed on his screen.

"You're way better at this detective shit than me."

I stifled another yawn, drained after my bad night. "How's this all work? How did you pull up a photo like that?"

"The MagiPol database," Aaron explained. "They have an online network called the MPD Archives that contains all their information about everything. Different mythics have different levels of access, but you can look up almost any mythic or guild. It's also where jobs, bounties, and bonuses are posted. The two guys we need to find are unguilded, meaning they're rogues with bounties for their capture."

"Unguilded? But didn't you just say you think they're part of a guild?"

"Sorry, I meant they aren't guilded with a legal guild. Just like there are rogue mythics, there are rogue guilds."

"Mythics gravitate toward group structures even without MagiPol's rules on guilding," Ezra told me. "It's tough to go it alone. We naturally form groups, and the same goes for rogue mythics. They band together into loose guilds that don't follow MagiPol's regulations."

"They're illegal as shit," Aaron added. "MagiPol does its best to stamp them out, but they're hard to pin down and harder to eradicate. Even if you take out some members, they form up again somewhere else."

Ezra tapped one finger on his stack of papers. "The sorcerer and the kryomage are probably part of the same rogue guild, but we can't look it up in MagiPol's guild registry since rogue guilds don't officially exist, let alone file paperwork."

"How will we find them, then?" I asked anxiously.

"MPD has ongoing investigations into every known rogue guild." Kai clicked rapidly on his laptop. "I'm pulling up all the available information on the rogue guilds in the area, then cross-referencing records of their crimes and activities against Peters's and Durov's charges to see if anything lines up."

"Oh."

"See?" Aaron remarked breezily. "That's why I let Kai do this stuff."

Since I was no help with the rogue research, I pulled out my laptop and got started on an assignment. After a few minutes, Kai retrieved a stack of papers from the monster printer in the corner. Highlighter in hand, he laid the pages across the table.

I tapped away on my hypothetical business plan for a dog grooming salon—not my choice; I fully intended to become a crazy cat lady by middle age—while Kai worked, Ezra assisted, and Aaron played a game on his laptop. Aaron didn't seem to be paying attention, but as Kai and Ezra quietly discussed possible connections between our culprits and the rogue guilds, Aaron piped up with further questions.

As the guys methodically cross-checked their information, I lost my train of thought on a reasonable marketing budget for my grooming salon and found myself observing them instead. On the surface, Kai seemed to be doing all the work, but the closer I watched, the more I saw their flawless teamwork. Kai's organization and intelligence, Ezra's sharp insight, and Aaron's outside-the-box probing.

The icky nervous weight in my gut lessened for the first time since the sorcerer's attack yesterday. Maybe this wasn't as bad as I thought. Maybe I wasn't giving Aaron, Kai, and Ezra enough credit. They knew what they were doing. They knew how to deal with this.

But what about me? *They* could handle criminal mythics and rogue guilds, but I didn't want to rely on them. Experience had taught me that relying on people led to trouble, pain, and failure. Nothing sucked more than counting on someone only to have them let you down. If I kept working here, even for a couple weeks, would I end up in trouble again? Aaron, Kai, and Ezra wouldn't always be there, and I wasn't equipped to protect myself.

Sabrina's voice rang in my memory, the spread of tarot cards clear in my mind's eye. *Though you've walked this far alone, others are waiting to join you.*

My attention roved across Kai and Ezra, then settled on Aaron. The Knight of Swords. Did the tarot card really mean them? Sabrina had warned that my past, my fears, would shape my fate. I wanted so badly to roll my eyes and call her reading a load of bullshit, but parts of it resonated with me in a way that was difficult to ignore.

Was I seriously stressing over tarot cards?

"Something wrong, Tori?"

I blinked and focused on Aaron. "Huh?"

He tapped a finger against my chin and I realized my mouth was hanging open like a gormless halfwit. I snapped it shut, but he was waiting expectantly.

"Do you know Sabrina?" I blurted. Super-smooth subject change, oh yeah.

"Sabrina? Of course. She's a diviner. I know everyone in the guild."

"She asked me for your phone number. And Kai's."

Aaron winced. "You didn't give it to her, did you?"

"Nope."

"Good. I don't want her to know I blocked her."

"You blocked her?" I glanced at Kai and he nodded. "You too? Why?"

Smirking, Aaron pulled out his phone, flipped to a messaging app, and passed the device to me. My brow furrowed as I stared at the screen for a long moment, then swiped up. Photo after photo flashed by, and my eyes got wider with each one.

"Oh. Wow. Okay." I cleared my throat. "She, um. She has … really cute … bunnies?"

Every single photo, spanning months of messages, featured three floppy-eared rabbits. Eating lettuce. Wearing little hats. Posing amidst flowers. Sabrina had interspersed the images with probing inquiries about Aaron's thoughts on her "bun-buns" and flirtatious invitations for him to come over some time to meet them. His responses, when he did respond, lacked enthusiasm for either subject.

"You blocked her over bunny photos?" I asked skeptically.

"*Constant* bunny photos," he complained. "Plus she keeps trying to get me to ask her out, but yeah. *Bunny photos.*"

Handing his phone back, I asked Kai, "Same deal for you?"

"Yep. Half the guild are lucky recipients of her photography."

I frowned. "But not you, Ezra?"

He shrugged, his attention on a printout. "She doesn't like me."

"What? Why not?" How could she not like Ezra? His warm, quiet smile had won me over right away. He merely shrugged again, and only then did I realize I'd asked a damn rude question. Mildly embarrassed, I pulled my laptop closer.

"Did Sabrina do a reading for you?" Kai asked as he shuffled papers around, tossing some aside.

My gaze snapped up. "Uh ... yeah. How'd you know?"

"You had that look."

"The 'this shit can't be real' look," Aaron added knowingly. "Anyone who isn't a diviner looks like that after a reading."

"Have you gotten a reading before?" I asked.

"A few times, but I'd honestly rather let the future surprise me. Did anything interesting come up in yours?"

"I don't know. It was all about conflict and deception and 'fear ruling my heart.' I thought it was kind of stupid."

Aaron turned on his chair to face me, his expression thoughtful. "What are you afraid of?"

"Nothing."

"It would have to be a prevailing fear for the tarot cards to pick it up," Kai remarked as he tossed a printout into his reject pile. "Something powerful or long term."

A chill washed over me. They didn't think her reading was bullshit, and I didn't like that. If they'd jumped on the skepticism bandwagon like I'd hoped, I could've discounted the whole freaky experience.

Kai shoved the last of the papers aside and dropped a single sheet in the center of the table. "This is it."

"It isn't Red Rum, is it?" Aaron asked warily.

"No." Kai spun the page toward me and Aaron. "Looks like a small operation. MPD records call them the 'East Hastings Gang' because that's where they're often seen. Eight to twelve rogue mythics, including a kryomage and at least one sorcerer who favors card-style artifacts."

East Hastings Street was only a few blocks south of our location. I shifted nervously.

"Any connection to the last rogue sorcerer we turned over to MagiPol?" Aaron asked.

"Not that I can see. Based on their known activities, I don't think they'd be after a ransom from your family, either. I'm betting someone hired them to muddy their tracks."

"So we need these guys to reveal who hired them, and why." Aaron cracked his knuckles. "Sounds like fun."

"Should be interesting," Kai agreed as he gathered the other printouts and chucked them in a recycling bin. "But you won't get to find out, because you're staying right here."

"What? No way!"

"*You're* their target. You'd be walking right into their hands. Ezra and I will handle them."

"Not alone," Aaron growled.

"I have a few people in mind. I'll get a team ready to go for tomorrow night."

Grumbling, Aaron sagged in his chair. "I should come. I owe them payback."

"Deal with it," Kai said implacably. "Besides, Tori works tomorrow. You need to be here with her."

While they talked, I pulled the single page closer, scanning the list of known and suspected criminal activity committed by the rogue guild's mysterious members. Magic mumbo jumbo took up most of the page, but some disturbingly familiar words jumped out at me: Assault. Arson. Robbery. Abduction. Murder.

This wasn't a sloppy group of troublemakers and minor criminals. This was organized crime. This was a gang in the real sense. They were hardened criminals who weren't afraid to kill—and they used weapons more dangerous and unpredictable than guns.

"Are you ..." I hesitated, then forced the question out. "Are you sure confronting these guys is a good idea?"

Halfway through standing, Kai gave me a searching look. He sank back into his seat, his dark eyes meeting mine. "The Crow and Hammer has a poor reputation. We're casual, disorganized, irreverent, and disobedient. Our ranks are filled with outcasts and former rogues. But every member of this guild brings something special to the table. We have some of the strongest mages, the most skilled sorcerers and alchemists, and the rarest psychics in the city. And none of us tolerate losing."

"Don't hit first," Ezra murmured.

"But always hit back. And we hit damn hard." Aaron grinned at his fellow mages. "Tori, they overpowered me last time because I was outnumbered, unarmed, and unprepared. But against our *guild*? Kai and Ezra aren't the only ones who are pissed that they jumped us. These East Hastings guys won't know what hit them."

My gaze shifted from Aaron's blazing blue eyes to Kai's dark stare to Ezra's mismatched irises. Under his simple black t-shirt were scars from injuries that would've killed most people. Behind Kai's cool competence was scary, calculating intelligence. Beneath Aaron's teasing grins was fiery confidence backed up by raw power I'd only glimpsed.

Releasing my fear on a long exhale, I gave Kai a fierce smile. "Give that bastard sorcerer an extra kick to the balls from me."

His answering smile was downright malevolent.

I LIKE TO THINK I'm a pretty chill person, but right now? I was fretting worse than a granny with her best china in a room of hyperactive toddlers.

Anxiously straightening the bottles in my well, I eyed the pub's patrons. Only a few were here for pleasure. The rest were ready and waiting for Kai and Ezra to arrive: the team that would be hunting down a rogue guild tonight.

Zora, the petite blond vampire hunter with a penchant for big-ass weapons, wore leather pants and a tank top, and strapped to her back was a sword that should be called Skull Crusher. It was probably called Skull Crusher. That's what I was calling it from now on.

At her side was Felix, her husband and the guild's third officer. He carried a backpack instead of a sword, and with his thick glasses and a comb-over to hide his receding hairline, he just ... yeah. Officer or not, he was nowhere near as daunting as his wife.

Sorcerer number three was Gwen, a tall, thin woman with a sleek ponytail who normally looked like she'd stepped out of a Fortune 500 executive office, complete with designer shades and tailored business clothes. Tonight, she wore black leather and carried a dozen sticks hooked on her belt—eight-inches long, glossy black, and inscribed with runes.

The last sorcerer on the team was Ramsey. He'd left off the eyeliner and his dark hair was tied back. Black clothes—as usual—but he was decked out in an odd assortment of weapons and magicky artifacts.

Kai hadn't recruited only sorcerers for his team. Two psychics completed their ranks: Taye, a suave man with warm umber skin and a South African accent, had an ability called telethesia that, according to Aaron, allowed him to "track" people; and Drew, a telekinetic like the unforgettable weasel Liam.

Said weasel was in the house tonight, holed up in the corner with his bookworm pal Tom, and seeing the two telekinetics in the same room was like looking at before and after pictures of Captain America: short, thin, and weedy versus tall, buff, and ready to beat up bad guys.

The four sorcerers and two psychics would join Kai and Ezra, and together the team of eight would hunt down as many members of the East Hastings Gang as they could catch before sunup. Kai was confident he'd pinpointed the rogues' location, but he didn't know how many mythics the gang included.

I nervously straightened my liquor bottles again, turning each label forward and angling the pour spouts.

"Relax, Tori," Aaron told me from his stool, laptop screen flashing as he blasted alien spaceships. "They know what they're doing."

"But what if there are more rogues than Kai's anticipating?" I muttered.

"They'll be fine. Damn it!" His screen flashed red as his spaceship exploded into pixelated flames. He shut his laptop and glanced across the casually chatting team. "Kai has all his bases covered. He, Ezra, and Zora make up the offensive point— they're bringing the firepower. Felix specializes in magic detection and dissolution, so he'll head off any traps or ambushes, and Ramsey's counter-magic game is insane. He has an artifact to counter almost anything. Taye's job is to track anyone who makes a run for it, and Drew and Gwen are the flex members—they can join in on the offensive or switch to defense as needed."

Biting my lip, I nodded. "I guess that's … but only three offensive team members against a dozen?"

"*If* there's a dozen." Aaron grinned. "Besides, you haven't seen Kai in action. Ezra is no pushover either."

As though summoned by his name, Kai walked through the front door. The cleaning cloth fell out of my hand.

Gone was the "well-dressed, high-class model" Kai that I knew. He wore lightweight boots and dark clothes, the long sleeves interrupted by small throwing blades strapped to his upper arms. A slim-fitting black vest held more small weapons, and two katanas hung from his hip—one short, one long.

I dragged my stare from the swords up to his face, reexamining the exotic features I'd never quite been able to place. But now I knew. Japanese heritage blended so smoothly with Caucasian that he didn't obviously resemble either, but instead had a unique look all his own.

Ezra came in behind him, and he had shed his boy-next-door guise. A thick strap crossed his chest, holding an unfamiliar weapon against his back. Dark, fingerless gloves ran up his arms, the knuckles shining with steel and the elbows reinforced with more metal. A black bandana was tied over his hair, and with the scruffy shadow of a beard edging his jaw, his face had a more dangerous cast to it than I'd ever seen before.

Kai headed toward his team and, gulping back my shock, I pulled myself together as Ezra joined me and Aaron.

The pyromage heaved a dejected sigh. "Can't believe I'm stuck here while you guys have all the fun."

"We'll tell you all about it when we get back," Ezra replied with a cheerful lack of sympathy, adjusting his glove.

"Are you sure you're ... properly armed?" I asked him doubtfully, eyeing his lack of weapons compared to Kai. The thing on his back looked like a two-foot-long black pole with silver caps on the ends and a silver section in the middle. "Shouldn't you have a sword too?"

"We aren't planning to behead anyone. MagiPol strongly discourages dead bodies."

"Show her the Twin Terrors," Aaron suggested. "She'll love it."

I scrunched my nose. "The what now?"

Stepping away from the bar, Ezra reached over his shoulder and pulled the short pole arm off his back. He spun it easily in his hand, and remembering how hard Ezra could hit with his bare fists, I wondered if maybe *this* weapon should be called Skull Crusher.

He grabbed each end of the pole and twisted. The weapon split in the middle and pulled apart with a metallic slither, revealing two foot-long blades attached to black handles of equal length. With terrifying grace, he whirled the blades, the steel whistling in the air, and brought the butt ends together with another twist. Just like that, it was one weapon again—except now it was four feet long with deadly blades at both ends.

"Um." I inched back, warily eyeing the double-ended spear. "How good is your depth perception again?" By "good," I really meant "bad."

He twisted the two blades apart and sheathed them inside each other so it was once again an innocuous metal pole. "Terrible, as usual, but it's rarely an issue in a fight. Moving people disturb the air, so I can tell how far away they are even if I can't see them."

"Oh, right," I said faintly as he slapped the weapon against his back. It stuck to the baldric on its own—magnets, maybe?

"All right," Kai called. "Any questions before we head out?"

"Whose car are we taking?" Felix asked dryly. "I'm not riding in the back of Aaron's pussy-mobile."

"Hey! Don't insult my baby."

"We're taking the van," Kai said. "Anything else?"

Zora folded her arm and cocked a hip. "Are any of the bounties DOA?"

"Dead on Arrival?" I muttered questioningly to Aaron.

"Dead or Alive," he corrected. "Not common, but it happens."

"No," Kai replied. "We take them alive, but don't hesitate to defend yourself with whatever force is required. Your lives come first, always."

That sick, lightheaded feeling returned. I gripped the edge of the bar, my knuckles turning white.

Kai waved at the team to follow him. "Let's go."

"Ezra," I said hoarsely as he moved to follow. "Be careful."

He smiled reassuringly. "We'll be back before you know it."

Aaron stood and clasped arms with Ezra, then the aeromage hastened after the other seven mythics, Kai in the lead. The door shut behind them, and my shoulders drooped. No matter what Ezra said, for me it would be a long, long night.

DESPERATE for a distraction, I would've loved a crazy Tuesday-evening rush, but the pub was dead most of the night. Sin popped by to chat, my favorite hag Sylvia ordered three Manhattans before stumbling out, and yoga-girl witch and two friends hung out for a while, but otherwise, my only customers besides Aaron were Liam and Tom, parked in a corner while Tom read a new sci-fi book and Liam played on his phone.

As midnight crept closer, I circled the front of house, straightening chairs and wiping already clean tables. Giving up on work, I sat on a stool beside Aaron. Hunched over his laptop, he was scrolling through an ugly white website that looked ten years out of date.

"What's that?" I asked, unable to take the silence anymore.

"Hmm?" He yawned, belatedly covering his mouth. "The MPD Archives. This is the job board. I'm checking for new listings with good bonuses."

Oh wait. I'd seen this site before, hadn't I? I'd uncovered the homepage during an otherwise fruitless Googling session on magic. "Find anything?"

"Not really. It's been quiet lately."

I watched him scroll. The page went on forever. "Are these all from MagiPol?"

"For the most part. They typically come from three sources: MagiPol, which makes up about eighty percent of the postings, then individual mythics who need help with something and guilds that want to pass off a job." He scrolled through another dozen listings. "Some are open bonuses, meaning they're always ongoing—stuff like exterminating vampires, tagging shifters, and confiscating artifacts from humans. Others are what we call the 'Wanted Ads,' which are postings about something suspicious that anyone can look into."

He tapped the screen. "Like this one. 'Claims of spiritual activity in abandoned warehouse.' Anyone can go check it out, and if they find something troublesome, they deal with it, report to MagiPol, and see if they can get compensated. It's hit or miss, but sometimes you land a jackpot."

"Interesting." I squinted at the screen, then pointed. "What about that one?"

"'Missing girl from Arbutus Ridge, suspected mythic involvement,'" Aaron read. He clicked the listing and a new page opened, dominated by a photo of a brunette with short hair and hollow cheeks, around sixteen years old. "Missing person cases are difficult, especially when they're human. As mythics, it's tricky to get involved. We can't just walk into a police station and demand to see the case file."

He resumed scrolling. "Me, Kai, and Ezra prefer hunting rogues. Excellent bonuses, opportunities to beat someone's ass, and no one else's safety to worry about."

I nodded absently. I could understand them not wanting to take on the responsibility of saving lives like that, but how could he forget that girl's face, her hopeless eyes? I couldn't shrug it off that easily.

"Someone else will take the job," Aaron added reassuringly, snapping my focus back to him. "There are guilds that specialize in this stuff."

"That's good." Somewhat relieved, I folded my arms on the bar top and pillowed my head on them. "How much longer until the guys get back, do you think?"

"Tough to say. If it went smoothly, another hour or two. If they have to chase down the rogues, could take all night. Kai will want to question these guys before turning them over to the MagiPol satellite office."

I closed my eyes, my head and neck throbbing from tension. "I want to know how that sorcerer tracked me down while I was shopping."

"Yeah, that's been bugging me too. I've also been wondering about their attack on the way to your apartment." He snapped his laptop shut. "They waited until I was alone— not with Kai or Ezra, I mean—but how did they know to target me that night? I'd never walked you home before, so how could they have known?"

"It seemed like they were waiting for us to show up." I raised my head. "Two guys followed behind, but the other four were ahead of us."

"It's weird. I can't even guess how they could've predicted our movements." He rubbed a hand over the stubble on his jaw. "They waited until I was basically alone to attack me the first time, but breaking into our house … and just the one guy, too? I don't get it."

"Maybe they thought you'd be alone again? They must know they'd have no chance against three mages, right?"

"But Kai and Ezra live in the damn house. Why would the kryomage think …" He frowned. "Actually, now that you mention it, Kai and Ezra were talking about scouting Stanley Park on Sunday night. There was a werewolf sighting, and they even cleared their plan with the Stanley Coven on Saturday. They ditched the idea after you were attacked."

We stared at each other.

"So," I said slowly, "if the sorcerer hadn't attacked me, and Kai hadn't brought me back to your place, and he and Ezra hadn't decided to stick around for the night, you would've been alone when Ice Guy snuck in."

Aaron nodded, unease shadowing his usual confidence. "He was using stealth spells to get around. Ezra is probably the only one who would've noticed him before he attacked." He pursed his lips. "Even then, Ice Guy might have made it through the house without anyone noticing if you hadn't woken Ezra."

My nerves twisted at what might've happened if not for a fortunate clash of coincidences. "Stealth spells are a sorcerer thing, though, aren't they?"

"Anyone can buy artifacts off a sorcerer. Same thing for alchemic potions. Sharpie—my sword—is technically an artifact." He drummed his fingers on his laptop. "Damn. Kai better catch that kryomage. I want to know how they know so much about our movements."

"Yeah," I agreed. "Otherwise, I'm going to develop an ulcer from all the anxiety."

Aaron's disquiet melted into a smile. "Don't worry, Tori. We'll protect you."

My stomach fluttered. Goddamn it. I didn't *want* protection. I wanted to not be hunted by murderous rogues. Aaron and his chivalrous declarations were messing with my head.

"Knight of Swords," I muttered under my breath.

"Hmm?"

"Nothing."

He propped his chin on his hand. "Oh, your tarot reading, right? Figured out any more of it?"

"What's there to figure out? It's so vague it could mean anything."

"Have you thought about what you're afraid of?"

"I dunno," I drawled. "Being murdered in my underwear by a knife-wielding sorcerer, maybe?"

"In your underwear?" he repeated with interest.

"I was in a changeroom. I could easily have been down to my undies when he burst in."

Aaron grinned as though enjoying the mental image. "The tarot reading wouldn't pick up on that kind of fear. Like Kai said, it's something that's been bothering you for a while."

"I have no idea what the reading means."

Chin in hand, he tilted his head, blue eyes meeting mine. "I think you know."

My stomach flipped again, but in a very different way—a not-fun way. Sabrina's warning about being blinded by my past flashed through my head. "Why do you say that?"

Staying silent, he waited.

My hands clenched and I looked away. Yeah, I knew what fear the tarot cards had picked up on, but I had no intention of sharing it, especially not with Aaron. He'd make fun of me, and then I would hate him. I didn't want to hate him.

"Tori," he murmured.

I squeezed my hands into tighter fists. Forcing myself to meet his eyes, I knew no matter what I said, he wouldn't tease me. Maybe … maybe if I told him part of it, the tarot reading would stop digging holes in my brain.

"My dad is a piece of shit," I said, going for a light and casual tone. "My mom had had enough by the time I was seven and took off. After that, it was just me and my brother. When Justin turned fifteen, he ran away from home. I was ten. Then it was just me and Dad …"

Grabbing my bar rag, I twisted the cloth into a knot, forgetting I was feigning nonchalance. "I ended up living with relatives for a while. When I was sixteen, Justin showed up again and got me out. I cut all ties with our relatives and started to get my life together."

Aaron tugged the rag out of my white-knuckled grip. Pulling my composure back into place, I forced a smile. It probably wasn't convincing, but I tried.

"Things were good. I was happy. But then Justin applied to the police academy here and when he got in, he …" I coughed before the faint tremor in my voice became too obvious. Why was this so hard to talk about? I mean, yeah, I'd never told anyone before, but it shouldn't be this difficult.

"It was fine," I concluded. "He was following his dreams. I'm happy he gets to do what he wants. I moved back in with my least revolting relatives, but then my dad started showing up, so I relocated here."

"And now you're living with your brother again," Aaron murmured. "You're afraid he'll abandon you a third time?"

"No, not that." Giving an overly careless shrug, I reclaimed the rag and wiped a few water droplets off the counter. "I know he won't always be there. He's got his own life to live and he doesn't owe me anything. When he's off again doing his own thing, I'll be okay this time. I don't need him."

"I see," Aaron said softly.

My wary gaze shot to him. "See what?"

"You still have my number, right? You should memorize it."

"Why?"

"So that no matter where you are or what happens, you can call me. I'll always be there to help you."

I didn't want help. Not his, not anyone's. If my mother would abandon me, and my brother would ditch me *twice*, and my relatives would only help when it was convenient, how could I trust a near stranger to be there for me?

The only person I trusted was myself. Once, I'd put my faith in Justin, my white-knight hero, to help put me back together. But when it hadn't been easy, when fixing my temper and my insecurities and my broken self-control had grown too tedious, he'd left me all over again.

Screw that. I wasn't giving anyone the power to crush me like that, not a second time. I would count on me to take care of me.

Before I had to come up with a response, Cooper stuck his head through the saloon doors. He'd taken over kitchen duty for the night since Ramsey was out hunting rogues with Kai and Ezra.

"Hey, Tori," he said, the stink of cigarette smoke wafting off him. "Will you be okay on your own? It's dead tonight so I'm going to take off. There's a Chinese place I wanna hit for dinner before they close."

"What time is it?" I asked, too lazy to get my phone out of my pocket.

"Quarter after eleven."

"Oh, yeah. No problem. I'm going to start cleaning up in a few minutes anyway." With a wave, he vanished back through the doors, and I stretched on my stool, rolling my shoulders. "I could go for some Chinese food too. Or even better, something sweet."

Aaron's eyes lit up. I'd come to discover he had a sweet tooth worse than mine. His ordering a margarita with a mandatory candied cherry on top should've been my first warning.

"Chocolate would be perfect." I sighed wistfully, remembering the box he'd given me as part of that dumb bet. "How far is the nearest 24/7 gas station?"

"Too far," he replied, sounding as disappointed as I felt. "Besides, your shift isn't over yet. And we're supposed to wait here, remember?"

"Damn it." I tapped my lower lip, considering my options. A genius idea popped into my head. "Aha!"

"What?"

"Nothing," I said brightly, hopping off my stool. "I'm going to clean up in the back."

"You've never been this excited about cleaning before," he observed with squinty-eyed suspicion. "What are you really doing?"

"Cleaning." I slid away from him. "You know, scrubbing ... things. You wouldn't like it."

"Uh-huh." Standing, he followed me. "You look guiltier than a kid with an empty cookie jar."

"You're imagining things." I speed-walked around the bar, but he strode after me. "Hey! You're not allowed back here."

He smirked. "Who's going to stop me?"

Scowling, I zipped through the saloon doors and across the kitchen to the dry storage room. Aaron scrambled after me, but

I beat him to the door, jumped inside, and shut it behind me. Holding the knob with one hand, I grabbed the box of milk chocolate stir sticks used to garnish chocolate martinis.

"You found chocolate, didn't you?" Aaron demanded through the door, the handle turning in my grip.

"Of course not!"

He pushed on the door and I dug my heels in. I was short the hundred pounds of muscle required to stop him, but I stuffed three chocolate sticks in my mouth before he got the door open.

His greedy stare found the box in my hand. "Is there a reason you can't share?"

"Mmphrm." I wanted to point out he'd eat twice as much as me if I let him, but three chocolate sticks was too much to talk through.

He reached for the box and I held it behind my back, frantically chewing before I choked. Dancing backward as he tried to reach around me, I darted for the door. He swung it shut, trapping me and my precious snack inside.

"You are a mean person, Tori," he reprimanded as I skittered out of reach. "Talking about chocolate then eating it right in front of me? Cruel."

I swallowed my mouthful. "You wouldn't have to watch if you hadn't followed me." To emphasize my point, I stuck another chocolate stick in my mouth, the end poking out as I grinned unrepentantly.

Growling, he grabbed for the box again. I dove away but he caught me around the waist and pushed me back into the closed door, then his head dipped down. He caught the other end of my chocolate stick in his mouth, his lips brushing across mine as he bit the end off.

I went rigid. Suddenly, I was intensely aware of his hands on my waist and his heat radiating into me. He swallowed his stolen bite of chocolate and licked his lips.

"Not bad," he remarked.

Then he kissed me.

His hot mouth pressed against mine and my stomach dropped. I almost crushed the chocolates in my hand, my breath gone from my lungs as he pulled me closer. My free hand found his arm, sliding over his bicep. He kissed me unhurriedly, the heat building, a slow fire stoked by each touch of his mouth.

Lifting his head, he arched an eyebrow. "Remember how I said I was going to ask you out?"

"Mm-hmm," I agreed, embarrassingly breathless.

"Do you want to get dinner together once the evil rogue guild is no more?"

"Sure."

"Excellent." His gaze slipped down to my mouth again. "Do I have to wait until after our date to kiss you again?"

I pretended to deliberate, distracted by his thumbs caressing my sides. "I don't think that will be necessary."

I'd barely gotten the last word out before his mouth closed over mine again. Blindly shoving the chocolates onto the nearest shelf, I wound my arms around his neck. He pulled me into him and I pressed as much of my body as possible against the warm, hard muscles I'd been admiring for weeks. God, he had an amazing body. I wanted to run my hands over his bare skin. I wanted him back in nothing but his boxers. Ever since waking up Monday morning with him and Ezra practically naked in the same room as me, I'd been fighting nonstop fantasies every time I closed my eyes.

Wrapping one arm around me, he slid his other hand up the side of my neck and into my hair, pulling my mouth harder into his. I parted my lips, inviting an even deeper kiss, and his tongue flirted with mine, tasting of chocolate. I ran my hands over his shoulders, then slid one under the back of his shirt, wanting to touch his feverish-hot skin.

Then something smacked into the top of my head.

My eyes flew open as the offending object bounced onto the floor. A lemon?

With dull thudding, an entire bag of yellow fruit poured off the top shelf and rained down on us. I yelped, ducking out of the way, and Aaron backpedaled, hauling me clear of the citrus avalanche. Wide-eyed, I watched another dozen lemons bounce across the floor. Uh ... oops. That was probably my fault. I may have been a bit rough when I rammed the chocolates onto the shelf.

Laughing at the absurdity of being interrupted by *lemons*, I started to pick up fruit. "Maybe you should get back to the front."

"I can help." He stooped to fish lemons out from under the bottom shelf. "And I'm not leaving without at least one whole chocolate stick to myself."

I snorted. "If I give you chocolate, will you go? I don't want to get caught making out with a customer in the back room. I've been fired for less."

"Clara wouldn't fire you for that, and besides, no one is around to catch us anyway. Who could possibly overhear us back here?"

I straightened, my hands full of lemons. "Please, Aaron. There are a couple people out front and I don't want to risk this job. I really ..."

Trailing into silence, I stared at nothing as a lightbulb went off in my brain.

"This job is important to you, isn't it?" Crouched by the shelves with an armload of fruit, he paused. "Tori? You okay?"

I opened my mouth, then closed it. My face felt cold. I must have gone pale.

Aaron rose to his full height. "What's wrong?"

"I think—I just realized—but—" I bit off the words. "I need to check something."

"Huh? But Tori—"

Dropping the lemons back onto the floor, I sped out of the storage room and through the kitchen. At the saloon doors, I peeked into the pub. All the tables were empty except one. Liam sat alone, his face illuminated by his phone and his feet resting on a nearby chair.

I shoved through the doors. "Liam, where's Tom?"

"Hmm? Oh, he left a few minutes ago. Decided to go home. I'm leaving too, just finishing—"

I spun on my heel and raced back through the kitchen. Aaron stood in the storage room doorway, his brow furrowed. "What—"

"When Kai and Ezra were arranging to go to Stanley Park on Sunday, did they talk about their plans while they were here?"

"Here?" He glanced around the kitchen. "Uh. Yeah, I remember Kai talking to the Stanley Coven on the phone. We were upstairs in the workroom."

I pressed a hand to my mouth, my heart hammering.

"Tori, what the hell is wrong?"

"I just realized ... we've been wondering how the rogue guild knew to ambush you near my apartment, and how they knew where I'd be on Sunday, and why they thought you'd be alone that night. We assumed they were predicting our movements, but it's way simpler than that."

His expression hardened with intensity. "How?"

I wrapped my arms around myself. "Last Saturday before we left, when you offered to walk me home, I mentioned West Georgia Street—and that's where you first noticed we were being followed. While here at the guild, Kai talked on the phone about how he and Ezra would be gone on Sunday night. And"—I swallowed—"on Saturday, I mentioned to Sabrina that I was going shopping and what my favorite store is."

Aaron's eyes widened.

"In the storage room, you said, 'Who could possibly overhear us?' But there *is* someone—"

"*Tom*," Aaron hissed. "Is he here? I saw him earlier."

"No, he already left. I just checked." I peered toward the bar as though I could see the corner where Tom had been sitting most of the night—and where he'd been almost every night. Clear as chiming bells, I could hear Liam's voice as he explained Tom's psychic ability, clairaudience. *Super hearing. He can hear people talking within a certain vicinity.*

Aaron raked a hand through his hair. "Okay, so Tom is probably the only person who could have overheard all three conversations, but that would mean he's been feeding information to the rogue guild. He wouldn't do that."

"How do you know?"

"He—he just wouldn't. He's a guild member. He wouldn't betray us like that."

I closed my hand around Aaron's arm, holding tight. What he was really saying was that a *guild member* wouldn't betray the guild. Aaron didn't believe any of his precious comrades-in-arms would deceive him.

Deception, Sabrina's tarot cards had warned. *Deception lurks in the shadows, calling the conflict ever closer.*

Calling the conflict.

Tom had left.

"Aaron," I gasped. "We need to leave. Right now."

18

"**WHAT?**" Aaron said blankly.

"We need to leave," I repeated, panic flaring through me. "Tom left. Liam was the last one here, and he just went home. We're alone—just like the first time we were attacked."

"We're in the guild, Tori. No one would be dumb enough to attack us here. Besides that, our team is hunting down the rogues as we speak. It doesn't matter if Tom tries to tip them off."

I sucked in a shallow breath to quell my anxiety.

Aaron rubbed my arms soothingly. "It's okay. We'll wait here." He pulled his phone out, thumbs zooming over the keys. "Felix will come right back after they're done, since he's on duty tonight, but I'll tell Kai and Ezra to return here too. We'll find out from them if Tom is really involved."

"Okay," I mumbled uncertainly.

"Message sent." He looked up from his phone with a smile. "I told you I would always—"

I didn't see it, but I heard it—the sickening crack of something hitting bone.

Aaron lurched sideways, then crumpled. As he hit the floor, my heart slammed to a dead halt, shock paralyzing my entire body. With a silent gargle that would've been a scream if I'd had air in my lungs, I stumbled toward him.

Something flashed past me, just missing my face. I reeled back, hands outstretched with no idea what I was defending against. I spun around and froze a second time.

People had appeared—three of them, standing casually at the back of the kitchen. A man, a woman … and Tom. His usually shy expression was lined with sadistic glee. I staggered a step away, my foot bumping Aaron's unmoving arm.

Three shiny orbs the size of billiard balls hovered in front of the unfamiliar man, each glowing a different color. As they stilled, floating serenely, the red splatters on one became visible. Horrified, I looked down at Aaron—at the blood running down the side of his slack face.

"He should have listened to you," Tom said conversationally. "If you'd run immediately, you might've escaped."

My hands clenched and I inched back another half step. "But then I wouldn't have gotten to tell you to your face that you're a shit-eating coward who deserves every bit of pain coming your way."

The woman laughed. "Take her out."

The other man canted his head, and I threw myself down as two orbs whipped past. Telekinesis. How the hell was I supposed to defend against a telekinetic?

Go for his eyes, Aaron had told me after Liam had messed with me. *He needs to see to use his telekinesis.*

Launching up, I sprinted for the saloon doors. The woman laughed again.

An orb struck my shoulder with the force of a major league pitcher throwing a fastball. The impact spun me in a half circle and I bounced off the counter but kept on my feet. Gasping, I slapped a hand against the light switch.

Darkness plunged over the room. Only the faintest light leaked in from the pub, but it did nothing to illuminate the kitchen. The three orbs glowed, hovering in the air near me, but they weren't moving. The telekinetic didn't know where to aim them.

"Get the lights back on!" the woman yelled.

Tom and the telekinetic growled at each other, clattering against counters and cupboards as they searched for a switch. Crouching, I slid an empty stock pot off the counter and crept toward the orbs. They glowed, allowing the telekinetic to see them, but maybe I could fix that.

Taking aim with my pot, I swept it through the air like a bug-catching net. *Clang, clang, clang.* The three orbs hit the bottom of the pot and I slammed it down on the floor, trapping the balls and extinguishing their telltale glow. The man swore furiously.

I shoved the pot under the sink where the telekinetic wouldn't spot it even if they got the lights on again, then threw my hands out, feeling for the sauce pans hanging over the range. Grabbing a handle, I charged. I'd been through this kitchen a hundred times. I didn't need light.

When I heard the scuff of backpedaling shoes, I whipped the sauce pan around in my signature baseball swing. It thwacked into a body. Skirting back a step, I wound up and swung again. This time I hit a bony limb and the telekinetic yelped.

A footstep clacked on the floor on my other side, and I whirled, ready to strike. A hand touched my shoulder.

The saucepan fell to the floor with a bang, and my arms dropped to my sides. I stood there, unmoving, the hand on my arm and a voice in my head. It commanded me to stand still—and that's what I did. I could do nothing else, the voice drowning out my thoughts, my consciousness.

Clattering sounds, then light bloomed, blasting my eyes. But I didn't move. I didn't know how.

Tom's face appeared in front of me, and he sneered. "You were right that I was passing on information about Aaron, but you were wrong about everything else."

"You two carry the Sinclair kid," the woman ordered.

Tom's face disappeared, and more scuffling sounds followed. Then the light changed—a surge of red and yellow, the crackle of flames, and an agonized howl.

The hand on my arm disappeared and awareness flooded my mind. I recoiled, hitting the door to the walk-in fridge and grabbing the handle for balance. The door swung inward and I almost fell, my legs trembling.

Aaron was halfway up, blood streaking his face. Fire blazed over his arms and his hands clenched around fistfuls of Tom's shirt. Tom screamed, grabbing at Aaron's wrists but unable to touch the flames that coated his skin.

The telekinetic thrust his hand out and an invisible force shoved Aaron backward. Tom tore free, sobbing as he scrambled away. With a wave of his hand, the telekinetic lifted my abandoned saucepan off the floor and it streaked toward Aaron's head.

He smashed it out of the air with his fist, flames exploding on impact. The telekinetic snapped his hand in a "come-hither" motion. A butcher knife zoomed across the kitchen and halted inches from my throat.

"Stop where you are, or she dies," the telekinetic barked.

Teeth bared and fear in his eyes, Aaron went still. The fire on his arms flickered out.

"If you move," the woman purred, stepping toward him, "you'll get to watch her bleed out all over the floor."

She reached for his arm.

"No, Aaron!" I yelled. "Don't let her touch y—"

Her hand wrapped around his wrist. The fury and fear in his face evaporated, and his expression went as lifeless as a plastic mannequin. The woman turned a simpering smile on me and flipped her blond hair over her shoulder with her free hand.

"Shall we, then?" she said to her accomplices.

The telekinetic, his eyes fixed on the floating knife pointed at my unprotected throat, smirked triumphantly. Openly weeping from his burns, Tom had staggered to the back entrance at the far end of the kitchen, and the woman started after him, her hand tightly gripping Aaron's wrist. He followed submissively, his eyes vacant. He didn't look at me as they passed. He didn't see me at all, and I knew why. She had control of his mind, just as she'd controlled me.

Tom disappeared through the back door, and the woman paused in the threshold. "Why don't we show Darius how serious we are? A dead body in his guild ought to get his attention."

Chuckling to herself, she steered Aaron out the door, leaving me with the telekinetic. As they vanished, the butcher knife floated away from me as though an invisible wielder were drawing it back to strike. I stared at the blade, unable to move, nowhere to go.

The knife shot for my throat—then veered off course, screeching across the walk-in fridge door.

"Tori!"

At the other end of the kitchen, Liam hung off a saloon door, one hand stretched toward me.

Swearing, the other telekinetic waved emphatically. Two more butcher knives whipped out of the block and catapulted for Liam. He ran toward the projectiles as a huge pot lid flew in front of him like a shield. The knives ricocheted off the lid and everything crashed to the floor.

Liam skidded to a stop beside me, hands outstretched as though waiting for the next item to command.

The other telekinetic glanced over Liam and sneered. A serrated bread knife pulled from the block's dwindling supply, then a thin-bladed boning knife. As the points swerved in our direction, Liam thrust his hands toward them.

The knives stopped where they were, vibrating in the air.

A third knife pulled out of the block and spun to face us. Liam gasped, muscles tensed like he was straining against a terrible weight. The three knives vibrated harder. Liam panted, his arms trembling from the effort.

The third knife wobbled, then flashed into motion. Liam flung a hand toward it, halting its movement—but the other two broke free and whipped across the distance.

Liam fell back, tumbling into me. I grabbed him and threw us into the open walk-in fridge. As I kicked the door shut, the third knife hit the metal with a shriek. Footsteps stomped toward the door and I wrapped my fists around the handle, determined to hold it closed.

"Leave them!" the woman called. "We have what we came for."

"Fine," the telekinetic snarled, his voice right outside the door. The handle shuddered under my palm and a terrifying metallic crunch sounded, then his footsteps thudded away. A door banged.

I whirled toward Liam. He lay on his back, hyperventilating as his hands waved helplessly around his chest where two knives stuck out of his body.

"Oh god," I whimpered. "Hold on, Liam."

I fumbled my phone out of my pocket, but there was no reception in the metal-lined fridge. Lurching to the door, I twisted the handle. It didn't move.

"No," I moaned, wrenching on it. "No!"

I battered my shoulder against the door but the impact didn't so much as shake the heavy, insulated metal. I twisted the handle until pain burned through my fingers, but I couldn't make it move. The telekinetic had jammed it.

Dropping to my knees beside Liam, the painful chill of the floor spreading through my jeans, I tried to remember a long-ago first aid class. Bright red blood trickled from around the knives, and the handles shifted with every frenzied breath he took.

"I'm sorry," he whispered. "I came back ... forgot my sunglasses ... heard you—"

"Shh, Liam." I wrapped his cold hand in both of mine. "Just hang in there. Help will be here soon."

He nodded, his face white, and didn't ask the question I knew he was thinking. The question I was desperately avoiding.

Help would come … eventually. But would it come soon enough to save Liam's life?

19

EZRA LEANED against the table, and I leaned against him. His warm arms banded across my back as though he could squeeze the shivers out of me. I tried to stop my teeth from chattering.

An hour. An hour trapped in the fridge, desperately hoping Liam wouldn't die before Ezra, Kai, and Felix returned. I'd heard them come in and screamed my head off until they broke the door open. Kai and Felix had rushed Liam away, taking him … somewhere. Kai had been on the phone with a woman named Elisabetta—the guild's best healer.

I'd already given them a brief rundown of what had happened, but while we waited for Kai to return, I told Ezra everything. As I spoke, he went more and more rigid, his arms like steel clamps. The air around us grew noticeably chill and the lights dimmed. I pretended not to notice.

Ezra's phone chimed. Keeping an arm around me, he fished it out of his pocket, the studded knuckles of his bad-guy-smasher gloves gleaming. He swiped the screen up and read a message.

"Liam is with Elisabetta," he murmured, his smooth voice soothing my anxiety. "Kai and Felix are on their way back, and they've called in the troops. Every guild member they could reach is on their way here."

I nodded against his chest, too exhausted and sick with worry to voice the questions piling up in my head. Ezra cocooned me in his arms again. My shoulder, struck by the telekinetic's murder-ball, throbbed nonstop.

When the front door snapped open, I jumped half a foot and Ezra clamped me tighter to him as though I might leap over backward and hurt myself. Zora swept inside, her pink-streaked pixie cut damp and her giant sword in hand, the sheath's straps dragging on the floor.

"Got Felix's message," she said tersely. "I'd just stepped out of the shower. What happened?"

Now that we had company, I tried to pull out of Ezra's arms but he didn't let go.

"While we were hunting the rogues," he said, an unfamiliar growl in his voice, "a different group attacked Tori, Liam, and Aaron. They took Aaron. Liam is with Elisabetta. Stab wounds."

Zora's eyes blazed. "They *took* Aaron? How?"

"From what Tori described, it sounded like a mentalist."

She swore with such vileness that I flinched. "You okay, Tori?"

"I'm fine." I pried myself out of Ezra's embrace. "What's a mentalist?"

Zora's mouth twisted with distaste. "A type of psychic who can influence the thoughts or actions of—"

She broke off as Lyndon the sorcerer strode into the building, followed a moment later by Sin, her hair a tangle and her t-shirt inside out.

"Tori! Are you okay?" Racing past Lyndon, she grabbed my hand. "Why are you so cold?"

"I got locked in the fridge."

"*What?*"

"What's happening?" Lyndon asked, rubbing the stubble on his usually shaved head. "All Felix's message said was Liam is in critical condition, Aaron is missing, and everyone needs to get their asses over here."

"Felix can explain when he arrives," Ezra replied. "He's on his way back."

Lyndon nodded toward Ezra's gear, his Twin Terrors lying on the table behind us. "How did the rogue hunting go?"

"Better than expected. They had no idea we were coming, which makes the rest of this even stranger."

The five of us waited without speaking as the minutes ticked past. More guild members arrived in ones, twos, and threes—familiar faces like Gwen, Ramsey, and Taye from Kai's rogue hunting team; Andrew, Cameron, and Cearra from the team that had exterminated a vampire nest; Sylvia, the Manhattan-loving sorceress; Riley, Sin's curly-haired alchemist friend; the yoga witch and her boyfriend. Others I hadn't seen since my first shift came in as well, gathering silently in the pub. It occurred to me I should offer them drinks or something, but I didn't move from Ezra's side.

The atmosphere was tense, the silence oppressive. Some asked what was going on, but Ezra gave the same answer: "Felix will explain."

Finally, the back door thumped and a moment later, Felix strode out of the kitchen with Kai right behind him, still clad in his black warrior gear, looking none the worse for having spent the last several hours tagging rogues. As Felix took a spot in front of the bar, facing the gathered mythics, Kai swept around the table and stopped on my other side.

"I'll get straight to business." Felix glanced at me, then continued. "A rogue guild dubbed the East Hastings Gang has been targeting Aaron for two weeks. Tonight, while Kai led a team against them, another group showed up here. Liam was critically injured in the fight, and Aaron was captured."

"Was that group part of the rogue guild?" Zora demanded.

"We're not sure." Felix's jaw flexed. "We learned from the rogues that they were hired to abduct Aaron. We also learned tonight that Tom Newburg, our clairaudient, has been passing information to either the rogues or the unknown party—or both."

Gasps rang through the group. "Tom? Are you sure?"

"Without a doubt," Felix said, raising his voice over the shocked muttering. "Our top priority is finding out who the other party is and why they've targeted Aaron. I haven't been able to reach Darius, but I sent him a detailed message. Same for Girard—he's in Seattle. For now, it's just us."

I counted the assembled mythics. Twenty-six. Just over half the guild.

"What do we know about the group who captured Aaron tonight?" Lyndon asked.

Felix, Ezra, and Kai looked at me.

I cleared my throat nervously. "Three people came in the back door. One was Tom. He mocked me for figuring out he was eavesdropping on conversations so the rogue guild could attack Aaron while he was vulnerable, but—"

"How is Aaron vulnerable?" Cearra interrupted, her tone suggesting I was an idiot for thinking Aaron could be exposed to danger.

"Anytime Ezra and I aren't with him," Kai answered shortly.

"I think Tom was passing his tidbits along to this other group, and they were giving it to the rogues." I tugged nervously at the hem of my shirt. "The two other people with him were a telekinetic man and a woman who can ... control people."

"A mentalist," Ezra added. "A powerful one with a touch-dependent gift. She forced Aaron to leave with them."

"Including Tom, that's three Psychica mythics," Zora pointed out. "Do we know of any rogue guilds with a heavy inclusion of psychics on their roster?"

"I can think of a few," Andrew responded grimly. "But I don't know why any of them would go after Aaron. They have no reason to—"

"Revenge." Tabitha's cool voice preceded her out of the kitchen. She pushed through the saloon doors, her jaw-length bob smooth and her ice-queen expression undisturbed.

"What?" Zora snarled. "Who wants revenge on Aaron? For what?"

"Not for anything Aaron has done, but revenge on the Crow and Hammer." Tabitha stopped beside Felix and held out her phone. A green call symbol glowed on the screen. "Go ahead, Darius."

"Good evening, everyone." The deep, vaguely familiar voice of the guild master echoed from the phone's speaker. "Thank you for coming on such short notice."

Felix's wide eyes darted from the phone to Tabitha and back.

"A few minutes ago, I received a call," Darius continued. "The caller demanded I present myself at a specific address in two hours. If I fail to arrive, or do not arrive alone, he will kill Aaron."

Lightheaded terror swept through me and I clutched the table for balance.

"Unfortunately, the caller did not give me the opportunity to inform him I'm three thousand miles away. I can't meet his demands, so we'll need a different approach."

"Who the hell are these guys?" Sin yelled, her hands balled into fists as she glared at the phone.

"Thank you, Sin. I was just getting to that," Darius replied dryly. "Six months ago, I instructed Girard, Tabitha, and Alistair to investigate the activities of a local guild—Kirk, Conner & Qasid."

At the guild's name, faint recognition pricked me.

"Ostensibly a law firm, the guild's membership is composed entirely of Psychica mythics. Though they present as a legitimate guild, their activities behind closed doors are distinctly unsavory. In short, it's a guild of predators, cheaters, and conmen. Over the past half year, Girard, Tabitha, and Alistair have done an admirable job of catching their members in numerous illegal activities. The MPD has cracked down on them, banning members and levying destructive fines. Any further charges and the guild will risk dissolution."

Darius paused as though gathering his thoughts. "The reason I assigned this task to our most experienced officers and most powerful mage is because of the threat KCQ presents. It was not a task I wanted other members involved in. Though psychics are often underestimated, KCQ has attracted some dangerous individuals. Tabitha?"

The second officer raised her chin. "Four weeks ago, Alistair and I tagged one of KCQ's most promising new recruits—an empath with a frightening ability to influence the emotions of everyone around him. He's now in MPD custody. After his arrest, all activity from the guild went quiet."

Her dark eyes flashed to me. "The moment I heard what had happened tonight, I knew who was behind it. We took a gifted and powerful young member from KCQ—and now they've taken our most gifted young member in turn. But that isn't the extent of their revenge. Aaron is Darius's protégé, and they're using him as bait to lure Darius into the open."

"They don't just plan to punish us by killing Aaron," Lyndon growled. "They want to kill Darius too."

"I believe that is their goal," Darius agreed, his voice calm but deepened by intensity. "We will not allow them to accomplish either goal. They will deeply regret every moment of their supposed vengeance."

A silent, restless shiver ran through the gathered mythics. I could taste the impending violence in the air.

"Tabitha has the address my caller provided, but we can assume that location is a trap. They are likely holding Aaron elsewhere. KCQ has two offices, one registered and one not." His tone shifted, becoming more businesslike. "Tabitha, in my and Girard's absence, you are in charge. Aaron's life is in your hands."

"I'll get him home safely," she promised.

"Good. I'll await your update." The line clicked.

Tabitha slipped her phone into her pocket. "We have no time to waste. Taye, contact all our Psychica members who aren't already here. Delegate others to go to their homes if you can't reach them by phone. Felix and Kai, pull up all the information you can find on the three addresses we'll be targeting. I already texted them to you. With one office downtown, one in the West End, and the shipping yard where they told Darius to go, we'll need to coordinate our movements carefully."

Felix and Kai sped toward the stairs to the second level.

"Andrew and Zora," Tabitha continued, "organize the combat mythics present into three teams. Sin, get a hold of our healers. Ezra, print off the profiles of every known KCQ member, six copies each."

Giving my hand a quick squeeze, Ezra hastened upstairs as well. Sin disappeared downstairs for a quiet place to make calls, and Zora herded the other mythics to the far end of the room. As the purposeful bustle consumed the pub, I squeezed my hands together.

No one protested the perils of the mission. No one questioned or complained about their assignments. They moved with determination, with anger burning in their faces. Every person here had come to help Aaron, and not a single one showed the slightest hesitation about going up against a guild Darius had deemed too dangerous for regular members to tackle.

Tabitha turned to me. "What happened this evening when Aaron was captured? I need all the details."

Stumblingly, I described every moment of the encounter, every word I could recall. When I finished, Tabitha nodded.

"Very well," she murmured. "You may leave now."

"L-leave?"

"Your home is the safest place for you." When I started to argue, her cold stare silenced me. "You are a liability, and I will not put any more lives at risk to protect you."

My whole body went cold, the chill sinking even deeper than hours in a refrigerator could inflict.

"Consider your employment terminated," she added without sympathy. "You were brave, but allowing you to set foot in this building was a mistake from the start. All else aside, I will not see you hurt or killed on my watch."

I glanced around desperately, but Kai and Ezra were upstairs and Sin was in the basement. Not a coincidence. Anyone who might have come to my defense was busy elsewhere.

Tabitha noticed my searching look. "Do you plan to distract them at such a critical time? Go home, Miss Dawson. You do not belong here."

My throat constricted so tightly it hurt to swallow. She was right. I didn't belong here. Even if I wanted to argue with her, I couldn't do it now. I couldn't distract Kai and Ezra from saving Aaron, who had less than two hours to live. Giving Tabitha my information about tonight's attackers was the extent of my usefulness. The best thing I could do was get out of the way.

Forcing my tight fists to open, I nodded and stepped away from the table. No one noticed as I walked around the bar and into the kitchen. The saloon doors swung shut behind me for the last time.

Working hard to ignore the splatters of blood on the floor, I got my purse from the office, then picked up the hot-pink umbrella Aaron had given me. My hands clenched around it, tears burning my eyes. Determinedly blinking them away, I marched through the back door. A black van was parked crookedly right outside, and a half dozen other vehicles were crammed into the small lot, including Aaron's red sports car in the corner.

The cool night air washed over me as I joined the sidewalk and headed away from the Crow and Hammer, my heart heavy and my lungs hurting. In my mind, I watched Aaron's face go blank as the mentalist woman took control of him. Two hours before they would kill him in retaliation against Darius.

I scarcely noticed the dark road, the boarded-up windows, the graffiti-marked walls. Normally, I would've been nervous as hell walking these streets alone at night, but I didn't care. All I could think about was Aaron. Had Ezra and Kai noticed I was gone? Even if they had, they didn't have time to waste on me tonight, not when Aaron's life was ticking away with each minute.

My shoulders drooped, my steps sluggish. My thoughts and fears were focused on Aaron, but at the back of my mind, pain throbbed. Another job, gone. Just like that, I'd been fired again. Even though my position had been temporary from the start, this one hurt more than any job I'd lost before.

Trying not to think too hard, I hurried my pace. My mind spun, jumping from topic to topic with lightning speed, wondering where Aaron was, how the Crow and Hammer mythics would get him back safely, how long it would take them to plan their attacks on three different locations. How—

I stumbled on a nonexistent crack in the sidewalk. Three locations …

Stopping beneath a flickering streetlight, I yanked my purse off my shoulder and dug into it. My sunglasses spilled out and hit the pavement, one lens shattering.

"Come on," I hissed.

I squirmed my hand through a tangle of receipts, then pulled a crumpled paper free. On it, three job listings were printed. One for a bartending position. One for a bank teller position. And one for a receptionist position at a law firm—Kirk, Conner & Qasid.

The psychic guild's name had sounded familiar. Now I knew why.

I tilted the page toward the streetlight, reading the address. Clark Drive. That was east of here, whereas the downtown and West End offices Tabitha had mentioned were in the opposite direction. *This* address was for a different office. A third office. And if I was remembering correctly, at the north end of Clark Drive was a gargantuan quay where ocean-going cargo ships loaded and unloaded their freight. Could that be the shipping yard where Darius was supposed to surrender himself?

The dark text on the page stared back at me. A third KCQ office, almost on top of a shipping yard. A location Darius and Tabitha didn't know about.

I whipped out my phone and pulled up Kai's number, then hesitated. What if they already knew about this address and it was a dud? Or worse, what if they didn't know—and they split their limited resources even more thinly to investigate it? What if Aaron died because they sent a team out to a meaningless address from a random piece of garbage I'd picked up?

But there was a chance, however slim, that it was a real location. Probably not a *secret* one, since they'd put up a public job posting for it, but maybe it was a new office—one so new it wasn't registered in MagiPol's database yet.

Turning on my heel, I strode in the opposite direction of home. Since I was otherwise unneeded for Aaron's rescue efforts, I would make myself useful. I'd check out the location from my printout and determine if it was worth alerting Kai to its existence.

No need to distract them. A quick investigation on my own, nothing dangerous—I wasn't an idiot, I knew I was no match against mythics—and then I'd either call a cab and go home, or I'd call Kai and tell him what I'd discovered.

I couldn't save Aaron, but if there was something I could do, no matter how small, then I would do it—even if it meant going alone to stick my nose in the business of a guild so dangerous even other mythics steered clear.

20

BENEATH a claustrophobic concrete ceiling, I crouched in a deep patch of shadows. Above me, a low bridge slanted upward, spanning a wide set of train tracks.

It had taken me almost twenty minutes to get here, and if I hadn't been busy fearing for Aaron's life, I would've been fearing for my own. Strolling through a slummy commercial area in the middle of the night wasn't the smartest thing I'd ever done. I was at the far end of the Downtown Eastside, the bustling city core thirty long blocks west.

I squinted across the road at a rundown two-story building with the address from my printout. Just north of it, the access street ended in a chain-link fence where the train tracks ran parallel to the quay beyond. The bridge above my head connected to the shipping yard. Assuming it was the same shipping yard Tabitha had referred to, I was ridiculously close to the "hostage exchange" location.

My stomach turned sickeningly as I scanned the formerly white office building that was now a dull piss yellow with tattered siding. Scaffolding occupied one ugly wall, and a section of siding had been stripped away. The windows on the lower level were brand-new, stickers and labels stuck to the pristine glass, and sturdy plastic barriers were taped over the square openings on the upper level.

Lights glowed through the plastic coverings. It was the only building on the block that showed any signs of life.

I flinched as a lone tractor trailer drove down the bridge, rattling the concrete above my head. Pressing deeper into the shadows, I pulled my phone out to check the clock—forty-five minutes until the two-hour time limit was up—and saw messages from Kai and Ezra blinking on my screen. My thumb hovered over them.

If I called Kai or Ezra now, they would try to include this new location in their plans. But how much would that throw off their current strategy? Did they have enough people to investigate a fourth building? If I was wrong—if KCQ wasn't using this building yet, if Aaron wasn't here, if the lights were from squatters or something—Aaron might die because I'd messed up their plans. I couldn't risk it. I'd check the location myself.

Slipping my phone back in my pocket, I focused on the building. Heavy metal gates barricaded the recessed front entrance. If I'd been a mythic, maybe I could've blasted them open, but I was a lame-o human with no magic. I considered the scaffolding, but it was set up against a window-free stretch of wall. No good.

Slipping out of my hiding spot, I jogged across the street to check the building's other side. Around the corner, a one-story welding shop butted against the office. On its far side, behind a chain-link gate, was a small lot littered with junk.

I eyed the scrap metal piled against the wall, then strode to the fence. Time for some good ol' breaking and entering.

Slinging my purse over my shoulder—maybe I should invest in a fanny pack—I hauled ass over the chain-link gate and dropped down on the opposite side. Keeping to the shadows, I climbed onto a rusting metal barrel, scrambled across a stack of rotting wood pallets, then used the top of a heavy-duty pipe to propel myself high enough to grab the edge of the rooftop.

I dragged myself up, groaning quietly. I needed to work out more. Lots of pull-ups. Biceps are sexy, right?

Rolling onto the rooftop, I scampered across it to the office wall. The four windows were covered in plastic and, unlike the others, devoid of light. I pulled my keys out of my purse, jammed one through the plastic, and tore a long opening. Parting the edges, I peered into the dark room on the other side. That was easy. Look at me, trespassing like I did this shit all the time.

I slid inside, my shoes landing on something crinkly. Faint light leaked through the half-open door, illuminating the plastic laid across the carpet. The empty room reeked of plaster and fresh paint.

With a deep, calming breath—my heart totally wasn't racing out of my chest—I stuck my head out the partially open door, discovering a short hallway carpeted in utilitarian beige. Somewhere ahead, quiet voices murmured.

I pulled out my phone, checked it was on silent, then crept down the hall one terrified step at a time. This wasn't my first experience with breaking into a building, but the delinquent phase of my youth was way behind me. I didn't remember being this jumpy back then, and I could have used some of my teenaged overconfidence as I crouched at the end of the hall and peeked into the room beyond.

The moment I saw what waited for me, I whipped back out of sight, shaking from head to toe.

The good news: I'd found Aaron.

The bad news: everything else.

Beyond the hall was a large-ish room with two rows of cubicles, brand-new and still wrapped in plastic, with an open space in the center. In that opening was a metal folding chair, and in the chair was Aaron, hands tied behind his back, blindfolded, his mouth duct-taped, and dried blood streaking his face. The mentalist woman stood beside his chair, her hand on the back of his head.

Aside from them was, oh, about a dozen other people. Probably psychics. Probably scumbags. At least three for-sure scumbags—the mentalist, the telekinetic, and Tom, his hands and neck covered in gauze.

Hands trembling, I withdrew my phone one more time. Why oh why hadn't I called Kai sooner? Thirty-five minutes until Darius was supposed to show up at the shipping yard.

I minced down the hall, moving farther from the psychics, and opened my messaging app. Barely seeing Kai's recent texts—asking where I was and promising to call after Aaron was safe—I typed into my phone and sent the same message to him and Ezra: the address of the office, and three words.

I found Aaron.

Holding my breath, I waited. Would Kai check his phone, or was he already on his way to one of the locations? Twenty seconds passed, then thirty, then a minute. No response. My finger hesitated over the call button. Tom was here. If I called

Kai, no matter how quietly I spoke, the clairaudient would hear.

"Rigel," a man called from the main room.

Jumping in fright, I shoved my phone into my purse and slunk toward the voices.

"Ivan just messaged me. A Crow and Hammer team is closing in on our Cypress office."

I peeked out as a man rose from a leather office chair and straightened his tailored suit jacket. His black hair was combed back, the style enhancing his stark features and the deep creases around his mouth.

"Then it's time," he murmured in a crisp English accent.

He positioned himself across from Aaron, who was uncannily still with the mentalist's hand on his head, keeping him under her control. From my angle, I couldn't see what Rigel was doing—then the sound of a phone ringing on speaker broke the silence. The psychics in the room waited, unmoving.

The line clicked.

"Have you decided to return my pyromage?" Darius's calm, deep voice echoed from the phone.

"Darius," Rigel said, ignoring the question. "I am disappointed."

"A mutual sentiment, Rigel."

"Guild etiquette is simple. We do not interfere in one another's business. Isn't that your personal maxim as well? Don't hit first?" A sneer coated Rigel's tone. "You broke your own rule, my friend. You struck first, and now I'm hitting back."

"I could remind you of the personal standards *you* once held," Darius replied coolly. "But I suppose the days we shared the same ideals are long past."

Rigel barked a laugh. "Those ideals you still cling to are the reason you'll never be able to challenge my place in the mythical and mundane hierarchy."

"Our estimations of your position in that hierarchy might differ."

"My firm's clients rule this city. Yet *you* chose to interfere with us. With *me*." His voice took on a quiet, dangerous edge. "You should have known you stood no chance against my guild. No power is sacrosanct when psychics can sway the people who wield it. Just look at your promising young pyromage, reduced to a puppet."

"Rigel—" Darius began, anger tingeing his voice for the first time.

"Perhaps watching him die will drive home the ridiculous arrogance that motivated you to strike at me. Are you watching, Darius?"

Rigel advanced on Aaron, helpless in the chair, and I realized it wasn't a call on speaker phone but a video call. Oh god. I had to do something. But what? I didn't have a weapon. Just my hot-pink umbrella and—

"You're making a mistake." Darius's voice came through the speaker in a low growl. "Whatever lines you've trampled before, this isn't one you want to cross."

Keeping the phone camera pointed at Aaron, Rigel slipped a hand into his suit jacket and withdrew a black pistol from a hidden holster—and this one definitely wasn't a paintball gun.

He leveled it at Aaron's head.

I dug into my purse, spilling my belongings across the floor. The Queen of Spades card fluttered to the carpet between my feet. The spell reflected magic, but it couldn't reflect bullets.

"You started this war, Darius." Rigel waved the mentalist aside, and she shifted out of the way, keeping one hand on Aaron's shoulder. "And you're three thousand miles too far to save anyone."

My head jerked up. Rigel *knew* Darius was on the east coast? Then he'd never intended to spare Aaron. The last two hours had served no other purpose than to make Darius and the guild frantic—a farce to punish them even more.

Card in one hand and umbrella in the other, I braced myself.

"If you kill him," Darius snarled, fury breaking through his calm, "I'll teach you what it means to fear power."

Rigel didn't react to the threat. "Any final words for your protégé? He can't respond, but he can hear you."

"Rigel—"

"No? Very well."

Rigel handed his phone to a nearby psychic, who stepped back to bring both Aaron and his executioner into frame for Darius. Rigel pointed the gun between Aaron's blindfolded eyes.

"*Rigel!*" Darius roared.

I sprinted into the psychics' midst.

Flying past the watching mythics, I whipped my umbrella up into Rigel's wrist. The gun flew from his hand and I jammed the umbrella's handle into his face. As he staggered, I lunged forward, umbrella held like a jousting lance, and jammed its metal top into the mentalist's sternum. She jerked back, her hand slipping off Aaron's arm.

"Aaron!" I screamed. "Light the room on fire!"

I was afraid he would hesitate, would delay for fear of hurting me, but he didn't. With a sizzle of heat, flames burst from him and exploded outward in a howling maelstrom.

Holy shit. When Aaron had said he could light a room on fire, I hadn't realized it would be this easy for him. I threw myself toward the bank of cubicles, and as the wall of fire rushed at me, I pointed the Queen of Spades at it. "*Ori repercutio!*"

The air rippled and the flames shot away from me. As Aaron lunged off his chair, the fire washed harmlessly over him and rolled toward the screaming psychics. The blindfold and gag had burned off Aaron's face and flames ate holes in his shirt. Half the room was burning and Rigel had disappeared. Psychics fled in every direction—but not everyone was running.

A familiar figure charged through the flames. The telekinetic who'd almost killed Liam flung two daggers into the air and they shot at Aaron.

Aaron grabbed the metal chair and swung it, knocking one dagger off course. The other grazed his arm, his blood sizzling in the flames. As the telekinetic waved his hands wildly, bringing the weapons back under control, I popped out from my hidey hole under the desk, grabbed a brand-new keyboard, and threw it at the telekinetic.

Snapping a hand toward the projectile, he brought the keyboard to a halt in midair—but, distracted, he let his two knives drop to the floor. Aaron tackled him, flames bursting everywhere. The man went down with a shriek.

A flash of movement in the corner of my eye. The mentalist, her face contorted with either pain or fury, reached for me.

"Oh no you don't!" I yelled as I grabbed the next piece of equipment off the desk.

Her eyes widened and she frantically backpedaled. Not fast enough. I smashed the shiny new computer monitor into her head and she dropped like a rock. She wouldn't be using me as a hostage against Aaron a second time.

Another psychic ran out of the smoke and rammed me into the desk. The cubicle wall collapsed, the whole desk smashing into the floor. As his hands closed around my throat, sound blared through my ears and light flashed in my vision. Screams of terror, hideous screeching, splatters of red blood, wide staring human eyes, glowing red monster eyes, vicious snarls—

The hands around my neck disappeared and the horrific sights and sounds evaporated from my mind. I gasped in a lungful of smoke as Aaron hauled the mythic off me and threw him into a burning cubicle.

I grabbed Aaron's offered hand and he pulled me up. Fire had completely consumed his shirt but his pants were still in one charred piece. The spreading inferno was out of control and smoke billowed from the burning walls. Eyes stinging, I searched for our next opponent but the dumb ones were on the floor and the smart ones had already fled.

"This way," I coughed, my throat burning as the smoke thickened. "We can escape out the window."

With Aaron on my heels, I shot into the hall and scooped my purse off the floor. Halfway through shouldering it, I hurtled through the door into the half-renovated office.

And almost ran into the gun aimed at my chest.

21

TOM, his bandages blackened and his eyes blazing with hatred, clutched the pistol in a white-knuckled grip.

"Um," I whispered, staring at the barrel too close to my heart. Behind me, Aaron radiated heat. "Hi, Tom."

"Don't move, Aaron!" Tom snarled. "If you even twitch, I'll shoot you both!"

I didn't move. I didn't even breathe.

"Bitch," Tom hissed bitterly. "Do you have any idea how exclusive this guild is? What it takes to get a *chance* to join? This was supposed to be my big break!"

I leaned back from the gun but he stepped forward, bringing it closer.

"Tori," Aaron said. He sounded calm. Way too calm when my innards were about to decorate the white walls.

"Shut up!" Tom barked, jerking the gun side to side like he wasn't sure if my heart was in the center of my chest or on the left. I waited for my life to flash before my eyes, but all I felt was terror so intense it hurt.

Aaron lunged for Tom—and the psychic pulled the trigger.

The gun clicked, then Aaron ripped it out of Tom's hand. As I bailed out of the way, Aaron dropped the gun and grabbed Tom by his bandaged neck.

"Interesting thing about guns," the pyromage said, his flippant tone marred by a growl. "Firing a bullet requires *fire*."

Tom gawked, panic straining his features. With a flex of his muscular arm, Aaron flung Tom into the wall. The clairaudient slid to the floor.

I picked myself up, hacking as tears streamed from my burning eyes. Too much smoke. The flames on his skin dying down, Aaron pulled me to the open window. I clambered out and sucked in a desperate lungful of clean air.

"You can suppress gunfire?" I asked incredulously.

"With effort, concentration, and close proximity." He pulled me across the rooftop—not toward the pile of junk I'd climbed up, but toward the street. "Not something I normally count on."

Leaving me standing at the rooftop's edge, he jumped. Hitting the ground in an easy roll, he shot up and held his arms out to me, one streaked with blood from the knife wound. I sat on the edge and pushed off. He caught me, set me on my feet, then sprinted across the access road.

I didn't question his rush—I had no intention of stopping either. We weren't out of danger yet. Over half the psychics had escaped the burning room and could be anywhere.

As we raced toward the bridge, I glimpsed the second-floor windows dancing with the light of flames, then a gunshot rang through the silence. Aaron flinched at the sound but didn't stop, leaping onto the bridge deck and hauling me after him.

From the office entryway, people streamed out—more mythics than had populated the upstairs room. My whole body went cold as I realized more of the guild must have been waiting on the lower level. And now they were chasing us down.

More shots rang out as Aaron and I sprinted up the bridge. Why did they have so many freaking guns? They were mythics! Where the hell was the magic? I'd really prefer fireballs and ice shards to bullets right about now!

Lungs burning, throat on fire from smoke inhalation, I clung to Aaron's arm as we crossed the midpoint of the bridge, a quadruple set of train tracks running beneath it. Dark blocky shapes spread out before us—the shipping yard.

More gunfire, muzzle flashes erupting as the psychics chased us onto the bridge.

I tripped and fell, my hands and knees scraping across the pavement and my purse tumbling away from me. Aaron grabbed my waist and heaved me up, but my left knee decided it didn't want to hold my weight anymore. Pulling me against his side with one hand, he flung the other backward, casting a wall of flame behind us.

Lunging toward the bridge rail, he pulled us onto it and jumped. Ten feet below, massive shipping containers were stacked five high. We landed on top, the metal booming from the impact, and my leg buckled.

"Hang on, Tori," Aaron panted, dragging me up again.

Clutching his arm, I glanced down at my lame-ass knee that didn't want to work—and saw the shiny wetness coursing down my calf. Blood. Oh, shit. I'd been shot?

Half carrying me, Aaron launched into a sprint. The container boomed as more people jumped onto it, and Aaron flung fire behind us, more to blind the enemy than to stop them. We ran the length of two containers, then jumped down to a lower stack—but we were still forty freaking feet above the cement quay.

Leg crumpling under me, I slumped back into the side of the container. Aaron launched another wave of bright flames at our pursuers, but the shipping container wasn't flammable and he couldn't keep the flames burning indefinitely.

I pressed a hand to my leg, blood squishing between my fingers, and wondered why I felt no pain. Too much adrenaline? Dizzy and shaking, I scanned the shipping containers and spotted a stair-like stack farther along where we could climb down, but we'd be exposed to our pursuers the whole way. If they had any bullets left—

"Tori." Aaron yanked me toward the container's edge. "Jump!"

"What? No! We can go that way and—"

He pushed me toward the edge and I dug in my heels, clawing at his arms.

"No!" I screamed, fighting for traction on the steel, the forty-foot drop to unforgiving concrete right behind me. "Let me go!"

Aaron grabbed my jaw with one hand, forcing my eyes to meet his as firelight flickered across his features. "Tori, *trust me.*"

Trust him? No, no, no. I didn't do that. It never worked out for me, ever. Other people didn't save me. I saved myself.

A gunshot blasted through the night and Aaron reeled, blood spraying from the graze across his shoulder. Flinging fire at the gunmen, he shouted, "Jump!"

I pried my hands off his arm, cast a terrified look across him, then spun around and leaped.

Screaming, I plunged downward. Wind howled, then gusted beneath me with insane force. My drop slowed, then I crashed into something much softer than concrete.

Arms closed around me, pulling me tight against a warm chest.

Light flared above and Aaron jumped off the container pile. As his shadow plunged down, Ezra flung his hand out. The wind whipped into a dense updraft, and Aaron landed in a neat roll—then flopped out of it with zero grace. Panting for air, he scrambled up.

Without a word, Ezra and Aaron bolted into the labyrinth of shipping containers. I hung in Ezra's arms, gawking uselessly. Where had he *come from*? How had Aaron known he was there, waiting to catch us?

We whipped around a corner, then Aaron and Ezra skidded to a stop.

Spread in a line, blocking our path, was the rest of the psychic guild. They must have crossed the bridge and entered the yard from a different direction—cutting off our escape.

Rigel, his face blistered and bleeding, stood in the center of the line holding a shiny pistol, and a new telekinetic waited behind him, daggers floating at the ready. Two other psychics pointed guns our way.

"You thought you could escape?" Rigel sneered. "I have telethesians who can track you no matter where you run. I have clairsentients who can see you no matter where you hide. I have clairaudients who can hear you no matter how quietly you whisper. I have telepaths to coordinate our every move."

Aaron stepped in front of me and Ezra, shielding us from the gunmen. Heat radiated off him, but he didn't summon his flames. The psychics were too far. They'd shoot us before he could burn them.

Footsteps clattered behind us and Ezra turned as our pursuers from atop the shipping containers ran out of the darkness, sealing off our escape route. Ezra set me down and pushed me between him and Aaron, their backs to me as they faced the two forces.

Mouth opening in a silent laugh, Rigel aimed his gun at Aaron. "It was futile from the beginning, boy."

All the hair on my body stood on end.

Lightning leaped out of the darkness in a blinding flash and slammed into Rigel's pistol. The bolt forked and struck the two other guns. The three men holding firearms went down, convulsing.

A black-clad figure shot from between two containers, sprinting toward the psychics with electricity rippling over his arms. Kai's hands bristled with small throwing knives, and he hurled them at the psychics without breaking stride. The blades found the vulnerable flesh of the mythics, striking legs and shoulders—then lightning leaped from Kai's hands to the conductive metal.

Behind me, Ezra launched toward the other group of psychics, yanking his pole arm off his back. A gust of wind whipped dust into the psychics' faces, then he hammered the weapon into the first mythic, throwing him into the nearest container. The hollow metal boomed louder than gunfire.

Kai spun through the larger group, his movements swift and decisive. A telekinetic sent a knife flying at him, but the electramage darted aside with eerie, silent grace. He closed in on the telekinetic—and executed a flying double kick straight out of a martial arts movie. Landing neatly, he cast his hand wide. Lightning burst off him, seeking his metal knives. It tore through the psychics again, half of them falling to the ground in convulsions.

Gunshots rang out but Kai was a flickering shadow, impossible to hit. Ezra smashed his last opponent into the ground, then ran toward Kai's larger group. The aeromage whipped his weapon in an arc, and a concentrated gust of wind swept the legs out from under another three mythics. Breaking under Kai and Ezra's combined onslaught, the psychics fled into the dark passage between shipping containers.

Light flashed.

A yellow glow spiraled up the monstrous sword held by a petite woman with a blond pixie cut. Zora stood with her feet planted, the point of her blade resting on the asphalt as she waited for the psychics to run within her weapon's reach. Arrayed behind her were six more sorcerers.

The psychics pulled up short. Kai and Ezra blocked any possible retreat. Trapped, the mythics clustered together, then with their heads drooping, they put their hands up in defeat.

"But," I gasped, goggling at Zora as I huddled against Aaron. "Where ... *how?*"

"The psychics aren't the only ones with a telepath to coordinate their teams," Aaron said, sounding smug despite his hoarse exhaustion. "Bryce has been yammering in my head since we hit the bridge."

I looked up at him, wide-eyed. *That's* how he'd known Ezra was waiting to catch us? I couldn't wrap my mind around it as Zora and her team advanced on the dejected psychics. Kai sheathed his handful of throwing knives.

"No!" Rigel's hoarse cry cut through the quiet. He pulled himself off the ground, his clothes still smoking from the last lightning attack, and lifted the gun he'd somehow held on to. He aimed the barrel at Kai.

Faster than should have been possible, Ezra veered toward Rigel. His pole arm twisted apart, one half in each hand, and light gleamed down the foot-long steel.

Then Ezra, soft-spoken Ezra with the gentle smile, rammed both blades into Rigel's back.

22

I PROPPED MY CHIN on my palm. "Are you sure you don't need help?"

"I'm good," Justin muttered distractedly. "I'm—oh, shit! Shit shit shit!"

He grabbed the pot lid as starchy water boiled over, spilling across the stovetop. Swearing, he scooped noodles into the sizzling wok full of chicken and vegetables. As he reached blindly for the bottle of teriyaki sauce, I nudged it into his hand.

"I've got this," he said, upending the bottle over his concoction. "This is my world-famous teriyaki stir-fry. You love it, remember?"

I remembered eating it, not loving it, but I nodded noncommittally while saying a silent prayer for the poor vegetables drowning in sauce. Rest in salty peace, carrots and broccoli.

Setting the bottle aside, Justin cheerfully tossed the contents of the wok. "This is great. I haven't made this recipe since you moved in."

"That's because I usually cook," I pointed out. "I don't mind."

His enthusiasm dimmed. "You cook for me even when I'm not home and leave me leftovers in the fridge, clean the kitchen, and keep the apartment spotless." His hazel eyes, twins to mine, assessed me. "And you pay half my rent and utilities on top of that, even though you're sleeping on the sofa."

I shifted on my chair, a twinge of pain running through my calf where I'd been shot. Not that Justin knew about that. He dished stir-fry into two bowls and slid one to me. I reached for the chopsticks but he grabbed them first, holding them hostage.

"Tori," he said seriously, "don't worry about rent this month, okay? Just let me help you out this one time until you find a new job."

Looking away from his earnest stare, I heaved a sigh. "Okay. Just this one month, though."

He handed me a pair of chopsticks and I dug them into my meal. Surprisingly, it wasn't too saucy and the vegetables were crisp. Not bad.

"Don't take this the wrong way," he went on, standing at the counter with his bowl in hand. "But I'm honestly relieved you aren't working at that bar anymore. The place was nothing but trouble."

My chopsticks paused, a piece of chicken hovering over the bowl. "I'll find something soon. Maybe another bartending position."

Justin slowly chewed his mouthful. "You liked that job, didn't you?"

I flapped one hand dismissively. "They were a bunch of kooks. Good riddance."

"I'm sorry, Tori."

Biting my lip, I fought back the gloomy shroud that had clung to my thoughts for most of the week.

After defeating the psychic guild five days ago, the rest of that night had passed in a whirlwind of activity as more Crow and Hammer members showed up to restrain the psychics and treat injuries. Aaron and I were rushed away to a fancy house in a snazzy neighborhood where I met the mysterious healer Elisabetta.

Unfortunately, I sort of passed out so I missed all the cool stuff and woke up with my leg already fixed, the gunshot wound replaced by a circle of smooth, pink skin. Literal sorcery. I didn't even know how bad the injury had been. All that was left was a slight twinge in the muscle, which Elisabetta assured me would pass within a week.

Since then ... life had gone back to normal. As in, pre-Crow-and-Hammer normal. I hadn't heard from Aaron, Ezra, or Kai, and even Sin had ghosted me. Was I surprised? Not really. I was just a human, after all. Non-magical nobody here. Why would they bother keeping up with me after I'd been given the boot?

I wasn't surprised ... but it still hurt. It hurt *a lot*.

As Justin piled dirty dishes into the sink, I slipped my hand into my back pocket, feeling the worn edge of a playing card. The Queen of Spades. My only souvenir of a vacation from reality that had come to an abrupt end.

I tried to help Justin clean up, but he shooed me away, reiterating that the meal had been his treat and he wasn't letting me lift a finger. After freshening up in the bathroom, I grabbed the folder I'd prepared that morning and called a goodbye as I headed out.

The early afternoon sun blazed in my eyes as I stepped onto the baking-hot sidewalk. My purse—recovered from the battlefield and painstakingly cleaned but still smelling of smoke—hung off my shoulder, and I missed the weight of my pink umbrella, lost in the fire.

As I walked into the Sunday bustle, I dejectedly flipped my folder open to the stack of résumés with my spotty employment history. I hadn't bothered including the Crow and Hammer on it. What was the point? I'd lasted less than three weeks.

Tucking the folder under my arm with my purse, I extended my stride. Before I started dropping off applications, I had one stop to make.

The only person to reach out since that night was Clara. She'd texted yesterday asking me to come in. That was it. Just to come in. She probably needed termination paperwork signed or something. And I needed to pick up my final paycheck.

The closer I got to the guild, the more my steps slowed. My stomach twisted, compacting my lunch into a queasy ball. I didn't want to go back. I just wanted to forget about the insane magical world I'd entered. Walking in there and seeing that everything and everyone had moved right along with their magical lives without me ... it was going to suck hardcore.

Mentally pulling up my big-girl pants, I marched onward.

I didn't hesitate again until I reached the guild door with the painted crow, perched on its hammer. Revulsion and the need to run away swept through me, triggered by the spell on the door, but I shoved it open and stepped into the dark interior, momentarily blind after the dazzling sunlight.

"Tori!"

I caught a glimpse of Sin's blue tresses before she swept me into a crushing embrace. After squeezing all the air from my lungs, she stepped back and laughed at my expression, her hair in a wild tangle.

"I'm so glad you're back!" she exclaimed, linking our arms. The pub was comfortably busy, most of the faces familiar. Mythics called out as we passed, but Sin towed me straight to the bar. "How've you been? How's your leg?"

"Fine," I said dazedly, setting my folder and purse on the bar top. "Um …"

"I'm sorry I didn't call you." She perched on a stool. "MagiPol was investigating us. They were all up in our business, snooping around, checking records of everything."

"They were? Why? The psychics were the psycho kidnapping murderers, not you guys."

"Yeah, but we have a reputation and MagiPol wanted to be sure we hadn't provoked KCQ." She shrugged. "They were prying into everything. Clara made us delete your contact info and conversation history from our phones in case MagiPol checked them."

My eyes widened. Was *that* why I hadn't heard from anyone all week? I glanced around the pub but a certain trio of mages was nowhere in sight.

"Liam will be happy to see you. He went home yesterday—full recovery." Sin smiled tentatively. "I'm glad you're back."

I didn't point out that my return would be short-lived. "MagiPol didn't find out about me, did they?"

"Nope, you're good. Everyone was really careful to keep mum about your involvement. It wouldn't have been good for the guild or for you."

Feeling weak in the legs, I sat on a stool. The bar was unmanned; Cooper must be in the kitchen.

"I can't believe everything that happened." Sin smirked gleefully. "You saved Aaron's life *again*. He owes you big time. Make sure you rub it in his face as much as possible."

I opened my mouth, unsure I wanted to explain all the reasons that wouldn't be happening, when Clara rushed out of the kitchen in her usual the-world-is-ending frenzy.

"Tori! You're here." She dropped a stack of folders on the counter. "Come with me."

I expected her to lead me to the back office. Instead, she headed for the stairs. Chewing my lower lip, I followed her past the second level work area and up to the third story. Just like my one and only visit to this level, we entered the shared workspace of the three officers, but their desks were empty.

At the back of the room was another door, and Clara knocked before opening it. Inside was an airy office with a single desk and two large bookcases on opposite walls, framing the space. Three chairs were lined up on one side, occupied by the guild officers: Girard with the magnificent beard, ice-queen Tabitha, and blond and bespectacled Felix.

Behind the desk, a vaguely familiar man sat—older, salt-and-pepper hair, a short and neatly groomed beard, and distinguished features. Darius, the guild master.

He gestured at the chair in front of his desk. "Welcome back, Tori. Please have a seat."

I minced forward and perched on the chair, my gaze darting from face to face as Clara took a spot behind Darius's right shoulder. Was I in trouble? They'd already fired me, but maybe Darius was going to turn me over to MagiPol for punishment.

Darius folded his hands and rested his chin on them, analyzing me from head to toe. At least I was dressed nice and not wearing my usual short-shorts. I'd hate to go to magic prison in less than my best.

"Tori," the guild master said, his words slow as though he were choosing them carefully. "Among mythics, unique abilities and strong personalities abound. It takes truly rare and exceptional strength to stand out among the crowds of intensely gifted mythics we encounter daily."

His gray eyes met mine. "You, Victoria Dawson, are the most surprising and remarkable young woman I have met in many years, mythic or otherwise. Thanks to your courage, determination, and trust in your own instincts, you saved Aaron's life where I failed to protect him. He, I, and this guild owe you a great debt."

I gulped silently, suppressing my surprise. Not what I'd been expecting to hear.

"That said," he continued, his voice hardening, "you put your life in severe danger. You failed to communicate your plan, acted alone without a support network, and nearly died. You disregarded the skills of other guild members and withheld crucial information."

Mouth hanging open, I shrank in my chair, as intimidated as a kindergartener being lectured by the school principal.

"This isn't a guild of independent contractors. At the Crow and Hammer, we function as a team—our strengths compensating for our fellows' weaknesses. No life is worth more or less than another, including yours." He leaned back. "Under different circumstances, this meeting would be to determine disciplinary action."

"D-discipline?" I stammered.

"I do not allow my guildeds to recklessly endanger themselves any more than I allow them to endanger others. However"—amusement sparked in his eyes—"since you are not a member of this guild, I can do no more than express my displeasure."

Straightening out of my cower, I attempted to piece my dignity back together.

He stroked his beard. "I understand Tabitha terminated your employment. Clara and I disagree with her decision."

Tabitha's dark eyes flicked to Darius then to me. "I made that call during a crisis with a guilded's life on the line, but perhaps I was hasty in removing you from the situation."

Was that an apology? I wasn't sure.

Darius lifted the sheet of paper lying on the desk in front of him. "Interestingly enough, according to the paperwork Clara failed to complete"—the AGM flinched—"you never officially worked for the guild. As such, I cannot rehire you."

I blinked.

"Instead," he murmured, sliding the paper toward me, "I would like to present this job offer for your consideration."

Numbly, I picked up the paper and skimmed it. My job, laid out in clear wording, down to my hours, wage, and perks. Darius's loopy signature already marked the bottom of the page beside a line awaiting my signature.

"There's still the matter of MPD's approval," Darius said. "But that's a bridge we can cross when we come to it."

My head buzzed. The guild master surveyed me, then said to the others, "Would you excuse us, please?"

Clara and the three officers filed out, leaving me alone with Darius. He rose from his chair and circled the desk. Unsure what to do, I jumped up, oddly wary. Authority figures normally inspired my smart mouth to run away with itself, but Darius wielded command and influence like an expert swordsman, and even I couldn't summon proper snark in his presence.

To my shock, he caught my free hand in both of his, his palms warm and calloused. "Offering you a job seems like paltry thanks. Without you, I would have lost Aaron. I would have watched him die, unable to stop it. I can't adequately express my gratitude, but know that whether or not you accept the position, you will always be welcome in any home of mine."

Unexpected tears stung my eyes. I blinked rapidly to clear them.

Darius released my hand and sat on the edge of his desk. "Would you like time to consider the job offer?"

"I've already thought about it." I raised a finger. "I'll accept on one condition."

His eyebrows crept up. "What condition is that?"

I turned the paper toward him and pointed. His eyebrows rose higher, and I smiled wickedly. With a quiet laugh, he reached for a pen.

Five minutes later, I skipped down the stairs, a copy of the signed offer in hand. As I landed on the bottom step, I reeled to a stop so fast I almost fell on my face.

Sin had disappeared, but lined up at the bar in her place, leaning casually against it with rum and cokes in hand, were Aaron, Kai, and Ezra. Déjà vu from our first meeting tingled through me, not helped by Aaron's mischievous smirk. I hopped down the last step, barely noticing the bustle in the rest of the pub, but before I could figure out how I wanted to react to their sudden appearance, Aaron pounced.

Looping an arm around my waist, he swept me over to Kai and Ezra. Next thing I knew, they were standing in a triangle around me, trapping me against the bar, and my paper was in Aaron's hands. He whooped victoriously.

"Rehired! And—whoa! A raise?" He pointed incredulously at my original wage, now crossed out with a new number written beside it in the guild master's neat print. "Nicely done! Darius is a stingy old badger."

Ezra smiled, his eyes warm. "Welcome back, Tori."

"About time, too," Aaron groused. "I was starting to think the MPD agents would hang around until Christmas."

Kai plucked the paper from Aaron and scanned it. "Excellent. Darius didn't include anything about supervision."

"Huh?" I said gormlessly.

"Aaron is off the hook for watching you every shift. Which is good, because we have a lot of work to do. Fourteen KCQ members are still unaccounted for and MagiPol has put out *very* generous bounties on them."

"But …" I looked at the paper, devoid of a supervision clause. "Is it really okay for me to … by myself?"

"Do you *want* me annoying you for eight hours a day?" Aaron's expression turned sly. "If we're going to spend that much time together, we should do it when you're *not* working. Don't forget I promised you a dinner date."

"You don't need him, anyway," Ezra jumped in. "If anything, Aaron should be asking you to supervise *his* work."

Aaron bristled. "What're you—"

"Yeah," Kai agreed. "Maybe the three of us should work out a rotating schedule so Aaron has a capable defender at all times."

"I don't need—"

"You never know when you might get abducted again."

"That was only once!"

As Aaron fumed, Kai and Ezra snickered. I stood between them, my brain frazzled by the sudden rearrangement of expectations. I'd thought the guys were done with me and I'd never set foot in the guild again. But now I was back, I was rehired, and …

Three pairs of very different eyes watched me, and it was like nothing had changed. Like Aaron's kidnapping, our terrifying escape, and our near deaths had been just another day on the job.

Another day in the life of a mythic.

Good thing I wasn't a mythic. Just a bartender. For a guild. Of mythics. Okay, it was a fine line, but whatever.

A grin spread across my face. Beaming back at me, Aaron spun us toward the bar. Ezra leaned against the counter beside me, and Kai took up the spot on Aaron's other side.

Returning from the kitchen in a waft of cigarette-scented air, Cooper waved in greeting. "Want anything?"

"Order a drink on me, Tori," Aaron said imperiously. "Least I can do."

"We can toast to Aaron's amazing talents as a kidnapping victim," Ezra suggested.

"No," Aaron sniffed. "We can toast to Tori being freakin' amazing and saving my life."

Kai bent forward to catch my eye. "And after that, we can have a little chat about how, next time, you'll call me and Ezra *before* you race off to save his helpless ass by yourself."

"Er, yeah." I flinched. "Can we just not do a next time?"

The three guys exchanged looks, then Aaron pulled me to his side. "That sounds boring as hell. We'll just make sure you're more prepared for 'next time.'"

My eyes widened. "Uh, hey now. I'm just the bartender."

"Nope." His laughing blue eyes captured mine. "You might not be an official member of the Crow and Hammer, but you're part of the family now."

I stared at him, speechless.

Cooper hurried over, carrying my purse and résumé folder from the other end of the bar. He set them down beside me. "So, Tori? What do you want?"

Picking up the folder, I looked from Ezra's mismatched eyes to Kai's dark gaze to Aaron's troublemaker grin. As I stood between the three mages, the question echoed through me. What did I want?

Reaching over the bar, I let the folder slide from my hand. It landed square in the garbage bin on the other side. Straightening, I gave Aaron a mischievous smirk to match his.

"Since this drink is on you," I told him, "I know exactly what I want."

He watched curiously as I turned to Cooper, my smile widening.

"How about a margarita?"

TORI'S ADVENTURES CONTINUE IN

DARK ARTS AND DAIQUIRI

THE GUILD CODEX: SPELLBOUND / TWO

When I found myself facing down the scariest black-magic felon in the city, practically *daring* him to abduct me, I had to wonder exactly how I ended up here.

It all started when Aaron, Kai, and Ezra asked for my help. Did they want access to my encyclopedic knowledge of cocktails? Oh no. They wanted to wrap me up in a pretty ribbon and plunk me in the crosshairs of a murderous rogue to lure him out of hiding.

So that's what we did. And that's why I'm here. About to be kidnapped. Oh, and our grand plan for safely capturing said murderous rogue? Yeah, that completely fell apart about two minutes ago.

Why did I agree to this again?

KEEP READING FOR THE FIRST CHAPTER

DARK ARTS AND DAIQUIRI

I

"THIS HOUSE," the landlord declared, "is *not* haunted."

Lifting my sunglasses off my eyes, I peered at the sweating man. His baggy shirt stuck to his beer belly and his bald head shone in the afternoon sun. Had I somehow implied I was concerned about paranormal activity? Because I definitely hadn't asked about any hauntings.

At my dubious look, he realized his mistake.

"There are rumors—I mean, a few people have—that is ..." He deflated. "It's not haunted."

Uh-huh. I perched my sunglasses on top of my head and surveyed the property. We stood in the backyard of a tired bungalow that wore its recent renovations like a venerable old lady done up in clown makeup. The back fence had been painted white, but the peeling underlayer was already lifting the new coat off. The postage-stamp yard had been sodded with green grass, and a new pergola sat atop cracked patio stones, but a monster-sized spruce dominated the space.

Blowing my bangs off my forehead, I scanned my printout for the rental. "Is this yard shared with the people upstairs?"

"Technically, yes." He wiped his hands on his baggy gym shorts. "The main level is rented, but they travel a lot."

"Hmm." I waited a moment to see if he'd offer up anything else. "Can we go inside?"

"Oh yes!" He waved enthusiastically. "The door's unlocked. Go ahead and take a look around."

I glanced at my apartment-hunting wingwoman. Sin scrunched her face, arms folded over her teal sundress, the airy fabric almost the same color as her wavy hair. With a shrug, I headed for the back door and she followed behind me. The landlord, blotting his face with a crumpled tissue, stayed where he was.

Once inside the drab entryway, Sin snorted loudly. "What is with the weirdo count on this outing? The first landlord invited you to move into his house instead of the apartment. The second lady asked *seven times* if you were a natural redhead. Now this guy? Ugh."

I started down the stairs to the basement. "You forgot the creeper at the bus stop who tried to snatch your purse."

"The one you called a swamp donkey?" Sin smirked. "And threatened to shove into traffic?"

"Funny how he decided he didn't need to take the bus after all." I stopped just beyond the entryway. "Oh, hey. This isn't half bad."

The simple open layout showcased a basic kitchen with cheap appliances in one corner, a living room with a fireplace and a long window that let in a surprising amount of light, and imitation-hardwood floors throughout. Excited, I checked out the bathroom, bedroom, and tiny laundry room. Returning to the empty, echoey living room, I spun in a slow circle, scanning everything.

"This is really nice," I gushed, unconcerned by the lackluster finishes. Beggars couldn't be choosers, and having spent the last ten months sleeping on my brother's sofa, I was ready to overlook anything less than holes in the walls.

Which, unfortunately, had been included in all the apartments we'd looked at so far, along with complimentary mold, cockroaches, and suspicious odors. That wasn't including the batshit crazy landlords. Did normal people not dabble in real estate investment, or did all the well-adjusted landlords have tenants already?

"It's clean," Sin observed. "Running water. Heat. Wait, *does* it have heat? It's cold in here."

"Well, it *is* a basement." I flapped my printout. "It says all utilities are included in the rent. How sweet is that?"

Sin wrinkled her nose suspiciously. "It's too cheap. There's got to be something wrong with it."

"Maybe there's a hobo living in the crawlspace." I pointed at a half-height door tucked in a corner of the living room. "That's a crawlspace, right?"

We crossed the room and I crouched at the door, Sin leaning over my shoulder. I pulled it open. Inside was nothing but impenetrable darkness.

"Use your phone's flashlight," Sin suggested. "There must be a light switch or—"

Chill air whispered over my skin and all the hair on my body stood on end—then arctic wind blasted me in the face.

I recoiled, crashing into Sin's legs. She landed on her ass as the wind howled out of the crawlspace, whipping dust through the room. My printouts went flying and we scrambled backward on our butts with the papers spiraling toward the ceiling.

The darkness in the crawlspace leaked out from the doorway and pooled on the floor like ink. Shadows writhed and something pale materialized in the threshold—a skeletal woman on her hands and knees, toothless mouth gaping, empty eye sockets dribbling black blood.

I took one look at the moaning specter and screamed like the sissy girl that I am.

Sin let out her own terrified shriek as the ghostly woman dragged herself out of the crawlspace, her long hair trailing on the floor. She stretched a hand toward us, blackened fingers curled like claws, and icy gusts lashed at our faces. Still screaming, Sin grabbed my arm, her fingernails digging into my skin. Sharp pain cut through my panic.

I jammed my hand into my pocket and whipped out my trump card—yes, a literal card.

My trusty Queen of Spades was more than it appeared: a sorcerer's artifact embedded with a spell that reflected magic. Was there any magic here to rebound? I had no idea. Would it work on a ghost? Also no idea. I wasn't a sorcerer. I was a crime-of-convenience thief and I had only the vaguest notion how to use the card.

But it was the only magical defense I had, so I thrust it at the phantom and shouted, "*Ori repercutio!*"

The air rippled and the gale-force wind reversed direction. It slammed into the woman, flinging her back into the crawlspace. Her head hit the door frame with a solid *whack*.

"Ow!" she squeaked.

Sin's scream cut off. In unison, we launched to our feet. We weren't screaming anymore, but I for one was even more freaked out. The woman was too solid to be a ghost, but holy freaking shit, that body did not belong to a living being—papery skin clinging to bones, empty sockets for eyes, stringy hair down to her knees.

The ghost woman sprang up, raising her hands like claws. "Begone from this place," she moaned. "*Begooooone* … or else!"

I tipped my head toward Sin, not daring to take my eyes off the not-a-ghost. "Hey, Sin. Is that … a vampire?"

"No." She pulled a handful of vials with colorful liquid contents out of her purse. "Not even close."

Selecting a bottle, she dropped the others back into her bag and unscrewed the top. A hideous smell like burnt iron singed my nose.

"No!" the woman shrieked—except she didn't sound like a woman anymore. Her voice was two octaves higher and painfully nasal. "Don't!"

Sin held out the bottle threateningly. "Show us your real form or I'll drench you!"

"Noooo! Go *away*!" The woman stomped her foot. "Stupid humans! This is my house!"

Raising her hand higher, Sin started to tip the bottle.

"*Uuuuugh.* Fine." The woman threw her hands up—and her body melted. It lost solidity and shrank, then reformed into something new.

The creature was dark green with skin the waxy texture of pine needles. Even with twigs sprouting off its large head in place of hair, it barely reached my waist, and a mixture of spruce branches and pine cones hid its torso. Thin arms and legs stuck out of the twiggy mess, its hands and feet comically oversized.

Its eyes, narrowed angrily, dominated its face, the crystalline green irises unnaturally bright and entirely lacking pupils—just giant green orbs.

The creature pointed an accusing finger at us. "This is my house! Leave or I'll turn you into bean sprouts!"

I cleared my throat. "Okay, not a vampire," I said to Sin. "What is it?"

"This," Sin said grimly, "is a faery. Some sort of woodland sprite."

"Ah. I see." Faery. Got it. I pursed my lips. How come no one had ever mentioned faeries before? What the hell!

"Why aren't you listening?" the faery demanded. "I said get out, you stupid mud-slinging apes!"

"Whoa, whoa." I put my hands on my hips. "What did you just call us?"

"Apes! Dogs! Slimy worms! Hairless monkey fre—"

Sin tilted her reeking bottle and the faery jumped back.

"No! Keep that away from me!"

"If you don't want me to dump this all over the house," she threatened, "then show some respect."

"Respect," the faery sneered under its breath. "Who would respect talking leaf shitters who can't even—no no no!"

The faery plastered itself against the wall as Sin advanced with the anti-faery potion. She glanced back at me, her mouth twisted in a scowl. "The rent on this place is probably so cheap because this dingbat has been terrifying all the potential tenants with its *The Ring* impression."

Remembering the landlord's declaration, I shook my head in disbelief. "Not haunted, my ass."

"Well, it's an easy fix. We'll just bring a witch out to exorcise the faery and—"

"Nooo!" the faery shrieked in its grating voice. "This is my house! Mine!"

"It's a human house!" Sin yelled. "Go back to the forest!"

The faery pulled its green lips back, revealing pointed canines like a cat's. Then it leaped.

It crashed into Sin's chest, knocking her down as it grabbed at the vial in her hand. I launched forward, swung my foot back, and kicked the little green bastard square in the face. The faery tumbled into the wall, yelping the whole way.

Sin sat up. The vial, and her hand, were wrapped in thin tree roots, preventing the liquid from spilling out. Tearing the roots off her hand, she clambered to her feet, shot the faery a murderous glare, then stalked to the door. "Come on, Tori."

"We're leaving?"

"Only witches can deal with fae."

The faery sat on the floor with its hair twigs bent on one side. It glowered furiously at me, its spindly arms crossed. As I trotted through the doorway after Sin, it stuck its green tongue out.

I stuck my tongue out in turn, then slammed the door shut.

Sin recapped her anti-faery concoction and hid it in her purse as we walked into the backyard, baking heat sweeping over us. I sighed, relieved to be out of the unnatural cold. The landlord was waiting in the shade of the fence, his shoulders slumped dejectedly.

Heard us screaming, had he? He'd sure embraced his inner hero when he came running to our rescue. Not.

I pulled my sunglasses down over my eyes. "I'll call later this week to set up a second viewing."

His head jerked up. "You—you want to come back?"

Assuming every visitor got the faery's horror-movie treatment, I'd bet an entire paycheck that I was the first person to ever suggest a second viewing. "Yeah. I'll call you."

With a farewell wave, I strolled out of the yard. Back on the sidewalk, Sin and I headed toward the main street.

"Well," I remarked, "that was interesting. Are you sure a witch can deal with the pine-cone prick?"

"It'll be no problem. That's a minor faery, nothing that would slow down a witch."

"Excellent." I smiled wickedly. "One little exorcism and I can rent the place at a haunted-house discount."

She returned my grin. "How convenient that you happen to know several witches."

"Very convenient indeed." I checked the clock on my phone. My shift started in thirty minutes, and all things considered, witches were a cakewalk compared to some of my clientele.

ABOUT THE AUTHOR

Annette Marie is the author of YA urban fantasy series *Steel & Stone*, its prequel trilogy *Spell Weaver*, and romantic fantasy trilogy *Red Winter*.

Her first love is fantasy, but fast-paced adventures, bold heroines, and tantalizing forbidden romances are her guilty pleasures. She proudly admits she has a thing for dragons, and her editor has politely inquired as to whether she intends to include them in every book.

Annette lives in the frozen winter wasteland of Alberta, Canada (okay, it's not quite that bad) and shares her life with her husband and their furry minion of darkness—sorry, cat—Caesar. When not writing, she can be found elbow-deep in one art project or another while blissfully ignoring all adult responsibilities.

www.annettemarie.ca

SPECIAL THANKS

*My thanks to Erich Merkel for sharing your exceptional
expertise in Latin. Any errors are mine.*

THE
GUILD CODEX
SPELLBOUND

Tori might have averted one disaster, but do you think that's it? Her penchant for minor catastrophes aside, the three mages all have the same middle name: *trouble*. Tori has fallen head over heels into the mythic world, and once you're in, you're in.

Welcome to the Crow and Hammer.

DISCOVER MORE BOOKS AT
www.guildcodex.ca

STEEL & STONE

When everyone wants you dead, good help is hard to find.

The first rule for an apprentice Consul is *don't trust daemons*. But when Piper is framed for the theft of the deadly Sahar Stone, she ends up with two troublesome daemons as her only allies: Lyre, a hotter-than-hell incubus who isn't as harmless as he seems, and Ash, a draconian mercenary with a seriously bad reputation. Trusting them might be her biggest mistake yet.

GET THE COMPLETE SERIES
www.annettemarie.ca/steelandstone

SPELL WEAVER

The only thing more dangerous than the denizens of the Underworld ... is stealing from them.

As a nymph living in exile among humans, Clio has picked up some unique skills. But pilfering magic from the Underworld's deadliest spell weavers? Not so much. Unfortunately, that's exactly what she has to do to earn a ticket home.

GET THE COMPLETE TRILOGY
www.annettemarie.ca/spellweaver

A destiny written by the gods. A fate forged by lies.

If Emi is sure of anything, it's that *kami*—the gods—are good, and *yokai*—the earth spirits—are evil. But when she saves the life of a fox shapeshifter, the truths of her world start to crumble. And the treachery of the gods runs deep.

This stunning trilogy features 30 full-page illustrations.

GET THE COMPLETE TRILOGY
www.annettemarie.ca/redwinter

Lightning Source UK Ltd.
Milton Keynes UK
UKHW011913101119
353270UK00001B/158/P